How could he not care enough to ask about his daughter?

"Nothing changes, does it?" The words shot out before Hannah could think about them. "Your daughter's doing fine, by the way."

He stared at her. "My daughter?"

"Yes, your daughter. Who will be six on Saturday. Probably just slipped your mind, huh?"

"You...you ended the pregnancy. You had an abortion."

Hannah blinked. "What are you talking about?"

"Your mother told me you had an abortion."

"My mother?" She gaped at him. "My mother told you that! And you believed her?"

"You were very upset the day you told me you were pregnant," he said, his voice devoid of inflection. "You said we were too young. We had a fight and you left. When you didn't come home that night, I went to see your mother. She said you'd gone away and she wouldn't tell me where. But she definitely gave me the impression that you'd gone to have—"

"My God, Liam. Why would she tell you that? There was never any thought of having an abortion."

"Obviously, that's a question you'll have to ask her."

Dear Reader,

As a parent or grandparent, we want only the best for our children and grandchildren. But conflicting opinions can result in a painful and emotional tug-of-war. In *Keeping Faith*, six-year-old Faith is the center of a universe that includes her mother, Hannah, her grandmother Margaret and three aunts. All would do absolutely anything for her. And so would Faith's father, Liam.

In this book I've tried to explore issues of trust and boundary setting, and the complexities—and, of course, the numerous joys and rewards—of the mother-daughter relationship.

I love to hear from readers and try to write back whenever possible. Please visit my Web site at janicemacdonald.com and let me know how you enjoyed this book.

Best wishes,

Janice

Books by Janice Macdonald

HARLEQUIN SUPERROMANCE
1060—THE DOCTOR DELIVERS
1077—THE MAN ON THE CLIFF

Keeping Faith
Janice Macdonald

HARLEQUIN®

TORONTO • NEW YORK • LONDON
AMSTERDAM • PARIS • SYDNEY • HAMBURG
STOCKHOLM • ATHENS • TOKYO • MILAN • MADRID
PRAGUE • WARSAW • BUDAPEST • AUCKLAND

ISBN 0-373-71132-8

KEEPING FAITH

Copyright © 2003 by Janice Macdonald.

This edition published by arrangement with Harlequin Books S.A.

® and TM are trademarks of the publisher. Trademarks indicated with
® are registered in the United States Patent and Trademark Office, the
Canadian Trade Marks Office and in other countries.

Visit us at www.eHarlequin.com

Printed in U.S.A.

To my mother, Dorothy, my daughter Carolyn
and my granddaughter Emily.

CHAPTER ONE

HANNAH RILEY HAD NEVER actually experienced a gun going off at close range, but when she opened the *Long Beach Press Telegram* Monday morning and saw Liam Tully's picture, she figured the effect would have to be pretty similar. Around her, all sound and movement ceased. Oxygen seemed sucked from the room. The picture blurred.

Liam Tully? It couldn't be.

It was. A little older than the last time she'd seen him—six years older, to be exact—but definitely Liam. Thin face, too thin to be conventionally handsome. Deep-set eyes. Terrific smile.

The caption beneath the picture read: *Liam Tully, lead singer for the Celtic folk group, The Wild Rovers. The group from County Galway will perform next Friday through Sunday at Fiddler's Green in Huntington Beach as part of a four-week California tour.*

Hannah read and reread the announcement. Stared at Liam's picture as though it might reveal something the caption didn't. Stared at the picture and saw herself as she'd been the last time she'd seen Liam. Twenty-five, pregnant and scared to death. Of everything. *God.*

Carefully, as though it might detonate, she set the newspaper aside and smiled up at the dark-haired woman who had just walked into her classroom. Hannah stuck out her hand and searched through her brain, suddenly gone blank, for the woman's name. *Becker.*

"Hi, Mrs. Becker." She glanced at her watch. "You're a little early, but if you give me a minute, I'll find Taylor's assessment results."

Four-year-old Taylor had flunked a mock prekindergarten screening test two days ago. The real test, in which he would be put through his paces—skipping, hopping, wielding scissors and filling in the blanks to questions like "A bed is for sleeping and a table is for..."—was a few weeks away, but his mother had called to ask Hannah what could be done to improve her son's performance.

As she retrieved Taylor's folder, Hannah had an insane urge to propose to Mrs. Becker, a brittle-looking blonde in a black pantsuit, that Taylor be allowed to be himself. An easygoing child who delighted in running through the sprinklers on La Petite Ecole's manicured lawn and showed little enthusiasm for mastering the alphabet.

She resisted the urge. Parents who paid thousands of dollars a year to send their children to La Petite Ecole, who crammed their kids' schedules with extracurricular classes in early math and classical music appreciation, did so in order to crush the competition when it came time for kindergarten.

And, as Hannah continually had to remind herself, most parents—however misguided their motives might seem—really only wanted the best for their children.

Most parents.

She dragged her mind back to Taylor Becker's mother, who had just asked her a question and was waiting for an answer.

"Sorry." Hannah smiled at the woman.

"I was asking if there's anything else we can do." She hesitated, her face coloring slightly. "I bought him this darling T-shirt to wear for the test. I'm sure it sounds silly to you, but I started thinking that if he were dressed in a really hip shirt it might set him apart from the others." Another pause. "We don't want him to fail again."

Hannah looked at her for a moment. "If I can give you a piece of advice, Mrs. Becker, I would strongly suggest that you don't use the word *fail*. Especially to Taylor. And I'd also suggest that *you* try to relax. If he sees you're stressed, he'll get anxious and maybe not do so well. Children pick up on negative emotions."

IT WAS CRAZY, but all afternoon—ever since she had read the article about Liam—she'd had the fantasy that when she got home, Liam would be waiting for her. At one point the feeling was so strong she'd actually picked up the phone to make an appointment at the beauty parlor—this was not one of her better hair days. And then, remembering that he was probably still a few hundred miles to the north, she'd put the phone down and revised the scenario. There would be a message to say he'd called. She could still recreate the sound of his voice. Even after six years, she could conjure it up. *Let's get together,* he'd say in her fantasy. *Let's talk about what happened. I miss you, I still love you.* But as she opened the front door, Hannah knew Liam wouldn't be waiting inside and, as she stood in the kitchen doorway watching her daughter, she knew, too, that there had been no call.

Faith, a week shy of her sixth birthday, sat at a large wooden table in the center of the room. Brow furrowed, she was squeezing pink icing onto a row of cookies. A California girl, all tanned limbs and sun-bleached hair, worn now in a tightly controlled ponytail that set off her clear skin and blue eyes.

Liam's eyes.

Children pick up on negative emotions.

Most parents only want what's best for their children.

Liam wasn't most parents.

Hannah didn't need Liam in her life.

Faith didn't need Liam in her life.

Children pick up on negative emotions.

Hannah consciously slowed her breathing, stayed in the doorway, smiling now as she waited for either her daughter or her mother, who was on the phone, to look up and see her.

Her parents had moved into the large Spanish-style house a block from the ocean in Long Beach just after Hannah's first birthday and, of all the rooms in the house, the huge square kitchen figured most prominently in her childhood memories.

She'd learned to walk by pulling herself up to the cabinet edges, knocked out a tooth on a pantry shelf after roller-skating across the polished floor on a dare from her sister Debra. A large cast of dogs had eaten from various bowls that were always set out by the back door, and litters of kittens had taken their first breaths under the kitchen sink.

Nothing much had changed. After her father died, her mother had traded in the avocado-green appliances and ditched the old wallpaper with its repeating pattern of yellow kettles and orange teapots. The walls were peach now, or as Margaret insisted, apricot bisque; the refrigerator and stove stainless steel, but something was always in the oven or on the stove and, until last week when he'd gone to doggy heaven, Turpin, the family's elderly black Lab, had still been eating from the bowl by the door.

The henhouse, her mother called it these days. Hannah and Faith and Margaret lived there. Sporadically, Margaret's sister Rose and her own sister Debra came to stay. Helen, the youngest of Hannah's aunts, had her own coop, a guest cottage behind the rose garden, but always joined them for meals. Males were conspicuously absent.

"Who needs them anyway?" Margaret would say. "We're just a bunch of hens cooing and clucking around our baby chick."

So while Margaret's friends were dealing with the empty-nest blues and converting extra bedrooms into sewing areas, Margaret kept busy as she had all her adult life—cooking, cleaning and caring for her brood. "My family is my life," she'd say when Hannah or Debra would urge her to expand her horizons with a part-time job or volunteering. "This is what makes me happy. My daughters and my granddaughter. Why would I want to do something else?"

If there were times when Margaret's fussing and clucking made Hannah question the living arrangement, Deb made no secret of the fact that Margaret drove her nuts. Deb's biggest fear was that she'd turn out like Margaret. "If you ever catch me acting like Mom," she'd say to Hannah, "just shoot me, okay?"

And Deb in turn drove Margaret nuts. Deb was the problematic chick in the nest; prickly and demanding, always flying away only to return a few months later, torn and tattered but still defiant. Margaret had been thirty-eight when she gave birth to Debra and had once, in Deb's hearing, referred to her youngest daughter as "an afterthought." Debra had never forgiven her.

Still the relationship had a weird kind of synergy. Debra could tell herself that however screwed up her life might be, at least she wasn't like Margaret, leading some nutso June Cleaver existence, ironing sheets and baking pies while her husband cheated with women half his age as Hannah's father had done. And Margaret's tales about her problematic daughter always got a sympathetic hearing from the women in her Wednesday Weight Watchers group. "I give Mom a sense of purpose," Deb would say, only half in jest.

So, too, did Faith. In fact, Faith was so thoroughly the center of her grandmother's life that Hannah worried what Margaret would do if she and Faith ever moved away. Not that she had any plans to do so. She was happy. Sort of, kind of, basically. A job she enjoyed— well, maybe she would rather be a landscape gardener, but somehow that hadn't worked out. A guy she liked. Allan was sweet and thoughtful and if he didn't make her heart beat faster, so what? Chemistry wasn't everything.

More importantly, Faith was happy.

And if Liam didn't care that his little girl was just about to turn six, that was his loss. Hannah tiptoed into the room and came up behind her daughter. Arms wrapped around Faith's shoulders, she nuzzled her neck.

"Hey, baby. Who loves you more than anyone else in the world?"

"Ow, Mommy, you're squeezing too hard and don't call me 'baby.'" Faith wriggled away. "Look." She held up a large colored tin for Hannah to see. "Grandma bought me these cookie cutters. They have all the letters of the alphabet. See, I'm writing my name with cookies."

"Wow, that's terrific." Hannah pulled up a chair and

sat down next to her daughter. The cooking gene had skipped a generation, gone from her mother to her daughter. Both loved long days in the kitchen, Margaret's cookbooks spread out across the table, the KitchenAid whirring. Impulsively Hannah brought her face up under Faith's. "I'm the kissing monster." She puckered her lips. "And I won't go away until I get ten thousand kisses."

"*Momeee.*" Faith pushed Hannah's head away. "I can't see what I'm doing." Up on her knees, she began fishing small vials of silver balls and candy confetti from the tin. "Look. Grandma bought me all these decorating things. We're having *so* much fun."

"I can tell." Hannah glanced over at her mother, still on the phone. Margaret, sixty, and the oldest of the three sisters, had wiry, gray-blond hair tied up with an orange scrunchy. From Margaret's careful tone and turndowned mouth, Hannah guessed that the caller was Deb and that the crisis du jour was gathering strength.

"God." Margaret carefully set the phone back on the wall holder, leaned against the sink and folded her arms across her chest. "I swear Debra will drive me to an early grave."

"*No!*" Eyes wide and troubled, Faith looked at her grandmother. "I don't want you to go to an early grave, Grandma."

"Oh, honey," Margaret laughed, and hugged Faith. "That's just one of those silly things grown-ups say. Grandma isn't going anywhere. She's having too much fun with you. Did you tell Mommy what a great day we had? We shopped and baked and talked girl stuff," she said, addressing Hannah now. "And next week—"

"We're making all the cookies for Grandma's friend's party." Faith sprinkled blue sugar onto a pink cookie and sat back to look at the results. "Six kinds. Chocolate chip, lemon bars and I forget the rest."

"Oh, all different kinds." Margaret started clearing the knives and spoons from the table. "Poor Bella, she's got the garden club coming and she's overwhelmed so I offered to make the desserts. Somehow I'll manage to squeeze it between the birthday cake I promised to bake for Rose's friend and...damn, I know there's something else. Please God don't let it be something I promised to do for Deb. She's already upset because I forgot to ask what happened with that job interview she went on..." Margaret wiped the table and waited until Faith had gone to watch cartoons, then slowly shook her head at Hannah. "Tell me where I went wrong with Deb. Why can't I do anything right for that girl?"

Hannah carefully set Faith's decorated cookies into a tin, resisting the urge to bite into an extra letter *A*. Deb was twenty-two and she was thirty-one, but to Margaret they were always the girls.

"So what's up with Deb now?"

"She says she's moving in with Dennis."

"The bartender who sells marijuana?"

"This isn't funny, Hannah."

"I'm not laughing, Mom." Actually she'd been wondering whether or not to mention the news about Liam. "I thought she was through with Dennis."

Margaret reached for a jar of hand cream on the windowsill and began massaging it into her elbows. Margaret was always slapping alpha hydroxy on her neck and face and complaining that everyone called her ma'am.

"I thought she was through with him, too," Margaret said. "Now she tells me she's moving in and when I start asking her about it, she accuses me of nosing into her business. I swear to God, I can't win. Either I'm not there for her—her words—or I'm nosing into her business.''

"She knows she can jerk you around and get away with it.'' Hannah reached into the cabinet for a box of chamomile tea. Easier to analyze her mother's problems than to figure out why she kept looking at the phone and willing it to ring. "Listen, don't we need to get this chicken going?''

"I'll take care of it.'' Margaret removed plastic-wrapped chicken from the fridge and carried it to the stove. "Rose said she had indigestion all night after that last thing you made.''

"Tuna casserole?'' Hannah looked at her mother. "How could she get indigestion from that? I used the same recipe you always use.''

Margaret grinned. "Well, doll-baby, no one ever accused you of being Julia Child. Faith made me promise that I'd never get old because she didn't know who would make the kind of food she likes.''

"Little brat.'' Hannah shook her head. "I tried really hard with those potato skins she wanted.''

"I know.'' Margaret's smile turned conspiratorial. The chicken breasts flattened out on a cutting board, she began slicing them into strips. "Don't worry, Hanny, you have plenty of other talents, my love.''

Feeling disgruntled now, Hannah resisted the urge to ask Margaret to name the other talents. She knew Margaret would list qualities like sweet and generous, which had never struck Hannah as much to crow about. They certainly hadn't been enough to keep Liam interested. Margaret was back on Deb again.

"…and she just didn't sound happy about Dennis, so all I said was I'd like to see her married and she im-

mediately flew off the handle and went on and on about
how she'll get married when she's ready and she's not
about to do something stupid like…well, you know what
I'm saying.''

"Yeah." Hannah put her teabag in a cup of water,
put it in the microwave and stood passively, watching
the seconds count down. She knew only too well. Something stupid like Hannah did when she ran off with Liam
Tully, then compounded the foolishness by marrying
him in a Las Vegas chapel, only to return home three
months pregnant and on her own.

Debra could run off with an Elvis impersonator and
set up housekeeping in a Ralph's supermarket parking
lot and no one would be surprised. But not levelheaded,
dependable Hannah. If she spent the rest of her life in
chaste contemplation, she would never live down what
the family referred to as her Liam Lapse. Her father's
death from a heart attack had been blamed on it and
Margaret, who had never previously touched alcohol,
dated the start of her evening consumption of wine to
that time. "We all suffered," her aunt Helen frequently
reminded her.

"Just talk to Deb, will you?" Margaret asked. "At
least she won't yell at you."

Hannah took her tea from the microwave. The temptation to remind Margaret that it was up to her to work
out her problems with Deb blazed briefly, then died.
Even feeling as she did right now, kind of let down and
confused about Liam coming back, her inclination was
not to cause an argument. Ms. Congeniality, Deb called
her. The downside was that Hannah often did things she
didn't really want to do. Like last Saturday, when she'd
gone with her aunt Rose to the World's Largest Singles
Mixer because Rose hadn't wanted to attend alone.

God, what a nightmare that had been. A guy with a toupee that looked exactly like a small furry animal napping across his scalp had refused to believe Hannah didn't want to dance with him. She'd stood her ground, though, and eventually he and his furry friend had disappeared into the crowd. It wasn't quite so easy to say no to her mother.

"I'll talk to Deb," she said. "This time. After that, you're on your own."

Lately, Hannah reflected, it seemed as if she and her mother had reversed roles. As a kid, Hannah had needed constant reassurance from Margaret that one day boys would pay attention to her, that the pimples would go away and that, as unlikely as it had seemed at the time, she would actually get breasts. Now *she* was constantly doling out reassurances to Margaret and monitoring her mother's wine consumption much as Margaret had once sniffed for signs of teenage drinking. She hoped to God that by the time Faith needed monitoring and reassurance, Margaret would need less.

She decided not to say anything about Liam.

AFTER THE GIG, Liam shoved the sweaty clothes and boots he'd worn during the performance into a duffel bag and joined the other musicians making their way to the bus. The equipment had been packed up and stowed while he and a few of the others had gone next door for a couple of pints. The mike stands, lights and speakers. The guitars and drums, the audio effects and mixing console, T-shirts and merchandise. Packed up, stowed away, ready to start all over again.

In the bus, he sat up front for a while chatting with some of the others, then made his way down the aisle to the lounge in the middle. Yawning, he stretched out on one of the couches, hands pillowed behind his head. As buses went, this one was pretty plush. Microwave cookers and hi-fi. Mood lighting and couches. A far cry from the VW van they'd use in the band's early days. That one had been reliable only for breaking down at least once a day.

But now they were touring internationally. The Wild Rovers, all eight of them. No chartered jets yet, but this wasn't bad. Three days out and, as always, he felt the rhythm beginning to develop. Another day, another town. Pile off the bus, pile onto the bus. Stopping sometimes in the wee hours to traipse into an all-night place in the middle of nowhere for hamburgers and chips. Blinking in the fluorescent lights, bleary-eyed and half-asleep. Then back on the bus, collapsing into the bunk to fall asleep, rocked by the motion of the road. Waking to blinding sunlight creeping in around the black window shades. On the bus, off the bus. Set it up, tear it down. Different day, different town. He loved it. If there was a better way to live, he didn't know about it.

Someone pushed his feet off the seat, and he looked up to see Brid Kelly, long red hair streaming down her back and skin so white that in the murky light of the bus she looked luminous. She had on jeans and a thin sleeveless top. If there'd been enough light, he knew he'd be able make out the outline of every bone in her rib cage. Brid could be a poster child for famine relief. He worried about her and not just—as she sometimes claimed—because he'd never find another singer who understood his music the way she did.

She was holding a large plastic bowl and a beer, which she held out to him.

"Thanks."

She smiled and dropped down beside him. "How you doing, Liam?"

"All right." He sat up and eyed the bowl. "Is that cabbage salad you're eating again?"

"It is." She waved the plastic fork. "D'you want some?"

He drank some beer. "Have you eaten anything but cabbage salad in the last three days?"

"I have." She grinned. "Yesterday, I ate a carrot and three radishes."

He shook his head. She'd nearly collapsed after yesterday's show and he hadn't bought her excuse that it was the heat. "You're a skeleton, already, for God's sake. You'll make yourself ill, the way you're going."

"Ah, come on." With a wave of her hand, she dismissed his concerns. "I'll be fine. Nice and slim for when I walk down the aisle with Tommy Doherty."

"Tommy Doherty." Liam swung his feet back up on the couch and over her lap. "You've been talking about walking down the aisle with Tommy Doherty ever since I've known you."

"This time I mean it. I've had it with all this." She dug her fork into the cabbage. "I'm ready to start making babies."

"Another thing I've heard at least a hundred times."

"Right, well, it's time now."

"I won't hold my breath."

"You'll see, Liam. I've had enough of it. On the road for weeks at a time. What kind of life is it anyway? Always away from your friends and family."

He didn't answer. He'd heard her sing the same song so many times he could recite it by heart. She'd get back to Ireland and insist she was through. They'd have to find a new singer. But then plans for the next tour would get underway, and he'd see her wavering. The truth was, the music was as much a part of her life as it was Liam's. She was every bit as addicted to the life.

"What about you then, Liam? You never feel like putting down roots somewhere? You don't miss being close to someone?"

With an elbow on the windowsill, he watched the road. "If I do," he said, "I take a couple of aspirin until the feeling goes away."

Brid pushed his leg and he turned to smile at her, then went back to watching the white lines flash past. Only one time had he ever considered packing it all in. About six years ago now. A marriage, brief as a blip in time. She'd missed her family, hated the long absences and frenetic craziness of his life. Because he'd loved her, he'd seriously considered settling down. Until he'd found out what she'd done.

He'd channeled his anger into the music and the following year he made the UK charts for the first time. *Betrayed.* That was the name of the single. And now, in a nice bit of irony, his next gig was in her hometown, where it had all started.

CHAPTER TWO

THE DAY AFTER HANNAH read about Liam coming back, she was standing in the kitchen making a salad for dinner when her sister Debra announced that she was pregnant.

"Don't tell Mom," Deb said. "I haven't decided what I'm going to do about it."

"You're kidding." Hannah dropped into the chair opposite her sister.

"Well, God, you don't have to say it like that. It was okay for you to get pregnant but no one else can?"

Hannah held up her hand. She wasn't in the mood for Debra. "If you want to talk," she said, "we'll talk. Otherwise, you can take your damn attitude and leave."

"Zowee." Debra's eyes widened. "Chill out, Hannah. What are you so steamed up about anyway?"

"Nothing."

"Come on." Debra peered at her. "It's something. You had a fight with Allan? You had a fight with Mom? You got fired?"

"For God's sake, Deb." She got up from the table, filled a glass with water from the fridge dispenser and sat down again. "Tell me what's going on with *you.*"

"I missed two periods and I threw up twice this week at work. Dennis freaked when I first told him, but once he got over the shock he thought it was kind of cool. Now he's saying I can move in with him until the baby's born. After that, who knows?"

"What do *you* want to do?"

Debra shrugged. "Not what I'm doing right now, that's for damn sure. 'Hi, my name's Debra,'" she said in a mincing voice. "'And I'll be your waitress tonight.' God. I am so sick of that job. I just want to have a decent job where I'm making some money and I don't have some jerk telling me to push the desserts and smile more. At least if I have the baby, it's something different, plus Dennis is being a whole lot nicer since he found out."

Hannah counted slowly to ten. Where did she even start? She traced the moisture on her glass and looked up at her sister. "What's happening with your classes at State?"

Deb rolled her eyes. "The instructors were such a bunch of idiots, I swear I couldn't even listen to them. I mean, I could learn more from surfing the Internet."

"But you're not going to get a teaching credential that way."

"Don't start on me about that, I've already heard it from Mom."

"Deb." Hannah put her elbows on the table. "You hate working where you are now, you hated working at Marie Callender's, you hated worked at Denny's—"

"Shut up, Hannah." Debra jumped up from the table, stomped over to the pantry in her clunky black waitress shoes and emerged with a bag of Oreos that she ripped open. "You think you've got it all figured out, don't you?" A cookie in one hand, she regarded Hannah as though she'd suddenly recognized something that hadn't been clear before. "You think you're so damn perfect."

Hannah snorted. "Right."

"No, you do. And Mom does, too. I am so sick of hearing how hard *Hannah* worked to get her degree, how wonderful *Hannah's* job is, what a great boyfriend *Han-*

nah has. 'Allan's an *attorney*,'" she said, mimicking Margaret's voice. "'And he lives on Riva Alto Canal and he's just so wonderful and Hannah's so wonderful—'"

"Maybe that's your interpretation, but it's not the way I feel…"

"Yeah, whatever." Debra eased the top off a cookie and bit into the cream filling. "I don't give a damn. Maybe you've got it figured out now, you know damn well the whole reason you got pregnant was to keep Liam around."

"No, I don't know that." Her face suddenly warm, Hannah held Debra's glance. She heard Margaret's car pull into the driveway and lowered her voice. "Look, Deb, having a baby is a huge decision—"

"Well, *duh*…" Debra was up from the table again. "Like I don't know it's my decision, too? God, I don't even know why I try to talk to you. Just because Liam was a jerk doesn't mean all guys are that way."

"Whoa…" Rose walked into the kitchen just as Debra stormed out. "What's the matter with her?"

WHILE MARGARET WORRIED aloud about Debra all through dinner, Hannah thought about Liam. Twenty-eight hours since she'd seen the article. Twenty-eight hours of thinking about practically nothing else. She didn't know his schedule—except for next Friday—but he was somewhere in California and it was making her crazy. Thinking of him in Ireland was one thing, thinking of him maybe just an hour or two away was something else. He *could* call. Of course, he could have called from Ireland, too. But he hadn't called. And he wouldn't call.

"Dennis is not a good influence on Deb," Margaret

was saying now. "I mean a bartender, for God's sake. And he bleaches his hair. What kind of guy would do that?" Her brow furrowed, she dug a fork into the gooey custard on her plate. "What is it with my girls?" she asked, glancing at Helen. "Why is it they both seem to have this thing for irresponsible men?"

"Well, hey, bad boys are more fun, huh, Hannie?" Aunt Rose, in a loose black silk shirt printed with beer bottles from around the world, winked at Hannah. Rose, a cosmetologist, was divorced from her second husband and staying at the house just until she got her credit card bills paid off. She'd recently had her eyelids tattooed with permanent liner because, she confided to Hannah, she hated to wake up beside a man and look washed-out. Rose was absolutely certain Mr. Right would turn up one of these days—for her and for Hannah. Rose had her money on Allan.

Aunt Helen shot Rose a disapproving look. "I'm quite sure that Hannah has already learned her lesson with…immature young men and I have no doubt that, before long, Debra will, too."

The youngest of the three sisters, Helen was small, pink and fair with a large soft bosom and a similarly proportioned bottom. Faith, who adored Helen, once confided to Hannah that hugging Aunt Helen was like hugging a great big marshmallow. Helen taught junior high school and everything she said had a sweetly reasoned tone as if she knew that, even under the most obnoxious and intractable behavior, goodness was just waiting to shine. Helen's husband had died years ago in a freak lightning storm back in Missouri where they'd gone to see his mother. Afterward, Helen had moved into the small guest cottage on Margaret's property and decorated it with Laura Ashley fabrics.

"What about that nice attorney?" Helen asked Hannah now. "Are you still seeing him?"

Rose shot up her hand. "If you're not, I get first dibs."

"Rose," Margaret and Helen said in unison.

"Hey, I like younger men." Rose grinned. "And he lives on Riva Alto Canal. What's not to like? Do your old auntie a favor, Hanny. See if he has an older brother."

"Well…" Helen smiled as if to say that particular subject was over. She looked at Faith. "Listen, sweetie, if you'll go bring me my purse over there on the couch, I've got a little surprise for you." Faith darted across the room and returned with a large canvas bag. "Let's see what we have here." Helen reached into the bag. "*James and the Giant Peach* and *Sleeping Beauty*."

"Oh, wow." All smiles, Faith clutched the books. "My absolute favorites."

"I knew they would be." Helen dropped a kiss on Faith's nose. "Now why don't you run off and read them? The grown-ups want to talk about really boring things." She gave Faith a few moments to leave the room, then produced a newspaper clipping from the bag. "This is probably something we should discuss."

Hannah felt her stomach tense. She watched Margaret, who was sitting next to Helen, reach for the clipping. Waited for the shock to register on her mother's face. The room felt hot and still suddenly. Margaret carefully set the clipping down on the table. Fingers over her lips, she looked at Hannah.

"Did you know Liam was coming back?"

"I just saw the announcement in the paper yesterday." She drank some water. They were all watching her. "It's no big deal, Mom." She looked at Margaret. "Really, don't worry about it."

Margaret drank some wine. "You're not planning to see him, are you?"

"Of course Hannah doesn't want to see him," Helen said.

"Why would Hannah give a hoot about Liam?" Rose asked. "She's got this hotty attorney boyfriend. Liam's ancient history. Right, Hannah?"

"ANY PLANS FOR A WEEK, Saturday?" Allan asked Hannah Wednesday morning when he dropped off his son at La Petite Ecole. "I have symphony tickets."

"Saturday?" She'd been sitting at one of the small painted tables selecting books for the afternoon's story session and she stood so that he wouldn't tower over her. Actually, she could stand on a table and he'd still tower over her. Allan was tall. She wasn't. Flustered now, mostly because next Saturday was Faith's birthday party and she was wavering back and forth about inviting him, she tried to find a way around the question. "Saturday." She frowned as though trying to picture her extensive social calendar. "Let me think."

Allan smiled indulgently. Allan always smiled indulgently. It was one reason she had trouble picturing them walking into the sunset together. That, and he called her "Kiddo." On the plus side, he was thoughtful, patient and sweetly romantic. As her Aunt Rose would say, she could do a lot worse. And, as her mother would add, in a not-too-subtle jab, she already had.

Allan and his ex-wife shared custody of four-year-old Douglas, who was in Hannah's class. A fastidious little boy, Douglas disliked getting his hands dirty and insisted on using a straw to sip his milk because he worried about germs on the glass. She'd been talking to Allan about his son's phobias during a parent-teacher conference and then somehow they'd moved on from Douglas to foreign films and she found herself accepting Allan's invitation to a festival. Half a dozen or so dates later, he was talking about moving in together. She felt him watching her, waiting for an answer.

"Actually, next Saturday is Faith's birthday party," she finally said, because she couldn't think of any way around it. "If you weren't busy…"

His smile broadened. "I'll give the tickets away. I'd love to meet your family and get to know your daughter."

"Well, I'm not sure you'll have much opportunity to get to know her. At last count, I think there were about fifty kids coming."

"Hey, it sounds like fun," he said. "I'm looking forward to it."

She smiled back at him. He really was kind of sweet, even if he didn't exactly make her heart turn over. "Okay, but don't pay any attention to my mother and aunts. They have this thing about me getting married, so they'll start asking you pointed questions about your intentions."

His expression turned thoughtful. "Really?"

"Yeah, so tell them you're just out for a good time and the last thing you'd ever want to do is settle down."

"But what if that's not true?" His eyes searched her face. "What if I tell them you're exactly what I'm looking for?"

"Uh…" She felt her face go warm. "Please don't, okay?"

He smiled. "Are we a little gun-shy, kiddo?"

"Not a little, and Allan…please don't call me

'kiddo.'" She picked at a piece of skin on her finger.
"Look, I screwed up once. I'm not about to jump into
it again."

"Perhaps you just married the wrong guy."

Hannah shrugged. Inviting him had definitely sent the
wrong message, she could see that now.

"One bad apple doesn't mean the whole barrel is
bad." Allan also mangled metaphors. "Any man who
could just turn his back on a daughter like Faith obviously has a severe character flaw. She's a wonderful
young lady."

"You've never even met her," Hannah pointed out.

"She's your daughter. How could she be anything but
wonderful?" With a quick glance over his shoulder, he
kissed Hannah softly on the lips. "And I've always
wanted a daughter."

AFTER ALLAN LEFT, Hannah couldn't get his words out
of her head. *I've always wanted a daughter.* And he
probably would be a terrific father to Faith. Attentive,
conscientious. There for her. Everything her real father
wasn't. With a sigh, she opened the book she'd selected
to read to the kids. A story about a cow who decides to
be an opera singer and moves to New York to take voice
lessons from Placido Domingo. As she held up the book
to show the kids the picture of the cow, all dolled up in
a sequined evening gown and warbling an aria, she
sneaked a quick glance at her watch.

Nearly noon. Right now, Liam was probably setting
up the instruments. No, he'd be sleeping still. Liam always slept late.

"Timothy is picking his nose, Ms. Riley," Morgan
Montgomery said. "It's revolting."

Hannah put aside the book to look at Timothy. He sat

cross-legged on the floor, hands clasped on top of his copper-colored curls, an expression of angelic innocence on his freckled face.

"He was, Ms. Riley. I think I'm going to vomit."

Morgan clutched her stomach dramatically. She had glossy brown hair, a heart-shaped face and, at four, was frighteningly precocious. Her parents were both psychiatrists and when they came to school to discuss Morgan's progress, Hannah always had the feeling they were analyzing her.

"He flicked it at me," she said.

"Did not," Timothy said.

Hannah watched Morgan pick up her floor pillow and move ostentatiously to the opposite side of the room, where she settled back on the floor with a flounce of her GapKids tartan skirt. After a moment, Hannah started reading again. She had discussed Timothy's nose-picking problem with his parents and knew she hadn't handled this latest incident very well. The La Petite Ecole method would have been to engage him in open discussion of social manners, but she felt distracted and irritable and in no mood for talk about boogers. Why the hell did she really want to see Liam?

At noon, she sat with Jen Bailey on the steps in the sun, eating a microwaved Lean Cuisine lunch and watching the kids wrestle around on the grass, hitting each other with paisley-patterned beanbags. Jen was the other teacher for the three-to-four-year-old group. She had cropped burgundy hair and a nose ring and lived in a funky apartment in Huntington Beach with her boyfriend who played in a band and designed surfwear. The only reason Jen was hired, she'd told Hannah, was her fancy degree in French Literature from Vassar.

Dr. Marberry, head of La Petite Ecole, was quite the

snob when it came to fancy academic degrees. She hadn't exactly sniffed at Hannah's Cal State Long Beach credentials but Hannah felt pretty sure one reason she was hired was that her father had, at the time, managed the bank where Dr. Marberry had her business loan.

"I'm thinking about doing something really dumb," she told Jen.

"How dumb?" Jen asked.

"Really, really." Hannah hacked at a piece of glazed chicken. "I want you to talk me out of it, okay?"

"You told Allan you'd move in with him?"

"Dumber." She mashed the back of her fork into the overcooked wild rice. "Faith's father is in Long Beach. He's playing at Fiddler's Green next week. I want to see him."

"Faith's father?" Jen turned to look at her. "I thought he lived in Ireland."

"He does. He's here on tour."

"Cool." Jen jumped up to stop Timothy from flicking a booger at Morgan. "Someone needs a time-out," she told him. "Please go and sit in time-out, Timothy, and think about why you need to do this." She dropped down on the step beside Hannah. "So he called you?"

"No, I read about it in the paper." Admitting aloud that Liam hadn't even bothered to call her made her stomach tense. "It's crazy, I know it. I mean, I can come up with a dozen reasons why I shouldn't, but I want to. Tell me it's a bad idea, okay?"

BUT JEN HAD THOUGHT a Friday evening at Fiddler's Green, drinking beer and listening to Irish music sounded like a hoot. In fact, she wanted to go, too. And Friday also happened to be Grandma's Night Out, a weekly excuse for Margaret to shamelessly indulge Faith with ice cream, movies, or whatever Faith wanted to do. Indulgence, Margaret always said, was part of the fun of being a grandma. Bottom line, it removed not having a baby-sitter as a reason to stay home and watch a cheesy movie instead of standing here in the Fiddler's Green washroom twenty minutes before the performance and feeling sick to her stomach with nerves at the thought of seeing Liam again.

Actually, Margaret hadn't even mentioned Liam as they all ate breakfast that morning. Hannah guessed that Debra's call, just as Margaret was pouring her second cup of coffee, had been a sufficient distraction. As soon as she heard Margaret utter the word *pregnant,* Hannah had gathered up Faith and made a quick retreat. Margaret and Debra could manage their problems on their own, she'd decided.

Damn. She looked at herself in the mirror. Why hadn't she worn something a little more hip than khakis and a white shirt? She rolled the sleeves up, undid another button, peered at her face. She screamed suburbia. Light brown hair cut in this wispy, tousled style around her face. "Blow and go," said the girl who had cut it. Easy and practical.

It had been white-blond and nearly down to her waist the last time she'd seen Liam. She'd bleached it herself one night while he was performing. The girls who were always hanging around his dressing room and throwing flowers up on the stage all had long white-blond hair. He'd been furious with her for doing it. "I thought you'd like it," she'd said.

It no longer matters, she told herself as she dug in her purse for a lipstick, dropping scraps of paper and grocery receipts and a stale Famous Amos cookie still in its crumpled foil wrapper into the washbasin. *You have*

*moved on from Liam Tully. Way, way on. You do not
care about Liam Tully. You have no emotional investment in Liam Tully. You have moved on. Look at me!*
She looked at her reflection again. *You are attractive,
you are well-adjusted and, Hannah, you are calm.*

Right. Deep breath. God, this lipstick was too dark.
She grabbed a paper towel from the holder, scrubbed it
across her mouth, dug around in her purse for a different
color and knocked her compact off the edge of the sink.
The mirror shattered into a cobweb of silver spikes.

Back at the table, she gulped down half a glass of
wine. Their table was closer to the stage than she would
have preferred, but the place was small and already
packed when they arrived.

Liam would see her.

There was no way he couldn't see her. Maybe she
should leave. On the other hand, maybe he wouldn't
even recognize her. *What if he didn't recognize her?* She
drained the glass and glanced at the door. Jen gave her
a quizzical look.

"You okay?"

"I don't know. I'm thinking this wasn't such a great
idea."

"You still have a thing for him?"

"No way." She picked up her glass, remembered
she'd finished the wine and glanced around for the cock-
tail waitress. "How could I? I haven't seen him for six
years. I don't even know why I'm doing this."

"How come you guys split up?"

Hannah picked at the edge of the coaster. "Jealousy."

"You or him?"

Hannah laughed. "What did he have to be jealous of?
I was this mopey, insecure, basket case. Whenever I
think about being married to him, all I remember is lying

awake in some apartment or hotel room, watching the clock, waiting for him to come home. Then he'd come in smelling like perfume.''

"He cheated on you?"

"I never caught him, but…" She traced the rim of her wineglass as she considered Jen's question. "There was so much temptation all around, how could he not?"

"So how long did you know him before you got married?"

"Not long. I met him in Ireland." She smiled. "God, I was so…smitten. We had this whirlwind thing and then I went back home. He told me all this stuff, he'd call, he'd write, but nothing. And then one day he just knocked at the door. I was blown away."

"He came over just to see you?"

"Not just to see me. He was on a six-week tour of California, all these small clubs and college campuses up and down the coast. He asked if I wanted to go with him. *Did I want to go with him?* It was like this fantasy. I'd wake up every morning beside him and pinch myself to make sure I wasn't dreaming."

"So who's idea was it to get married?"

"I can't even remember. Probably mine, but it was one of those spur-of-the-moment things. We just decided to do it. No thought about the future, or him going back to Ireland. It was all just in the moment. For a while, anyway."

"So what went wrong?"

"I guess we didn't really know each other. Everything was fine while it was this big adventure, but then that started to wear off…. When I look back on it, it feels as though I woke up one day and the dream was over. He was totally into his music and I sort of tagged along. There were always girls fawning over him. I'd wonder why he was with me when he could have any woman he wanted. And then I found out I was pregnant and the dream really *was* over.''

"He didn't want to be a daddy, huh?"

"Well, it wasn't just him. He had to go back to Ireland and he expected me to go with him…. I mean, he wanted me to go, or I thought he did, but the idea of having the baby so far away from home terrified me. Plus, he didn't really seem ready to settle down—"

"Yeah, that's like Rocky." Jen lit a cigarette. "I mean there's no way he's ready to do the family thing."

Hannah nodded sympathetically, although she was pretty sure Jen wasn't in any hurry to go the kids-and-suburbia route either. The difference was that Jen and Rocky were in agreement. Jen understood what Rocky wanted, recognized his limitations. With Liam, she'd always had this idea that he would magically turn into a responsible father figure. She'd wanted it so much she couldn't see that it was clearly not what Liam had wanted.

"Everything probably turned out for the best," she said. "Faith's really happy and well-adjusted, and…" The lights dimmed and the crowd was looking expectantly at the stage. Her heart started banging so hard she felt dizzy.

Transfixed, she watched a slim dark-haired guy in black jeans and shirt walk slowly across the stage, his face caught in the white pool of a spotlight. *Liam.* Without a glance at the audience, he sat down on the stool, picked up a guitar and began to sing.

"Wow." Jen leaned close to whisper in Hannah's ear. "What a babe."

SOME SHOWS WERE MAGIC, Liam knew that. The energy of the crowd, the music, voices from the audience singing along, filling the room until it literally seemed they could raise the roof. Others never really got off the ground. Something was missing. He would go through the motions, sing the songs that had always worked, but the magic wasn't there. Before he'd finished the first set, he knew that tonight was one of those times.

"Thanks." He smiled out at the audience, acknowledging the subdued applause. The club was smaller than most they'd played on this tour, the crowd jammed against the far wall or seated at the small tables in front. Intimate, but the lighting made it difficult to pick out faces.

"It's good to be in California again," he said, trying to warm them up. "You've some very strange weather here. That hot wind as though the devil himself is breathing down your neck. We've nothing like it back home. Except for my dog's breath, that is."

Polite laughter. He glanced over his shoulder, nodded to Brid to join him. Worrying about her wasn't exactly helping things. Half an hour earlier she'd had another fainting spell and he'd thought they might have to cancel the show, but she'd insisted she was fine. As she came over to stand beside him, he felt the crowd respond to her as they always did. Smiling, he held out his hand to her.

"A few years back," he told the audience, "I met a beautiful woman who completely changed my life. Brid Kelly." This time the applause was much louder. From the back of the room, someone whistled.

And then they held hands to sing a song they'd written together. Face-to-face, bodies swaying. She had on a filmy white dress that he'd joked looked like the lace curtains in his auntie's parlor, but it swirled around her and her red hair streamed all over her back and shoulders and she looked as if she'd just floated down from a cloud to join him.

She smiled into his eyes as they sang and he knew that at least half the audience would decide they were lovers. The press back home had come to pretty much the same conclusion, which meant that whenever he was seen with another woman, he was accused of cheating on Brid. It didn't exactly make for long-lasting relationships. Brid found the whole thing hilarious. "You're like my brother, for God's sake," she'd say. Still the stories persisted. Finally, he'd stopped trying to deny them.

They did a couple more songs together and then he brought Brid's hand to his lips and the audience applauded enthusiastically. As they broke for intermission, he heard a crash from the side of the room and looked over to see what was going on. A woman in a hurry to leave the room had toppled one of the small tables, sending glasses crashing to the floor.

"Obviously not a fan," he said with a grin at Brid as they left the stage.

HER HEART THUNDERING, Hannah stood in the lobby, back against the wall, waiting for Jen to come out of the rest room. All she wanted now was to get the hell out. Forget the second act. She'd seen all she needed to see.

At that moment Liam walked through the swinging doors of the bar and looked straight into her eyes. Her brain froze. Had he recognized her? His eyes flickered and widened.

"Hannah?" He shook his head slightly. "Hannah. My God, I don't believe—"

"Hi, Liam." Suddenly she didn't know what to do with her hands. Liam. She was talking to Liam. Close enough to touch him. His hair was different. Shorter, trendily mussed on top. A few lines around his eyes that hadn't been there before. Wiry still, with the same street-smart look that used to excite her, even though she'd never seen him in as much as a scuffle. Her parents, sensing the same quality, had been less enamored of it. He wore a watch now—something he hadn't done then—with a heavy black leather strap. Other than that, he looked pretty much as he had the night she had told him she was pregnant.

God, she couldn't think of a thing to say. None of the dreams she'd had of what she'd do if she ever saw him again—what she'd say, how she'd look—had her just standing there, tongue-tied.

She found herself studying his mouth, something vulnerable about his upper lip that had always gotten to her; the lower lip she'd once taken in her teeth. How was she supposed to talk calmly and rationally to him? The bar was emptying, people milling around, talking in clusters. The red-haired singer and a couple of the band members drifted by, cast glances at Liam, then at her, and disappeared. Jen emerged from the washroom, started over, saw Liam and stopped. With a wave at Hannah, she made her way back through the swinging doors.

"So…" Liam nodded slightly. "It's been…how long?"

"Six years…thereabouts."

"I didn't recognize you at first." He kept watching her, as though he were cataloging the changes the years had produced. "The last time I saw you, your hair was down past your waist."

"It's been short for a long time now," she said. "Easier to take care of." He nodded again, his gaze fixed on her. Self-conscious under his scrutiny, she touched her hair, remembered how he'd always liked it long. All her old insecurities were bubbling away just below the surface. She'd been thinner then. Younger. Was he thinking that? Comparing her to the redhead? Damn it, what did it matter what he thought? Someone with a hell of a lot more going for him than Liam Tully wanted to marry her. That said something, didn't it?

"So why are you here?" Thumbs hooked into the pockets of his jeans, he rocked slightly on his feet. "You've developed a taste for Irish music you didn't have a few years back? Is that it?"

"I've always liked Irish music, Liam." Her face went warm. "That wasn't one of our problems."

"Right." His mouth hardened, then he glanced over his shoulder at the double doors to the bar. "Well, I hear the band starting up again. I'd better get back. Good to see you again."

Stunned, she stared at him. He looked so much like Faith, it was unnerving. His mouth curved exactly like hers so that even when they were serious, a smile always seemed to be lurking. The identical way they both held their heads off to the side, a little quizzical. The same dark, dramatic brows. A total stranger would immediately see the resemblance. How could he not even care enough to ask?

"Nothing changes, does it?" The words shot out before she could think about them. "Music always came first. Obviously it still does. Your daughter's doing fine, by the way."

He stared at her. "My daughter."

"Your daughter. Who will be six on Saturday. Probably just slipped your mind, huh?"

"You had an abortion," he said.

"An abortion?" She blinked. "What are you talking about?"

"Your mother told me you had an abortion."

"My mother?" Incredulous, she gaped at him. "My mother told you I had an abortion?"

"The day you told me you were pregnant," he said, his voice devoid of inflection. "You were more than a bit upset about it. Something about being too young for the responsibility, as I recall. We had a fight and you left. When you didn't come home that night, I went to see your mother. You'd gone away, she said, but she wouldn't tell me where. The impression she gave me was that you were off having an abortion somewhere."

"My God, Liam. I...I can't believe this. There was never any discussion about an abortion. Why would my mother tell you that?"

"Obviously that's a question you should ask her," he said. Then he turned and walked back into the bar.

CHAPTER THREE

AFTER THE SHOW, there was a party at a big house on the beach. The friend of a friend of a friend. Liam stood out on the deck drinking a beer and watching the palm trees and the play of lights on the water while the festivities roared on in the lighted room behind him. The music had turned Paddywhack Irish, a great deal of whooping and diddly-diddly dooing. Mick, the Wild Rovers' fiddler, had launched into "McNamara's Band," a tune he would never deign to play sober, and the accompanying clapping and foot stomping was so enthusiastic, Liam could feel the vibration under his feet.

He had a daughter. He repeated the words to himself, trying to make them seem real. A daughter. And he didn't even know her name. Hadn't asked her name.

"I have a daughter," he told Brid when she came to see what he was doing out there all by himself.

"God, they're banging saucepan lids in there." She cupped her hand around her ear. "You have a what?"

"A daughter."

Brid looked at him for a moment, then disappeared and returned a moment later with a plate of carrots. With a nod, she directed him down to the far end of the deck, away from the noise. "All right, what's this about?"

"That girl I was talking to tonight." He drank some beer. "We were married for about a year. She got pregnant, and I thought she'd had an abortion. Tonight she tells me that wasn't so. Apparently, her mother lied to me.''

Brid leaned her elbows on the railing, staring out at the water. ''So this girl,'' she said after a minute, ''what's her name?''

''Hannah.'' Actually, he'd always called her Hannie. Now he thought of her as Hannah. He eyed the plate of carrots. ''You didn't eat any of the barbecue stuff?''

She wrinkled her nose. ''The chicken had a sweet sauce all over it, and I don't eat beef. So Hannah didn't know what her mother was telling you?''

''That's what she claims.'' He forced his mind away from Hannah and her news. ''Brid, you're worrying me with this food thing. There's enough in there to feed an army. If you don't like the chicken, find something else. Some bread or cheese or something.''

''For God's sake, Liam.'' She tossed the carrot she'd picked up onto the sand. ''What's it to you what I eat? You're getting on my nerves, always watching me.''

''Who will, if I don't? You're not exactly doing much of a job yourself.''

''I'm fine. Leave off, will you? I swear, you're like the bloody food police.''

Liam said nothing. Inside, they were singing ''The Belle of Belfast City'' and someone yelled for Brid to join them. She glanced over her shoulder but didn't answer. Moments passed and then she put her arm around his shoulders, pressed him close.

''Sorry.''

He shrugged. She was a grown woman and it wasn't his role to watch over her, but he couldn't help how he felt.

''Do you believe that she didn't know?'' Brid asked.

''I'm not sure.'' His thoughts back on Hannah's

bombshell, he picked at a bit of peeling paint on the railing. "You'd have to know her family. When one of them sneezes, the others not only know about it, they're there with hankies and cough mixture. Hannah was always close to them. I can't believe she didn't know all about her mother's conversation with me."

"But she came to the club to see you," Brid pointed out. "And she told you about your daughter. If she'd wanted you to think she'd had an abortion, why would she do that?"

Liam looked at her. Brid had a point. On the other hand, if Hannah wasn't in on it, why had she never tried to communicate with him? She'd never sent so much as a single picture. Nothing. A daughter—and he had no idea what she looked like.

"It sounds to me as though the mother was trying to get rid of you," Brid said. "Probably thought the abortion thing would do it."

He considered. It wasn't hard to imagine Margaret's thinking. The family—to put it mildly—had never been particularly fond of him. Being a musician was bad enough, being an Irish musician was worse. Easy enough to imagine their thinking. He would take Hannah back to Ireland, leave her barefoot and pregnant in an unheated shack while he traipsed off around the world drinking and womanizing. Maybe they'd thought rescuing her from him was their only option.

"Did you love her?"

He shrugged.

"Come on, Liam. It's me, Brid."

"I used to."

"Not anymore?"

"I don't know. It's been a long time."

She laughed. "You should see yourself. Furiously

picking the paint off the wood because this whole thing makes you squirm, doesn't it? Talking about feelings?''

"'Feelings,'" he sang, trying to distract her. There *was* nothing he hated more than rambling on about what was going on in his head. It was one of the things he and Hannah used to fight about. She was always trying to drag him into long, drawn-out talks. "Tell me what you're thinking," she'd say. "Tell me you love me. Why is it so hard for you to say it?"

He eased off another chip of paint, realized what he was doing and stopped. Hannah. He'd spent years hating her for what she'd done, or what he thought she'd done. Seeing her tonight was…he couldn't believe it. She looked different…great, really. Enormous green eyes and a wee little face. He used to pull her leg about looking like a kitten. Now she looked all grown-up. The way you'd expect the mother of a six-year-old to look, he supposed.

"What now, then?" Brid asked. "What will you do?"

"I don't know. I'm still trying to get used to the idea I'm a father."

"Does she know about you? Your daughter, I mean?"

"I've no idea what they've told her."

Brid lit a cigarette, waved out the match and tossed it onto the sand. "Want to know what I think you should do?"

He grinned. "Have I a choice?"

"No." She spoke through a cloud of blue smoke. "If you've any sense, you'll forget tonight ever happened. Getting involved will only cause trouble. The child's here. You're in Ireland. Music is your life. You spend half of it on the road and you know nothing at all about being a daddy."

"That's your opinion, is it?"

"It is. But from the look on your face, I've the feeling I might as well be talking to the wind. You'll regret it though, Liam. I'm telling you. You're not a daddy sort of fellow."

HANNAH STOOD OUTSIDE her mother's bedroom, trying to tell from the sounds inside whether Margaret was sleeping. The house had been in darkness when she got home from Fiddler's Green. A note from Margaret on the kitchen table said she'd dropped Faith off at a friend's house for a slumber party. Hannah raised her hand to knock, then stopped. Back in her own room, she sat on the bed. Maybe she needed to sort things out in her own mind before she spoke to Margaret.

Including why seeing Liam tonight made her want to run around locking windows and doors. She got up, went down to the kitchen and microwaved a cup of chamomile tea, carried it up to her room and set it on the bedside table. Fully dressed, she lay down on the bed. Even in the familiar security of her room, she felt shaky and anxious, as though the stability of her life had been physically threatened.

Jen had advised her to move out immediately. "Your mother lied to you, Hannah. She told Liam you'd had an abortion. There's no way you can go on living there."

Most parents really only want to do what's best for their children.

However misguided their motives. How many times had she had to remind herself of that when dealing with the parents of her students? But she hadn't been a child. How was she ever supposed to trust Margaret again? She picked up the phone to call Deb. Changed her mind and set it down. Swung her legs off the bed and wandered over to the window. Stared out at the dark night.

The room overlooked the rose garden her father had started shortly after she was born. There were something like thirty or forty plants out there. He would mark special occasions with a new variety. She'd lost count of all the roses planted for her and Deb. A pink Tiffany when she graduated from high school, a yellow one whose name she could never remember when she got her degree from Cal State. Three or four, all white, to mark Faith's various milestones.

The only occasion never commemorated with roses was her marriage to Liam. When she'd asked her dad about it, he'd said something about poor-quality roses that year, but she knew the real reason.

Liam. His music still played in her head, but the evening had already taken on a dreamlike quality. One minute he'd been there, close enough to touch. And then he was gone. Elusive as smoke.

It had always been that way with Liam. She'd met him during a trip to Ireland, a birthday present from her parents. He'd been playing in a Galway club that she'd wandered into one evening. During a break in the session, he'd come over to talk to her. He'd quoted poetry, made her laugh, hummed songs in her ear. Looking back, she knew she'd fallen in love with him that night.

Still, she'd left the club never expecting to see him again. The next morning her landlady had knocked on her door to say she had a caller. Barefoot, in a red tartan robe, she'd walked out to the top of the stairs. Liam stood at the foot, smiling in the pale sunlight, a bunch of daisies in his hand.

On her last day in Ireland, the countryside had bloomed with hawthorn hedges and primrose and the air had smelled of mowed hay and turf smoke. They'd taken a boat to Clare Island and stayed until dark. On the beach, with the moon beaming down on them, they'd made love. Afterward she'd looked up at the crescent of a new moon, like a fairy tiara in the dark sky; watched the silvery light on Liam's face. Felt the fine sand slip between her fingers.

They'd kissed goodbye at the airport and, despite all his promises to stay in touch, she'd again had the feeling that this was it. That as magical and wonderful as the whole experience had seemed, it wasn't quite real. Like trying to hold on to the memory of a dream. But, once more, Liam had surprised her. The day she'd opened the door to see him standing there had been as mind-blowing as opening the paper to see his picture. "Come with me," he'd said.

In a celebratory mood after a show one night, they'd driven to Las Vegas. The wedding chapel was so hideously tacky, they'd both dissolved into fits of laughter. As they walked back out into the garish night, Liam had dumped a bag of silver paper horseshoes on her head. Her father had been incensed. Margaret had cried for days, a mini nervous breakdown, according to Helen.

After Liam went back to Ireland, the family quietly and efficiently fixed up the wreckage of her life. A family friend had taken care of the divorce. Helen had arranged the job at La Petite Ecole. The nursery, where Faith had slept until she was five, had been decorated by Margaret and her sisters who, when Faith decided she was too old for rainbows and kittens, had redecorated it to look like a tree house.

Liam's name was seldom mentioned and, except for Faith, it sometimes seemed to Hannah that she'd dreamed the whole relationship.

Until tonight. She got up from the bed, padded out into the hallway and tapped on her mother's door. Nothing. She started to knock again, then stopped. It was nearly one. Margaret would be groggy. Better to wait.

THE NEXT MORNING, Saturday, Hannah doubled her usual three-mile run. At the bottom of Termino, she glanced both ways at the traffic then sprinted across Livingstone Drive and Ocean Boulevard, past La Petite Ecole, around the end of the pier and the new Belmont Shore Brewery with its ocean-view patio; down along the footpath that paralleled the edge of the beach.

She'd started running soon after Faith was born, and her route never varied. A sprint along the beach then up the slope that led to the art museum on Ocean Boulevard, twice around Bixby Park where, as kids, she and Debra had been taken by their parents to hear Sunday afternoon concerts on the grass, then back down the slope for the return trip.

Helen and Rose had given her an expensive headset for her last birthday so that she could listen to music while she ran. She'd used it a couple of times, but preferred the natural fugue of ocean sounds: the steady crash of the waves, the screeches and coos of gulls and pigeons and the slap of her feet on the asphalt.

These morning runs were hers alone, a time to think. Anything, from musings on what she'd eat for lunch to more profound matters such as whether she really wanted to spend the rest of her life teaching overprivileged and precocious four-year-olds.

This morning, her thoughts were dominated by Liam.

When she jogged up Termino twenty minutes later, she could see her mother outside the house, down on her knees, using a trowel to dig around the bird-of-paradise plants along the steps leading up to the front door. Margaret saw her and leaned back on her heels, trowel in hand.

"Damn nasturtiums, they run wild." Margaret gestured with the trowel at the offending pale green tendrils. "Every year I pull them all out, and every year they come back more than before. God knows why your father ever planted them in the first place."

Panting from her run, Hannah looked at the pile of orange calendulas and green nasturtium leaves her mother had yanked out. Neither plant, in Margaret's opinion, was in keeping with the Spanish architectural style of the house and she waged an ongoing and futile battle to eradicate them. Hannah bent and picked half a dozen blooms. "We need to talk, Mom," she said.

Still on her knees, Margaret glanced up. "Debra called this morning. I guess you know she's pregnant."

Hannah nodded. Dennis had refused to put Deb on the phone when Hannah called earlier.

"Now she's saying Dennis doesn't want her to have the baby. She's come back here with her suitcases." Margaret gathered up the discarded plants and dumped them into the trash can at the side of the house. She ran her hands down the sides of her sweats, brushed the back of her arm across her face. "I don't think she has the vaguest notion of what she really wants—"

"Mom, I don't want to talk about Debra right now."

Margaret eyed her warily.

"I saw Liam last night." Arms folded across her chest, she looked at her mother. Margaret's face was unreadable, her eyes hidden by the baseball cap she wore, but Hannah sensed that there was a battle brewing. "I don't even know where to start," she said.

"Then don't, okay?" Margaret's stance mirrored Hannah's, arms folded, feet slightly apart. "I've got enough on my mind with Debra. I don't need you giving me a hard time about something that happened years ago.''

Hannah stared at her mother, incredulous.

''I know for sure I'm not paying for her to have an abortion,'' Margaret said, ''but she's so headstrong, I don't even want to think what she might try. Rose and Helen are in there talking to her now. I had to come outside, I couldn't listen to her anymore. This is my grandchild she's casually talking about destroying.''

''For God's sake, Mom. This isn't about you. It's about Debra and what she needs to do for herself.'' Hannah took some deep breaths. Debra could fight her own battles. ''You lied to Liam.''

Margaret looked at her for a moment. ''You know what, Hannah? I don't intend to discuss this with you. I've got enough on my mind.'' She started for the house. ''Helen put a coffee cake in the oven and it's probably done now. It's a new recipe she clipped from the *Times*. You mix up sour cream and—''

''Damn it.'' Hannah grabbed her mother's arm. ''You are not just walking off. I want some answers.''

''Why don't you tell me what's really wrong?'' Margaret jerked her arm from Hannah's grasp. ''I've never seen you so worked up.''

''You told Liam I'd had an abortion, Mom. That's what's really wrong. Do you even realize the consequences of what you did? By lying to him—''

''Okay, Hannah, we've covered the lying issue. Let's talk about the consequences of your going to see him last night. Let's talk about the fact that he now wants to take Faith back to Ireland.''

''What?''

''He called this morning while you were running.''

"He said he was taking Faith back to Ireland?"

"Not in so many words. He said he wants to talk to you. But it's like Rose was saying, he's a troublemaker. If he tries to get Faith… Well, Helen gave me the name of an attorney who specializes in this sort of thing. When you've calmed down a bit, we need to give him a call."

"Mom." Hannah held her hands to her face for a moment, then took them away. "I don't believe this, I just don't believe it. You lied to Liam, deprived him of his daughter. Deprived Faith of her father and *you're* talking about legal action?"

Rose called from the kitchen, and Margaret glanced up at the house. "I'll be there in a minute," she said. "Listen, Hannah…" Her voice broke, and she swiped at her nose with the back of her hand. "Don't make me the enemy, okay? Any of us. Helen, Rose—"

"So they were in on it, too?"

"Don't say it like that. We were out of our minds with worry about you. Your father, too, to the point that it killed him. Imagine how you'd feel if Faith's life was in danger. Wouldn't you do whatever it took to save her?"

"Faith's a child, Mom. I was a grown woman. It's not quite the same thing."

"We found you walking along the side of the freeway," Margaret said. "Distraught, irrational, talking about killing yourself. And for what? For a fly-by-night musician, a womanizing jerk who wasn't aware enough to recognize the state you were in."

"That still didn't give you the right to lie. To me, or to Liam."

"To hell with Liam." Margaret's voice rose. "Liam isn't my concern. You are. You're my daughter and I was scared to death for you. You were clinically depressed. That's the term the doctor used. Maybe it was wrong, maybe I should have stayed out of it and just thrown up my hands and said 'oh well,' but I couldn't do it. If you're mad at me, so be it.''

"Margaret," Rose yelled from the doorway. "Hannie. Come and have some coffee cake. Debra has something to tell you." She winked at Margaret. "Good news."

"Come on, sweetie." Margaret touched Hannah's arm. "Please understand that this worked out for the best. You're happy now. You've got your life back together. Faith's happy. All of this other stuff is in the past. Just let it go. It's not important."

Hannah shook her head. What was the point? Her mother absolutely couldn't see the enormity of what she'd done.

"Hannie." Margaret peered into her eyes. "Please tell me you're not going to see him again. What possible good can come out of that?"

"Liam deserves a chance to know his daughter, that's all I know. And I'm going to see that he gets it."

THE DOCTOR IN THE E.R. had a high forehead and a pinched-looking mouth and he wanted to know if Brid was Liam's wife. Dazed and groggy from too little sleep and God knows how many black coffees, Liam shook his head.

"No, but I'm her best friend."

The doctor raised a brow. "Then you should have gotten treatment for her long before this."

Liam swallowed the words he'd been about to say. He didn't like this doctor with his condescending attitude. He was in a foul enough mood that it was all he could do not to pick up the little prat by the lapels of his starched white coat. He'd been on the phone with Hannah's mother when someone yelled out that Brid had collapsed. In an instant he'd dropped the phone and, ignoring Brid's protests, had driven her to the emergency room.

"What are you?" the doctor asked. "Some kind of band?"

"That's right," Liam said. "Some kind of band."

"She said you're on tour."

"She's right," Liam said. "How is she?"

"She needs treatment," the doctor said. "She has an eating disorder. I'd suggest you get her into some kind of program or she won't be doing much touring anymore."

"AH, THAT'S A LOAD OF COD," Brid said when Liam told her what the doctor had said. "I've let myself get a bit run-down, that's all. I'll start taking my vitamins again." She sat up on the narrow cot, reached for the tie at the neck of the cotton hospital robe. "Now, clear out of here, Liam, while I find my clothes. We've got a show tonight."

"The show's canceled tonight," he told her. "Probably the next few nights, too. No more shows until you're well enough."

"CANCELED?" Hannah stared at the bartender, who was polishing glasses in the dimly lit main room of Fiddler's Green. A couple of guys sitting at the bar looked her way then returned their attention to the televised basketball game. "But I thought they were supposed to be here for three nights."

"They were." The bartender picked up another glass. "One of them called a while ago to say the girl singer was sick. Strung out on drugs, or something, would be my guess. Anyway, tonight's going to be karaoke.''

Hannah bit her lip. Okay, this was a sign. A warning that maybe her mother was right. Maybe nothing good could come from seeing him again. Margaret had been crying when Hannah left the house. ''Think of what's best for Faith,'' Margaret had begged her. ''That's exactly what I intend to do,'' she'd replied.

Now she wasn't so sure. What was the point of having Liam breeze in and out of Faith's life? And why risk all the rebuilding she'd done of her own life? Why upset everyone and everything? Because she owed it to him. Simple as that. He'd been lied to and the least she could do was try to make some kind of amends.

''Do you have any idea where I can find him?'' she asked the bartender.

''Him?'' The bartender grinned. ''The singer? Liam something or other?''

She nodded and felt her face heat up. God, this was embarrassing. ''Look, it's not what you're thinking…''

''Hey.'' He flicked the towel across the top of the bar. ''I'm not paid to think. All I can tell you is what I told the other girls who came in asking about him. I think the band's staying at some place in Huntington Harbor.

Hannah checked the urge to ask, *What other girls? How many other girls?* Liam had always drawn girls. Well, so what? He could bed a different girl every night, and she wouldn't care.

''Do you have the address?'' she asked.

''Yeah…'' The bartender grabbed a napkin and drew a map of Huntington Harbor. ''There's a party there tomorrow, that's how I know where they are. Huge house on the water with a yacht the size of the *Queen Mary* on the dock outside. Some big cheese from L.A. owns

the place. A record promoter, or something." He
winked. "Told me to invite hot-looking chicks."

Go home, Hannah thought. You don't need this.

"Hell…" With a sigh, he threw down the pen he'd
been using and reached for another one. "I should probably photocopy these damn directions." He handed her
the napkin. "You'll probably have to take a number."

"BRID WILL BE FINE, Liam." Miranda Payton, the record
producer's wife, sat next to him, feet dangling in a pool
that had been built to look like a tropical lagoon. "I sent
my own daughter to Casa Pacifica when I realized she
was spending half her life in the bathroom with her finger stuck down her throat. They straightened her out in
no time. Quit worrying about her and enjoy yourself."
She brought a frosted glass to her lips, eyed him over
the rim and smiled. "You could be in a lot worse
places."

Liam laughed. An understatement if he'd ever heard
one. Beyond the purple bougainvillea-covered wall that
separated the property from the private beach, he could
see the Pacific Ocean. The sun was hot on his back, and
Miranda had brought out a jug of something icy that
tasted like rum and bananas. The exotic scent of it mingled with the suntan lotion she was massaging into her
legs. If he had to take a week off in the middle of a
tour, this definitely wasn't a bad place to while away the
time. Certainly none of the band had complained. A couple of them were off taking surfing lessons, the others
had gone to see the sights.

He'd thought about calling Hannah again. Thought
constantly about his daughter, whose name he still didn't
know. Off on a trip, Hannah's mother had said. Another lie?

"You're *soooo* serious." Miranda trailed one perfectly manicured fingernail down his arm. "Are you always this way?"

"Always," Liam said. "A right wet blanket, that's me. I cast a pall on any party I go to."

Miranda laughed with disproportionate enthusiasm. "I don't believe you. I think you're just deep."

"Wrong," Liam said. "Shallow as a puddle. Ask anyone who knows me." He reached for his shirt. Miranda was making him uneasy. She was about forty, thin, tan and attractive in what Brid would call a high-maintenance way. Lots of curly hair streaked in different shades of blond, plum-colored lips and nails. She was Bert Payton's third wife, considerably younger and obviously bored. Which definitely wasn't his problem. He got up and started for the house.

Miranda followed him. Her hand at the small of his back, they made their way through the open French doors into the blue-and-white living room just as a housekeeper was leading Hannah into the room through a door off the hallway.

Startled, they all eyed each other. Hannah's focus went from Miranda, who was clutching her bikini top as though she'd been caught in risqué underwear, to Liam's opened shirt and bathing trunks.

Hannah had on a short, sleeveless cotton dress patterned with small pink and orange flowers. Her hair was pulled back in a band and she looked young and a little uncertain. He wanted to tell her the thing with Miranda wasn't what she thought it was, which was a bit stupid because he had no idea what she thought and what difference did it make anyway?

He started to speak just as Hannah did, and then Miranda chimed in and there was a flurry of introductions. Hannah, he noticed, was avoiding eye contact with him.

"I wanted to talk to you." She addressed his left shoulder. "If this isn't a good time…"

"It's fine." He looked at Miranda, who fluttered her fingers at him and disappeared. "So…" He waved at the cluster of wicker armchairs upholstered in blue canvas. "Pick a seat." She did and he sat down opposite her. Music drifted in from somewhere in the house. Hannah sat with her knees close together, her hands in her lap. A silence hung in the air between them, thick with ghosts and recriminations. Hannah. Hannie. Hannah. Formal as a stranger now.

She cleared her throat. "Look, I just want to explain—"

"What's her name?" he asked. "What's my daughter's name?"

"Faith."

Faith. He said it again to himself. Then he looked at Hannah. "Why? Where did that come from?"

"When I was in the hospital having her…everything seemed so hopeless. You'd walked out—well, I thought you had—and my world was falling apart. And then I saw her and…" Her face colored. "I know it sounds kind of hokey, but she gave me the faith to believe in myself again."

He leaned his head against the high back of the wicker chair and stared up at the white-painted ceiling beams. So many questions were rattling around in his brain. Where to start? Finally he looked back at Hannah.

"Do you have any pictures with you?"

She pulled an envelope from her bag and handed it to him.

"She looks like me," he said after he'd studied the

first one. "A right little terror, I bet." He looked to Hannah for confirmation.

She smiled. "She can be pretty strong willed."

Slowly he leafed through the stack. Pictures of a baby Faith in a cradle, on a rug gazing wide-eyed at a Christmas tree. School pictures of a little girl, smiling obediently for the camera. A snapshot—recent, he guessed—of Faith riding a red bike. Laughing, the wind in her hair. Unable not to, he smiled at the image. God, how incredible to look at this child and see his own face reflected in hers. And yet, beneath the wonder, an old anger, smoldering now with new intensity. She'd been stolen from him.

He should have been there. He should have been the one teaching her to ride the bloody bike, not sitting here now looking at pictures. They'd stolen her from him, robbed him of her childhood. And then a voice in his head spoke up. *Ah, catch yourself,* it scoffed. *Can you really see yourself playing the suburban daddy? Bikes and kiddies and lawn mowers. Telly and slippers and "keep the music down, love, you're waking the baby." That's not you and it never will be.* Without a word, he returned the pictures to the envelope and held it out to Hannah.

"They're yours," she said. "I brought them for you."

He stuffed the envelope into the pocket of his shirt and felt her watching him as he did. In the first few weeks of their marriage, he'd come home one day and found her ironing his shirts. He'd started laughing. Never in his life had he worn an ironed shirt, and the sight of her carefully pressing the creases in the sleeves struck him as so touchingly funny, he couldn't help himself. Now he had an urge to apologize for hurting her feelings.

"What does she know about me?" he asked. "What have you told her?"

Hannah looked at him for such a long time that he thought she wasn't going to answer. "She thinks you're in heaven," she finally said.

"In heaven?"

"See, we didn't think she'd ever see you and—"

"No…" He shook his head, no explanation needed. It wasn't difficult to imagine the scenario. Given the lie he'd been told, he could well imagine that her family had believed they'd seen the last of him. Certainly his parting shot to Hannah's father would guarantee he'd never be welcome in their home again. And truth was, it was probably kinder than letting Faith think she had a father who had no interest in her. But heaven. Of all the places to pack him off to. He felt a grin spread across his face. "My God, Hannah. Wouldn't it have been more like them to tell her I was in hell?"

"Yeah, well…" She smiled back at him, clearly relieved by his reaction.

"That's no doubt where your da would consign me."

"My father died," she said. "A few months after you left. A heart attack. Needless to say, my mom was pretty devastated. The family were all there for her, of course, but she still gets lonely."

"Sorry," he said. "I had no idea." He recalled meeting her father for the first time, the look of clear disapproval on the man's face. A tall, imposing man, obviously accustomed to having control over most things, including his family. Which must have made it pretty tough when his daughter ran off and married a ne'er-do-well Irish musician.

"You never tried to contact me," she said.

"I was too furious with you. I thought you'd had an abortion. Why didn't you ever try to reach me?"

"Because..." She shrugged. "I just figured it was over. I didn't especially want to hear you confirm it. I'm sorry," she said after a moment. "For everything."

So am I, he thought. *For everything.* They sat in silence for a while. The memories were all coming back to her, he guessed, just as they were for him. The cheap apartment, the car that spent more time up on blocks than on the road, tins of beans and fried-egg sandwiches for supper. Happy enough until those last few weeks, or so he'd thought. One night he'd woken from a dream about Ireland, starving for the sort of lamb stew he remembered his gran making. He'd roused Hannah out of sleep, and at two in the morning they'd found an all-night market and spent all the money they had on the stuff to make it. By the time they'd got everything home, he was no longer in the mood for stew, and they'd made love on the kitchen floor instead.

"What happened?" he asked her now.

Hannah traced a bit of the wicker weave on the arm of the chair. "Short version?"

"Let's begin with that."

"I fell apart, and my family had me hospitalized. That's where I was when you came to look for me."

"Let's hear the longer version," he said.

She covered her face with her hands, took a deep breath then took her hands away. "Oh God, Liam, I don't know. I was such a mess. I hated your being gone all the time. I hated the clubs and the girls always hanging around. I was miserable, lonely. I missed having my family around me. Mostly I was terrified of going back to Ireland where I didn't know anyone. My life would have been tagging around after you, or staying home by myself.''

He looked at her, wanting to argue but resisting. He knew his version of what went wrong; he wanted to hear hers.

''Not that we didn't have some good times,'' she said. ''I don't mean that. It was just…I felt like I was disappearing. That last tour you had in San Francisco, I stayed home, remember? In our apartment, I mean. Anyway, I started going through the drawers in your dresser, and I found these letters from some girl…''

''God, Hannah—''

''No, let me finish. It's a chapter in my life that I'd just as soon never think about again, but I want you to know so you understand…about Faith and everything. I just went to pieces. Everything is a kind of blur. I guess I called my mom and she was on her way over to pick me up, but I'd already left. I don't even know what I was thinking. She found me walking along the freeway. At that point, she decided to take matters into her own hands.''

He thought of those last couple of months with her. He'd come home late from a gig to find her sleeping. She'd be sleeping still when he went off again the next day. When she wasn't sleeping, she was crying. For days on end it seemed she'd do nothing but sleep or cry. He'd alternate between racking his brain to figure out why she was unhappy and losing patience with her for doing nothing to help herself. ''For God's sake, snap out of it,'' he'd say. ''Stop feeling so bloody sorry for yourself.'' And then he'd blow money they didn't have on hothouse roses.

Her expression clouded, and she picked at the fabric on her dress. ''The thing is, my family still worries about me and Faith. My mom especially. Although lately, the tables have kind of turned and it seems I'm always worrying about her…'' She smiled slightly. "Another story. Anyway, they all know how bad things were after we split. I mean if it hadn't been for them…''

If it hadn't been for them, he'd know his daughter today. On the other hand, he hadn't recognized the severity of her depression and they had, so maybe he didn't deserve to know his daughter. He stood, restless, fighting a barrage of competing emotions.

"I was a real mess,'' she said again. "I couldn't even take care of Faith. So now, every time I feel smothered by my family, I remind myself of that.'' She laughed, a short, humorless sound. "Or they do.''

"But you're all right now?'' He turned to face her again, studied her for a moment. There was a confidence and strength about her that she hadn't had before. "You look great,'' he said. She smiled and he was reminded again of all the good times they'd shared. "No, I mean it. Back then, a good wind would have blown you away. You've…filled out.''

Her grin widened. "Are you saying I'm fat?''

"No, not at all. And I like your hair the way you have it now. It suits you.''

"You used to like waist-length, white-blond hair.''

"Ah, well, we all change.''

"Listen, Liam…'' She leaned forward in her chair. "About Faith. It's her birthday next Saturday, a week from today. We're having a party for her. If there's some way you can make it…''

He looked at her for a moment, tried to imagine himself in a room full of six-year-olds, one of them his daughter. Tried to imagine what he would say to her. *Happy birthday! You don't know me, but I'm your daddy. Thought I was in heaven, didn't you? Well, surprise! Sorry I can't stick around to see you grow up. Nice meeting you though. Drop by if ever you're in Ireland.*

Hannah was watching him. He felt the tension, hers and his own, as she waited for his response. "Listen, I um…" He rubbed the back of his neck. "Maybe it's better we leave things as they are."

"You don't want to see her?" A moment passed. "That's what you're saying?"

"Right." He hardened himself against the look in her eyes. "Thanks for inviting me, though."

CHAPTER FOUR

LIAM HAD REJECTED HIS DAUGHTER. The thought lodged in Hannah's brain for the rest of the weekend and was still there Monday even as she sat through another session with Taylor Becker's mother, who absolutely could not understand why she wouldn't be allowed to sit in on her son's prekindergarten readiness test.

Hannah tried to keep her voice free of irritation. Her personal problems didn't belong in the classroom, but it just seemed so damned ironic that she was dealing with parents who made themselves crazy trying to be perfect while her own daughter had a father who didn't give a damn.

That night, she took Faith to see *Harry Potter*, a movie Faith had been clamoring to see since the day it came out. Afterward they went for Faith's favorite cheese-and-sausage pizza with extra mozzarella. Dairy Queen brownie sundaes, another of Faith's favorites, were planned for dessert. A splurge, but tonight Hannah wasn't dwelling on economics. *Liam had rejected his daughter.*

Hannah sprinkled hot pepper flakes onto her slice of pizza. Not that Faith knew anything was wrong, but it seemed important to compensate for Liam's lack of paternal interest. She smiled across the table at her daughter. *You don't need him anyway, sweetheart. I can love you enough for both of us.*

Faith, in a pair of sixty-dollar denim overalls pur-
chased by Helen "Just because she's our own little prin-
cess," grinned at Hannah across the table, a study in
perpetual motion. Up on her knees to carefully pick up
a piece of pizza, then down to a sitting position, her head
swiveling to watch a man with two small children in the
booth on the other side of the aisle.

And then her smile dimmed and the slice of pizza in
her hand dripped a sticky stalactite of mozzarella. She
lifted the pizza high above her head and opened her
mouth wide to catch the cheese. Her expression contem-
plative, she chewed in silence for a while. Then she put
the pizza down. "Mommy, Grandma was sad today."

Hannah sipped at a glass of Diet Coke, thought guilt-
ily of Margaret's tearful entreaties not to be mad at her.
"My only thought was what was best for you," she'd
said last night and again this morning. And then Rose
had taken up her sister's cause. "Give your mom a hug
and tell her you love her," Rose had urged. "Between
Debra's pregnancy and your no-good ex-husband, the
poor thing's going out of her mind."

"People get sad sometimes, sweetie, for all kinds of
reasons," Hannah told Faith.

"I was sad two days ago," Faith said.

"You were?" Hannah thought back over the last couple of days to what might have made her daughter sad.
Nothing came to mind. "How come?"

"Because Beth wouldn't play with me. It made me
feel sad."

I hate Beth, Hannah thought. She reached for another
slice of pizza, then decided she wasn't hungry. *I hate
Liam, too.* She watched the man who had caught Faith's
attention a moment ago bundle a small child into a
sweater, watched Faith staring at him buttoning up the

sweater. The child said something and the man bent down and kissed the end of her nose. Something squeezed at Hannah's heart, and she looked away.

"Maybe Beth just felt like playing with someone else that day, honey," she said.

"But *I'm* her best friend." Faith stabbed at her chest. "She's supposed to play with *me*. She hurt my feelings."

"Ah…" Not trusting her voice, Hannah reached across the table, and caught her daughter's face in her hands. "People do that sometimes, sweetie," she said as Faith wriggled out of her grasp. "They behave in ways that hurt and make us feel sad. We don't always know why they do it, but it's kind of how life is."

"I have another best friend now." Faith's expression cleared. "Her name is Tiffany."

"Tiffany's a pretty name," Hannah said. God, it was uncanny how exactly like Liam Faith looked right then. Serious one moment and then a smile like a sudden burst of sunshine dissipating the clouds. She banished his image.

"Don't be sad, Mommy." Faith leaned across the table, bringing her face up close to Hannah's. "Tiffany's only my friend. I still love you best."

"And I love you best." Hannah felt her voice crack and she covered with a wide smile. "You're my very best sunshine girl, and I love you better than anything else in the world."

"Better than three million chocolate bars?"

"Three million chocolate bars with almonds," Hannah said.

Faith grinned. This was her favorite game. "Three million and one hundred million chocolate bars and two million Little Debbies?" she asked.

"Well, now you're making it difficult." Hannah pretended to consider. "What kind of Little Debbies?"

"Raspberry Zingers," a voice behind her said. "Or maybe Pecan Sandies."

Hannah turned to see Allan holding the hand of a scowling Douglas. She smiled at the boy, then looked up at his father. "Someone obviously doesn't know his junk food," she said. "Raspberry Zingers are not Little Debbies. And, if I'm not mistaken, Pecan Sandies are actually cookies."

Allan grinned. "Hey, kiddo."

Hannah bit back the urge to remind him how much she hated the nickname.

"My mommy's name is Hannah," Faith chimed in as though she'd picked up on her mother's irritation. "And my name is Faith." She smiled up at Allan. "I know what your name is. It's Allan. Want to know how I know?"

"Because I'm wearing a name tag?" he suggested.

Faith gave him a scornful look. "I don't see any name tag."

"Then I give up," he said. "How do you know what my name is?"

"Because my mommy has a picture of you by her bed, except you're wearing a blue shirt in the picture and now you've got a…" Clearly stumped by the color, she frowned over at Hannah. "A green one?"

"Kind of green," Hannah said, sorry that Faith had told him about the picture by the bed. Allan had insisted that they exchange pictures. She'd left his on her dresser and forgotten about it until she noticed that the housekeeper had set it by the bed. She couldn't decide whether or not she was pleased to see him. Allan had what Jen referred to as a high irritation factor. Extremely solicitous, he always opened doors, pulled out chairs and held her arm as they crossed the street. Rose couldn't see how being polite was a problem, and she'd just rolled her eyes when Hannah complained that she felt smothered by him.

Still, as she kept reminding herself, he really was a nice guy. And definitely cute. Blue eyes like his son, sandy blond hair a shade or two lighter; sun-bleached from his hours on the tennis courts. Preppy in khakis and Top-Siders. She shifted her glance to his casual but obviously expensive shirt. "More olive, I think," she said, referring to the color. "Or sage, maybe."

She noticed the children casting wary glances at each other and made the introductions, aware as she did of Allan watching her. Her face felt warm. Maybe she needed to squelch this before she got swept into something she didn't want. Helen had once confided that she'd married her husband because the family liked him. By the time she realized she had some serious doubts, the wedding invitations were in the mail. Never underestimate the power of family pressure, she'd told Hannah.

"Hey, Dougie—" Faith slid out of her seat "—want to go play?" Douglas moved closer to his father, his expression doubtful. "Come on." Faith grabbed his hand. "I'll show you something really cool, but you have to take off your shoes."

After the kids had disappeared into a giant plastic tube through which other children were crawling, Allan slid into the seat Faith had vacated.

"Neat little girl," he said. "Lots of confidence."

"Thank you," she replied. "I'm kind of attached to

her." *Her father doesn't give a damn, but that's his loss.*
She sipped her Diet Coke. "Your week to have Douglas?"

Allan nodded, started to speak then stopped as the kids came running back. Breathless, her cheeks flushed, Faith addressed Hannah.

"Mommy, I invited Douglas to my party. And he wants to come." Her ponytail had come loose from the red scrunchie, which she was now wearing around her wrist. "Actually, that's good because three other boys are coming." She pushed back a long strand of hair. "Holden Baxter and Timothy Jones, except that Timothy might not come."

"You said three boys," Allan pointed out.

"Oh, right." She thought for a minute. "James Bowen, that's the other one. And his sister Michaela. Mommy, please fix my hair?" She scooted into the seat next to Hannah and handed her the scrunchie. "It keeps getting in my eyes."

"Okay, sit still for a minute." Hannah pulled her daughter onto her lap and tied the ponytail. "There you go." She grinned as Faith slid back out of the seat and darted across the room. "Hey," Hannah called. "Wait for Douglas."

"Oh, right." Faith returned to grab the boy's hand. "You know what, Mommy? He's just like my little brother. Come on, Dougie. Let's go check out this really neat video game."

"Maybe a little brother would be good for Faith," Allan said after the kids had gone again. "And a big sister would definitely be good for Douglas." He held Hannah's glance for a moment. "Not to mention how much I would personally enjoy an expanded family. Or a wife. What you might call a win-win situation all around, don't you think?''

"Allan…" *Tell him, for God's sake. There's no connection, no chemistry. We're not destined for togetherness.* "Look, we've talked about this before. We've known each other, how long? A couple of months?" It was a cop-out, but she couldn't bring herself to hurt him. "It's way too soon."

He smiled. "For you, maybe. As far as I'm concerned, I knew the first day I saw you in the classroom." A moment passed and he gazed off toward the video area where the children were playing. "I do worry about Douglas," he said. "He needs to socialize with other children a little more." With a look of distaste, he glanced down at the congealing pizza on the table. "Which is why we came here instead of going to Felippi's, where at least you get edible crust and a decent Chianti to wash it down."

Hannah smiled. "The pizza's okay. A little overpriced, maybe."

"It's revolting." He smiled back at her. "But, hey. No sacrifice is too great for my boy. Even plastic cheese and cardboard crust."

Hannah started to speak, then realized she was on the verge of tears. She excused herself to check on the children. God, she was surrounded by models of fatherly behavior. Over there, a guy in blue jeans was hoisting a small boy up on his shoulders to give him a better look at the screen. Another man, down on his knees, was urging a tyke in a cowboy hat and boots to blow his nose. Allan, talking to Douglas now, was enduring cardboard pizza so that the boy could be around other kids.

Everywhere, reminders of what fathers were supposed to be and what Liam wasn't.

MIRANDA'S HOUSE WAS a nonstop party scene. Booze and, Liam assumed, pretty much anything else a person might want. Girls coming in and out at all hours. Twice over the weekend, he'd started to phone Hannah then changed his mind. That afternoon he'd finished the pitcher of banana rum punch that Miranda had made, then wandered up to his room and fallen asleep. When he woke up, it was dark outside and the party was going full swing downstairs.

He rolled over onto his back and held the pillow over his head, trying to block out the noise as well as the image of Hannah climbing into her little red car and driving away.

But nothing blocked out the noise or the thoughts. Hannah and Faith, hands extended, had even invaded his dreams. He stumbled out of bed, splashed water on his face and wandered, bleary-eyed downstairs.

Miranda spotted him immediately and thrust a cold beer in his hand.

"Party pooper." She wore black leather trousers and a black silk shirt, and her hair was piled up on her head, strands of it down around her neck and shoulders. "Where have you been, you naughty boy?"

"Escaping," he said.

"Escaping?" She gave him a pouty-mouthed smile. "Not from me, I hope."

"From me."

She laughed. "Why would you want to escape from you?"

"Because I'm a no-good, lily-livered coward." He'd heard John Wayne or someone say it on a Western. It seemed applicable. "A pathetic, quivering mass of in-decision," he added for good measure.

Miranda laughed louder. "Oh my. Well, not to worry.

No-good, lily-livered cowards are my favorite type of men.''

Liam drank some beer. Through the windows on the far end of the room he could see the sparks from bonfires on the beach, glowing and sputtering like fireworks in the dark night. Miranda had invited half a dozen or so bands, including his own, and the music throbbed from everywhere in the house. He stared at a girl with long, white-blond hair, who was drinking tequila straight from the bottle. She looked very young, sixteen or seventeen maybe. A thought buzzed across his brain. Someone's daughter. Abandoned by *her* father, too?

''Okay, I'm dying of curiosity.'' Miranda smiled her sultry, insinuating smile, keeping her voice low so he had to move closer to hear. ''Who was that girl who came here to see you?''

''She used to be my wife,'' Liam said.

''Your wife.'' She took a step backward, her eyes widened. ''Oh my. I wouldn't take you for the marrying kind.''

''I'm not,'' he said. ''Which is why she used to be my wife.''

Miranda appeared to be absorbing this new piece of information. ''She's cute,'' she said after a moment. ''Although I wouldn't have thought she was your type.''

''How is that?'' he asked, genuinely curious.

''Oh, I don't know.'' Miranda's eyes narrowed as she considered. ''She seemed sweet and wholesome. A homebody. You strike me as a more adventurous type. Dark and mysterious.''

Liam laughed. ''Right, that's me all over. But terrible husband material.'' *Terrible father material, too. I have a daughter who is going to be six tomorrow. She's hav-*

ing a birthday party, but I'm scared to meet her. "My wife's lucky she got out when she did," he said.

"Oh, I think perhaps you're being a little too hard on yourself," Miranda said. "You're obviously concerned about Brid. That says something."

"All it says is I need her for the band. If it weren't for that, Brid could starve herself to death for all I care." It wasn't true, but he felt so bloody awful about himself at the moment, he didn't want Miranda, or anyone else, trying to make him into something he wasn't.

Across the room he could see Pearse O'Donnaugh, who sometimes sang backup vocals with Brid, talking to the girl with the white-blond hair. Pearse was also a virtuoso on the tin whistle and held the title for bedding more girls during a single tour than anyone else in the band. He attributed both accomplishments to exceptionally agile tongue and lips. He would have the blonde on her back before the evening was through. *Someone's daughter.*

Miranda was giving him one of those looks. "Sometimes, I'm not really sure where you're coming from, Liam," she said.

He gave a laugh. "That makes two of us, Miranda."

An hour later, he had Miranda drive him to a toy shop, some overpriced place in a shopping mall as big as a town. When they got back to the house, he almost stumbled over Pearse and the blond girl half-naked on the beach. Without thinking, Liam grabbed the whistle player and punched him.

"I don't know what's gotten into you, Liam," Pearse said as he staggered to his feet, "but I'd take something for it if I were you, because you're acting like a bloody nutcase."

"WHEN I WAS PREGNANT with you," Margaret was telling Debra. "I was sick all the time. Morning, noon and night, all I did was throw up. Not like with Hannah, I wasn't sick once with her."

Debra rolled her eyes. "Even in the womb, Hannah was perfect."

Hannah said nothing. Debra was clearly back in the fold, and Margaret was just as clearly glad to have her there. They'd been sitting at the kitchen table when she and Faith had returned from their evening out.

She'd put Faith to bed, then gone back down to bake the cake for the birthday party Saturday. By that time, Rose and Helen were also seated around the table; Helen busy decoupaging paper flowers onto a ceramic teapot, Rose with the Dating Opportunities page of the *Long Beach Press Telegram* spread out in front of her.

Someone had sliced a pound cake and set it on a plate, next to a tub of Cool Whip and a full gallon jug of Burgundy. Margaret and Rose were both holding wineglasses. No one mentioned Liam, but whenever Hannah looked up from decorating the cake, she'd catch one of them watching her, their curiosity almost palpable.

"So, what was it like with Faith?" Debra asked. "Did you get sick?"

"A little in the morning." A tube of chocolate frosting in one hand, Hannah stood back to inspect her handiwork. She'd cut and frosted the cake to look like a grandfather clock. When it was finished, six marshmallow mice, which she still had to assemble, would run up the sides. And then she'd freeze it until Friday night. She glanced at the clock over the microwave. Nearly ten and she wasn't completely satisfied with the way it looked.

"I only wanted chocolate milkshakes when I was

pregnant with you,'' Margaret told Hannah. ''Remember that, Rose? That time, I sent you out at two in the morning to look for a Jack in the Box that was open?''

'''Distinguished professional gentleman,''' Rose read. '''Owns own home.''' She looked at Margaret. ''Do I remember what? Oh right…two in the morning and I'm driving around looking for a goddamn Jack in the Box. All I could find was a McDonald's, so I bought one of their shakes—''

''You said it would taste just the same,'' Margaret interrupted, ''But it didn't.'' With a smile, she moved on. ''Hannah was *so* cute when she was pregnant with Faith.'' She looked at Hannah. ''What were you, sweetie, about three months along? You were craving carrot cake. I'd barely got it out of the oven and you were going at it with a spoon. You couldn't even wait for the frosting. Remember that?''

''Yeah…'' Hannah nodded. Eating carrot cake and being fed lies about Liam. She couldn't bring herself to meet her mother's eyes. Earlier, when she'd walked into the kitchen, Margaret had tried to hug her and Hannah had felt herself withdraw. Right now, she felt like a stranger in the middle of her family.

''How about this one?'' Rose circled an ad with a pink magic marker. '''Divorced, Dynamic and Dedicated desires to meet'…nah. Sixty-four, too old.'' She broke off a piece of the pound cake. ''This is kind of stale. I had some of it at breakfast.''

''Well, you shouldn't eat cake for breakfast,'' Margaret said. ''Your taste buds aren't set up for it.'' She cut a sliver and stuck it in her mouth. ''Okay, that's it for me. Next week I'm going back to Weight Watchers.''

''I made a pound cake last week with pureed prunes

instead of oil." Frowning in concentration, Helen dabbed glue on a paper rose. "You wouldn't know the difference."

Rose peered at Helen over her red harlequin reading glasses, a sly smile curving her mouth. "An example of having your cake and losing it, too." She drank some wine. "Nothing like pureed prunes to keep you regular."

"I've tried that," Margaret said. "The cake, I mean. They ran the recipe in the food section." She looked over at Hannah. "You're kind of quiet, sweetie. Are you feeling okay?"

Hannah waited a moment. But the anger—simmering since the night at Fiddler's Green—flared. "Yeah, Mom, I'm fine. Terrific."

Margaret gave her a long look. "You don't sound fine." She got up from the table, put her arm around Hannah's shoulder. "Come on, sweetie. You're not still mad about...the Liam thing?"

"As a matter of fact, I am." Her hand shaking, Hannah dipped the knife into the bowl of hot water. "I think it's great that you guys are all yakking on about cakes and pregnancies. To hell with the fact that you lied to me and you lied to Liam. I guess that's in the past now, not even worth discussing, right?"

"Fine, Hannah." Margaret sat back down and pushed her chair away from the table. "I thought I'd explained already. What would you like from me now? You want an apology?"

"An apology for what?" The decoupage brush in one hand, Helen looked at her sister. "For acting in your daughter's best interests?"

"Your mother was worried sick about you," Rose told Hannah. "Liam would have taken you back to Ireland and God knows what would have happened then."

"You were a mess," Debra said. "You know you were. Mom just recognized you needed help. Which is a damn sight more than Liam did."

Margaret dismissed further comments with a wave of her hand. "We all know why I did what I did. Now I want to hear what Hannah thinks I should do next. You want me to talk to Liam? Explain why it all happened? Fine. Tell you what, why don't you invite him to Faith's birthday party?"

"Margaret," Helen and Rose protested in unison.

"For God's sake, Mom," Debra said.

"I'm serious." Margaret said. "Invite him. We don't have to tell Faith who he is. It'll be a learning experience for him. He'll discover that six-year-old children are so removed from the life he knows he won't be able to get away fast enough. Do you have a number where you can reach him?"

Hannah shook her head. "Forget it, Mom."

"No. Let's clear the air and move on. Give me his number."

"I already invited him, Mom." She heard her voice shake and waited a moment. "I gave him some pictures of Faith and invited him to the party." Her eyes filled. "He wasn't interested."

CHAPTER FIVE

EVERYONE HAD HUGGED HER after that. Told her they loved her; made hot chocolate, poured wine, plied her with brownies and assured her she was better off without a jerk like Liam anyway. After a while she began to feel a little better. By the time Margaret and the aunts had gone to bed, it was two in the morning. Hannah and Debra still sat around the table talking.

"To hell with Liam anyway," she told Debra. "Allan's looking better and better."

"Mom would be thrilled to hear that."

"I'm not about to marry him just to please Mom." Elbows on the table, face propped in her hands, Hannah decided it was time for a change of topic. "Are you really happy about the baby, Deb? This is what you want?"

"Yeah..." Debra mashed a cake crumb with her finger. "I am. I mean, I was kind of freaked at first, telling Mom and everything. But Rose and Helen and Mom were all so sweet. They love this little thing already and then they were talking about how much happiness Faith had given them and..."

Hannah looked at her sister for a long time.

Debra returned Hannah's look. "What?"

"You can't base your decision on what makes Mom or Rose and Helen happy. It's your life."

"I know that..." Deb folded her arms across her chest, stared down at the table cluttered with glasses and plates and brownie crumbs. "But nothing is ever really one person's decision. I mean, almost nothing. It's like…I don't know, we're all threads in this family tapestry. You can follow one thread, pull it out and separate it from the rest, but it's part of the design. If you remove one strand, you mess up the whole thing.''

Hannah grinned. ''Remind me to ask you about that theory when you and Mom are fighting and all you want to do is get away.''

''Yeah, I'll probably say to hell with the design and yank the damn strand out.'' She yawned. ''So is the birthday cake all done?''

''Except for the marshmallow mice. I can make them in the morning.''

''No, let's do them now.'' Debra got up again and returned with a bag of marshmallows. ''Cut them in halves? Or quarters?''

''Halves.'' They worked in silence for a few minutes, gluing pieces of marshmallow together with vanilla frostings. ''So is it really all over with Dennis?'' Hannah asked.

''His official name is now Dennis the Menace.'' Debra reached for another marshmallow. ''I guess I wanted the relationship to work so much, I couldn't see what a jerk he was. You know, I used to wonder why Mom stuck with Dad when she knew damn well he was running around on her, but you make yourself believe what you want to believe.'' She looked up at Hannah. ''Like you and Liam.''

''Actually, my situation with Liam was different,'' Hannah said. ''Maybe when we got married I kind of hoped that one day he'd turn into this family man, but deep down I never really believed he would. Liam's into his own world and there isn't room for anyone else. On some level I guess I've always known that, I just couldn't accept it before.'' She lifted one of the mice for Deb to see. ''What d'you think? Are the eyes too big?''

Deb glanced over at the mouse in Hannah's hand and laughed. "Kind of. Unless he's got thyroid problems. Maybe if you cut the chocolate chips in half."

"I'll put them in the blender." Hannah squatted to remove the blender from the cabinet. "It'll be quicker than trying to chop the damn things."

"Can I say something?" Deb asked.

Hannah dumped a handful of chips into the container and pressed the pulverize button. "Go ahead."

"I mean this is small-minded and mean and I know I'm going to be sorry I said it, but I'm kind of glad about what happened with Liam. You gave him a chance to see Faith and he turned it down, which means he's a jerk."

"Yeah..." Hannah looked at Debra. "And..."

Head lowered, Debra pressed her finger into the ground-up chocolate Hannah had dumped on a paper towel. "Sometimes I hate that everything always turns out well for you. After Liam, you went back to school, got your life together and it just kills me sometimes that mine gets so screwed up. If Liam had turned out to be this great father and you guys had just waltzed off into the sunset, I would have been so damn jealous."

"God, Deb." Hannah shook her head, equally touched and stunned by what Debra had said. "I really, *really* don't think I've ever had it all together. In fact, lately I've been wondering why I'm thirty-one and still living at home."

"Because of Faith," Deb said. "Mom and Rose and Helen are always here for her when you're at work, and there's no way you could afford to rent a place that's even half as nice as this."

"That's what I tell myself," Hannah said. "But sometimes I think maybe it's just an excuse because I'm too scared to be out on my own."

"Nah." Deb dismissed the idea with a shake of her

head. "You're just putting Faith's welfare first, which is good because her father obviously isn't interested."

Hannah sighed. "Let's not talk about him anymore. He's like a tornado that blew into town and tore everything apart. Even though things with Mom are okay again on the surface, deep down, I'm still mad at her. I almost think I was better off not knowing about the lie."

"Listen, Hannah, no one gets under my skin like Mom does." Deb scooped some chocolate, dumped it into her coffee. "Sometimes she just looks at me the wrong way, and I yell at her. But in this case, she was only thinking of you. Screwed-up thinking maybe, but she was truly scared. Not that I knew what was going on at the time, I was only fifteen or sixteen." She grinned. "I thought Liam was cool."

"You and every other woman." Hannah picked among the bits of chocolate for eye-size pieces. "Well, he had his chance."

"Exactly. Hold on to that thought," Deb said. "By the way, I forgot to tell you, Allan called just before you got home. He wanted to know if there was anything he could bring to the party Saturday. Or if you wanted him to stop by early in the morning to help set things up."

"He came in with his son while we were having pizza tonight." Hannah ran warm water over her hands, melting the sticky frosting from her fingers. "After the kids went off to play, we sat there talking about this and that and it was…nice. The way parents are supposed to be."

"And?"

"And I kept thinking, why can't I just fall in love with a guy like Allan?"

"No chemistry."

Hannah sighed. "I tell myself what a great guy he is, thoughtful, considerate. A good father."

"Listen, if there's no chemistry, there's no chemistry," Debra said. "If you don't like broccoli, covering it with cheese won't make a bit of difference. It's still broccoli and it still does nothing for you." She grinned. "Kind of like Allan."

ALLAN ARRIVED four hours early on the day of the party. Hannah was tying a bunch of multicolored ribbons to the mailbox, when his Volvo wagon pulled up at the curb. She watched as he walked around to the passenger side and opened the door for his son.

Douglas emerged slowly, his face solemn beneath a black felt pirate hat emblazoned with a gold skull and crossbones. A breeze filled the full sleeves of his white shirt, which was tucked into a pair of red-and-white-striped pants. The silver papier maché sword he held in one hand glittered in the sun.

"Hey, cool costume." Hannah bent down to hug him. "And those boots are terrific."

"They make my feet sweat." Douglas looked up at his father, then down at his black rubber boots. "Do I have to wear them, Dad?"

Allan, who had been gazing at Hannah, turned his attention to his son. "Would you rather wear your flip-flops?" he asked.

"Did you wash them?"

"They weren't really dirty, pal." Allan moved to the car, produced the rubber sandals from the trunk and helped Douglas remove the boots. "There," he said after Douglas had first inspected, then stepped into a pair of blue thongs. "Better?"

Douglas nodded, the faintest trace of a smile on his face. "I need to get the presents," he said. "Okay, Dad?"

"I told him it wasn't a costume party, but he was determined to wear it," Allan said after Douglas went off into the house, his arms full of lavishly wrapped

gifts. "He's been so excited about seeing Faith again.
It's all he's talked about."

"Good." Hannah smiled brightly and, suspecting Allan was about to take her in his arms, moved a few steps
backward. "So. We need to find you a job to do."

"Just a moment." Once again, he opened the Volvo
trunk and lifted out a paper grocery sack. "Ingredients
for lunch. I thought you'd probably be too busy with
party preparations to find time to eat."

"Actually, we were going to order pizza."

Allan grimaced. "Well, I'm here to spare you. I have
in this bag all the ingredients for a salad Nicoise."

Hannah looked at him. "That sounds kind of ambi-
tious, Allan. I was thinking of something quick."

"This will be. Quick as a wink." The bag in his arms,
he started up the path to the house. "Birds-of-paradise
are blooming nicely," he said as he passed the orange
plants lining the driveway. "A few nasturtiums lurking,
I see."

"Yeah, they're the bane of my mother's existence.
The more she pulls them out, the more they seem to
come back."

"You could use the leaves in a salad," Allan said.
"Only the new ones, of course. And the blossoms are
quite nice, too. They impart a rather pleasant peppery
taste."

"I'll have to try it," Hannah said, knowing she was
about as likely to add nasturtiums to her usual salad of
chopped iceberg and grated carrot as she was to whip
up a salade Nicoise. But Allan considered himself a mas-
ter chef. He'd cooked dinner for her at his house once,
an elaborate feast that he'd chopped and cut and sautéed
for hours. She'd stood in the kitchen as he'd lovingly
described everything he was doing and then given her a
little tutorial on clarifying butter. Another time, he'd

promised, he would show her how to butterfly lamb. *Right.*

One of the few things she'd had in common with Liam was their very basic approach to food preparation. They'd lived out of cans. Except for the time he'd gotten a crazy urge to make an Irish stew at three in the morning. After they'd bought all the ingredients, neither of them had wanted to make the stew. Instead they'd ended up making love. On the kitchen floor. She wondered whether Liam remembered that.

With Allan behind her, she took the steps up to the house. *Go away, Liam.*

"I COULD GET USED TO THIS." Brid pressed a button to open the sunroof of Miranda Payton's butter-colored Mercedes and tipped up her face to the sky. "Riding around in fancy cars, the sun all nice and warm. Maybe I'll find a rich American at the party."

"Tommy Doherty will be heartbroken." Liam craned his neck to read the green street sign at the intersection of Pacific Coast Highway. Second Street. He turned left. Everything felt familiar. The palm trees and oil derricks, the milky pale sky. Across a bridge now; a marina and boatyard on one side, on the other, a small stretch of beach where Hannah and her sister used to play as kids. She'd told him about the time she'd lost a little wooden dog in the water. A painted dachshund with red wheels that clacked as she pulled it along on a string. She'd been walking it along the edge of the sand and a wave had carried it away. He drove on through Naples, past a steak restaurant he'd gone to with Hannah and her parents. Over filet mignon, her father had once again made it clear that a Las Vegas marriage to a visiting Irish musician was definitely not what he'd had in mind for his daughter.

"I put some rice cakes in there, too," he told Brid. "And bananas."

"So you've said already," Brid reminded him. "Three times."

"Well, I don't think you should have checked yourself out so soon. Miranda didn't think so, either. She said her daughter was in there for nearly a month."

"Miranda's telling you that because she wants to keep you around."

Liam turned his head to look at her.

"I'm serious. She fancies you."

"Miranda has a husband who could buy and sell me a hundred times over."

"She's bored to tears with him. She asked me if the two of us had anything going. You and me."

"What did you tell her?"

"I told her we were at each other every chance we got."

Liam grinned. "Did she believe you?"

"She might have if I could have kept a straight face."

Without taking his eyes off the road, Liam reached for the bag in the back seat and tossed it onto Brid's lap. "Eat. It's not just me and Miranda who think you left the place too soon. The doctor said you needed at least two weeks."

"The doctor wants money. I'm fine, Liam. Stop worrying."

"Eat a rice cake then."

"Nag, nag." She put the bag on the floor by her feet. "Are you sure you want me to come along? You wouldn't rather go alone?"

"I want you to come, I already told you."

Brid brought her feet up onto the leather seat, and put her arms around them. "You just want to keep an eye on me," she said. "Force food down my throat."

"Not at all," he said. "It's your company. There's no one I'd rather be with."

She grinned and punched his arm. "Liar."

He turned on the radio and flipped through the preset stations. Miranda's taste ran to soft rock and easy listening. Billy Joel was singing "An Innocent Man." As they came into Belmont Shore, the traffic congealed into a slow-moving mass. Trendy little shops lined both sides of the street.

Liam thought of the pink stucco cottage Hannah had called her dream house. There'd been a strip of blue ocean at the foot of the street, the powdery dust of sand in the air. And flowers everywhere, the colors like a kid's box of crayons. Purple bougainvillea and red geraniums, bright blue daisies with yellow centers and pink-and-white-striped petunias spilling out of terra-cotta pots. "Could you see us living in a place like this?" she'd asked him.

"I think you should have phoned her first," Brid said. "It might be a bit awkward, just showing up."

"I'll take my chances." Second Street ended and merged into Ocean Boulevard. A street—whose name he couldn't make out—forked to the right. He waited at the stop sign, unsure which direction to take. A car honked behind him. Liam rubbed the back of his neck, let the clutch out too soon and killed the engine.

"You're nervous, aren't you?"

"Don't be daft." He craned his neck to read the street sign. There was a supermarket at the foot of Hannah's street, he remembered. They'd walked from her house to a long pier with a fishing tackle shop at the end. "Nervous about what?"

Brid laughed. "Come on, Liam, it's me you're talking to. I mean about seeing your daughter. You're scared to death." She reached over and put her hand on his arm. "You don't have to do this, you know, Liam."

"I can't remember the name of her street," he said.

"That's why you should have phoned."

"I'll know it when I see it." To his right, he saw a street with large two-story homes winding up a hill. He craned his neck to get a better view. "This is the one, I think. It's a big brown house with turrets in the front like a castle. When I used to visit Hannah, I'd half expect them to pull up the drawbridge."

"That one?" Brid pointed to a turreted structure several houses up the hill with long, narrow windows and a heavy wooden door. "Looks like money," she said as Liam pulled up outside.

"They do well enough," he said. "Or they did."

"They must have been thrilled with you."

He shrugged and stretched across Brid to peer at the house. Everything looked much as he remembered. The house was built on a slight incline so that it sat about six feet higher than street level. Sixteen steps led up from the street, made a turn, then twelve more ended in a meticulously clipped lawn edged with orange tropical flowers. Her father had been an avid gardener. Hannah had given him a tour of the old man's rose garden. Every rose, she'd told him, marked a special occasion in her or her sister's lives. She'd told him she'd argued with her father because he hadn't planted a rose for her marriage.

"Are we just going to sit here then?" Brid asked.

"No." As he opened the car door, he could hear children's voices and laughter coming from the back of the house. A bunch of colored balloons bobbed from the mailbox on the street.

Brid put her hand on his arm. "Liam..."

"It's all right," he said. "I've come this far..."

By THREE, the party was in full swing. Hannah watched her daughter, who sat at one end of a long trestle table covered with white paper. All around her, a dozen or so children with newspaper aprons were applying spots of black paint to cardboard dalmatians. Aunt Rose, sporting a pair of faux fur dalmatian ears, supervised the activity, regaling the kids with a tale about a dalmatian who'd managed to misplace his spots.

"Any ideas what he might have done with them?" Rose asked.

"Maybe they got dirty and he had to wash them off," Douglas suggested.

Hannah smiled and headed across the yard to where the food was being set up. A neighbor, in a tall white chef's hat and a navy-blue apron presided over the barbecue; Margaret and Aunt Helen were filling Tupperware bowls with chips and cheddar cheese goldfish. Smoke from the grill hung in the air and mingled with the laughter from the children. Margaret leaned over to say something to Helen, then all three turned and smiled at Hannah.

Her throat suddenly thick, Hannah bent down to adjust the strap of her sandal. The image of the picture-perfect happy family—something she'd seen countless times—suddenly seemed false. She could tell herself she'd forgiven her mother for lying to Liam, but something had changed. This house—filled with people who loved her—suddenly didn't feel like home.

"Hannah." Margaret waved her over, then smiled conspiratorially at Helen. "We both think Allan is a doll."

Helen smiled broadly. "Nice, too. Very polite and friendly."

"He said I looked too young to have a thirty-one-year-old daughter," Margaret said.

"That's all it needed for your mother to fall in love with him," Helen added.

"Not true," Margaret protested, pink-faced. "I liked him the moment I saw him in the kitchen wearing my apron and whipping up a salad. I thought, there's the guy for Hannah. Now if only we could find someone like that for Deb."

"Where is Deb?" Hannah asked.

Margaret's happy expression faded. "We argued again this morning, and she stormed out. I don't know if it's the pregnancy that's making her so touchy or what. All I asked was whether the baby was going to have Dennis's last name."

"Maybe she thinks that's her business," Hannah said.

"I'm her mother," Margaret said. "If she's living in my house, I think I have the right to ask a simple question without her jumping down my throat." She sighed. "If you could have a little talk with her, I'd really appreciate it."

"Where's that guy of yours?" The man tending the barbecue waved a spatula at Hannah. "Tell him to come and give me a hand. I could use a little break from women's yak-yak-yak."

Margaret peered across the yard. "I see him over there with his little boy. Allan," she called. "Get over here. We want to put you to work." She smiled at Hannah. "He is *so* cute."

"Goodness." Tupperware bowl in hand, Helen stared out at the crowd on the lawn. "Is that who I think it is? Over there by the steps."

"Damn." Margaret exhaled loudly, then turned to look at Hannah. "I thought you said he wasn't coming. I'll go and talk to him—"

"No, Mom." Hannah put her hand on Margaret's arm. "I will."

CHAPTER SIX

"I THINK THIS IS WHERE I go find the ladies' room or something," Brid told Liam. "Good luck."

As he watched Hannah approaching, Liam had an irrational urge to bolt. To drop the presents, wrapped by Miranda in silver paper with big yellow bows, and return to a place where he knew what he was doing.

Beyond Hannah, he could see a group standing around a barbecue. One of the women might have been Mrs. Riley, he wasn't sure. And then Hannah was standing in front of him, color flooding her face. She wore a short white skirt and sandals. Her pale pink lipstick was almost the same color as her sleeveless blouse. No smile.

"I didn't think you were coming," she said.

"Neither did I." The three square boxes were stacked one on top of the other, the top one brushing his chin. Hannah's brown hair curled around her face. She looked very young, hardly old enough to have a six-year-old daughter. The group at the barbecue were watching with undisguised curiosity. The woman in the blue dress was Hannah's mother, he was sure of it now. He shouldn't have worn a tie. Sweat trickled down the back of his neck, beaded on his forehead. He should have bought flowers, chocolates or something. "These are for...I don't know if it's the kind of thing she'd like. The girl in the shop had a little girl though..."

Hannah gave him a faint smile, then seemed to men-

tally shake herself. "Here, I'll take them." She reached
for the boxes, held them against her chest, but kept staring at him as if she thought he might be a figment of
her imagination. "I'm stunned, Liam. I don't know what
to say. I haven't... Faith doesn't know. I mean, I haven't
said anything. Why did you change your mind?"

"I don't know." He followed Hannah's glance to a
long trestle table, where a dozen or so kids sat daubing
black paint on paper and each other. He saw Faith. A
little older than she'd looked in the pictures Hannah had
given him, a pair of white fur dog ears on her head.
Hands raised like claws, she was barking at a boy in a
pirate's outfit. Liam grinned. *My daughter.*

"You spotted her," Hannah said. "Looks like she's
getting in a little practice for a game of My Dog Says.
It's like Simon Says," she added after Liam gave her a
puzzled look. "But the kids bark and growl instead."

Liam watched Faith chase the pirate across the grass.
Groups of adults in summer clothes stood around the
yard, talking and watching the kids play. Hannah tapped
his shoulder.

"I'm going to take these inside." She indicated the
presents. "Do you want to come with me?"

He followed her into the kitchen.

"The wallpaper's different," he said. "It used to be
little yellow teapots."

Hannah set the presents down on the table and looked
up at him. "You remember?"

"And the cooker and fridge were green."

"Avocado," she said.

"And the fridge was covered with snapshots and
newspaper clippings. You could hardly see the space between them."

"Yeah, well..." She gestured at the front of the current fridge, a pristine stainless steel, unmarred by even a magnet. "My mom finally moved out of the sixties. Want something to drink? Soda? A beer?"

Liam shook his head and saw disappointment covered by a quick smile. "Changed my mind," he said. "A beer would be nice." He moved to the window and stared out at the kids on the lawn. Faith appeared to be issuing commands to the other kids who were tearing around the yard on all fours. As Hannah handed him the beer, he caught a whiff of something familiar.

"Your hair," he said. "It still smells the same."

She touched her hair, blushed a little. "Same shampoo. I'm a creature of habit."

"It's nice. Brings back old memories." Back in Ireland, after they'd split up, he would lie in the dark and think about her and remember exactly the way her hair had smelled, the way traces of the aroma had lingered on her pillow. Once, in a particularly low moment, he'd gone out and bought a bottle of the same shampoo she'd used. And then he'd felt like an idiot for moping over a woman who'd aborted his child.

He stayed at the window, Hannah beside him. Watching his daughter. *Their* daughter. With something that felt a lot like envy, he watched the pirate's dad come to the rescue of his son. Faith, he noticed, was now wearing the pirate's hat.

"Oh, God." Hannah, who had apparently caught the switch, too, started laughing. "Faith's never been the shy type."

"That's good." The surge of pride he felt surprised him. "She goes after what she wants."

"Yeah..." She nodded, still smiling.

"Do you remember the last time we were at a birthday party together?"

"Yep," she answered. "The one you had for me. My twenty-first."

"And I forget to post the invitations so no one showed up."

"Yeah, but you made a great cake."

"If you like them flat as a pancake. And burned."

"Well, it was your first try."

"I'm not sure I'd have done any better after a dozen tries," he said. "You can't have forgotten the chicken?"

"The chicken?" Her expression puzzled, she looked at him for a minute. Then she clapped her hand to her mouth. "Oh, the chicken," she said, laughing now. "I remember."

He'd been trying to cook dinner for her. But he'd forgotten to look in the oven before he turned it on and hadn't seen the bags of potato chips she'd kept there to keep them from the mice that had overrun the apartment. After he'd put out the fire, he'd stuck the chicken back in—its innards still wrapped in plastic—and turned the temperature up high.

"God, the smell." Hannah was still laughing. "I mean, it would have been hilarious if we hadn't been so broke. I can still see you standing by the stove with this little tiny black thing the size of a sparrow."

"But the gravy was all right though. Nothing like a nice gravy dinner. Ah, well…" he said a moment later.

Hannah's smile faded and she stood looking out of the window at the children on the grass. A few seconds passed, and then she turned to him. "I'm glad you decided to come, Liam. It feels strange to be standing here with you, watching Faith. But it feels good, too."

"It does." He looked down at the beer can in his hand. "Strange but good."

"How long will you be around?" she asked.

"It depends on Brid. My singer. She's out there talking to the tall blond guy. She's had a few problems. If she's well enough to tour again we'll leave in three or four days. We have a gig up near San Francisco next week. A big music festival. I'd like to make it."

"So the band's doing well?"

"It is." He glanced at her. "We made the UK charts a couple of years in a row. And we've got a European tour coming up soon after we get back."

She smiled. "Fantastic. I'm happy for you, Liam."

"Thanks." Something in her eyes told him she meant it. "And yourself? Things are going well for you, too?"

"Yeah…pretty good. I teach in a preschool."

He caught the hesitation in her voice. "And you're happy doing that?"

"Sure, it's great."

He looked at her. "That's not really what you want to do, is it?"

She grinned. "No. I have this dream about doing landscaping design. Drought-tolerant plants. Rosemary, lavender, sage. Things that grow well in California." Her face grew animated. "People are always surprised at how colorful that kind of garden can be."

"So why are you teaching preschool if what you really want to do is grow plants?"

She shrugged. "I don't know, lots of reasons."

"That's a mistake, Hannah. You only live one life. Don't waste it doing things that don't make you happy."

"That's a nice thought, Liam," she said, an edge to her voice now. "And it's an easy thing to say, it's just not so easy to do. Happiness isn't always about just doing things for yourself. There are other people to consider."

"You're right," he said. "As long as you don't make

other people an excuse for not taking responsibility for your own happiness.''

''Well,'' she said brightly, after a moment of heavy silence. ''I guess I should get out there and do my hostess duties.''

''Right.'' Liam drank some beer and Hannah didn't move. They stood watching the children, queuing up for hot dogs. Brid and the pirate's dad were at the edge of the crowd, laughing about something. Faith had made her way to the front of the food line. He wondered what Hannah was thinking. He wondered if she was in love with the pirate's dad. He wondered if she'd had any thought of telling Faith that her daddy wasn't in heaven after all. He wondered if he needed his head examined. He decided he didn't care.

''Does she like…'' He started to ask, and then Hannah's mother walked into the kitchen, holding the arm of the pirate's dad. For a moment, they all stood looking at each other. Hannah's face was like thunder; Margaret's all flustered surprise—real or not, he couldn't be sure. The pirate's dad looked slightly amused and perfectly at ease. He had the kind of haircut that the men in the magazines Brid read all sported. In fact he looked a bit like someone in one of the ads—tanned and expensively dressed. Definitely a son-in-law candidate. Liam decided it was time to make his exit.

''OF COURSE I DIDN'T PLAN IT.'' Margaret held a glass of pinot noir as she moved around the kitchen, putting away bowls and serving platters. ''Allan suggested we all have dinner at Kelly's tonight, I'd told him I love the steak there, and we came to look for you to tell you about it. How would I know you were with Liam?''

"I wasn't *with* Liam, Mom. You make it sound like…
We were *talking*."

"Excuse me," Margaret poured more wine into her
glass. "I don't think I suggested you were doing anything other than talking. I just said—"

"I know *what* you said. It was *the way* you said it."
Hannah scooped leftover potato salad into a plastic container. What was the point of arguing? Margaret would
continue to claim innocence and Hannah would continue
to believe that her mother knew exactly what she was
doing when she brought Allan into the kitchen. She put
the container into the fridge and picked up a bowl of
baked beans. "You want to save these? There isn't much
left."

"Toss them," Margaret said. "Listen, I can finish
cleaning up here, if you want to go and get ready. Allan
said he'd be here at seven."

Hannah scraped the beans into the trash. Faith had
gone home with Allan and Douglas. This had also been
arranged while she'd been talking to Liam. Allan would
return with the kids, pick up Hannah and Margaret and
drive to Kelly's, where they'd meet Rose and Helen. In
the span of one afternoon, Allan had become part of the
family.

"Who was that woman with Liam?" Margaret asked.

"His singer."

"She was all over Allan," Margaret said. "Not that
he was doing anything to encourage her. Actually the
opposite, I think he was a little embarrassed."

"He'll get over it." Why *had* Liam brought Brid to
the party? And what was his relationship with the
singer? And why the hell did any of it matter? Once
again, Liam had just walked away. Not a word about
wanting to see Faith again or keeping in touch. Nothing,

just that faint, inscrutable Liam smile and then he was gone—down the road in a yellow Mercedes. With another woman.

"I suppose he didn't say anything about wanting to contribute to Faith's support," Margaret said.

Hannah felt her pulse kick up a notch. The thought had occurred to her, but she didn't want to discuss it with her mother. If Liam chose not to support his daughter, it was probably because he didn't really feel he had a daughter and so felt no obligation. She could tell herself this, but Margaret's question brought all the disappointment and simmering anger to the surface. Anger at Liam, at her mother, at herself for being taken in, once again, by Liam.

"No, Mom, he didn't say anything about it," she snapped. "Maybe he would have though, if he hadn't been cheated out of the first six years of Faith's life."

"Oh, for God's sake." Margaret dismissed Hannah's comment with a wave of her hand. "How many times are we going to play this same refrain? Okay, maybe I should have handled things differently, but I didn't. Get over it. It's time for everyone to accept what happened and move on. Liam knows he has a daughter now. What he does about it is his decision." She wrapped aluminum foil around a plate of sliced tomatoes and set the plate in the fridge. "Does he want to see her again?"

"No."

"Just no?"

"He didn't say anything, Mom. He just left. So, you can breathe easy again."

Margaret turned to glare at her. Arms folded across her chest, blue eyes bright with anger. "Sure, blame me for Liam's irresponsibility. What is it with you and Deb? Has she been giving you lessons in hostility? I'm tired of the two of you making me the enemy. How *should* I react to Liam? First he says he doesn't want to see Faith. Then he just shows up. And then he just leaves again. Who knows what the hell he's thinking?''

"Maybe he's confused about things," Hannah said. "Maybe it isn't so easy for him to just move on and forget the six years he spent believing he didn't have a daughter.''

Margaret shook her head. "Hannah," she said softly.

"What?''

"That's you, isn't it? Always giving him the benefit of the doubt. In your book it's poor Liam, the injured party." She refilled her wineglass. "I worry about you, Hannah, I really do. One of these days you're going to have to stop making excuses for other people's failings and start paying attention to your own feelings.''

Hannah opened her mouth to speak, then stopped. Her heart thundering, she picked up the saltshaker. Studied the grains crusted around the chrome top as she thought about all the things she couldn't bring herself to say to her mother.

But maybe Margaret was right. Maybe it *was* time for Hannah to focus on her own needs and stop accommodating everyone else's. For starters, she should stop going to singles dances with Rose just because Rose didn't like to go alone. And she should stop worrying that Helen's feelings would be hurt if she quit her job at La Petite Ecole. And maybe she should stop running interference between Margaret and Deb. And, on the subject of Margaret, she should find a place for herself and Faith and stop worrying that her mother would drink herself into a stupor as a result. And Liam. She needed to know Liam's intentions regarding Faith. Either he wanted to be a part of his daughter's life, or he didn't. And if the latter, she didn't want to hear another word from him.

"I'M DEPRESSED." Brid stared gloomily into her glass of beer. "God, but he was a lovely man. And I thought he liked me, too."

Liam watched the play of sunlight on the water. They were sitting in green plastic chairs on the outdoor patio of Belmont Shore Brewery where they'd driven, although it was just at the bottom of Hannah's road, after the party. At the next table, a middle-aged couple was discussing the price of real estate in California. Shot through the roof in the past year, one of them said. Astronomical, the other agreed.

Brid grinned. "I mean, I was all but working out the colors the bridesmaids would wear. D'you think maybe he's gay? That could explain it."

"He has something going with Hannah," Liam said.

Brid gave him a skeptical look. "She told you that?"

"Not in so many words," Liam said.

"How do you feel about that?" Brid asked.

"It's her life."

She kept watching him. "I can't tell whether it bothers you or not. You're a difficult read, Liam."

"Probably because there's nothing there to read."

"So how was it? Seeing your little girl?"

"Strange. I told Hannah that. Good, but strange."

"And now you've seen her," Brid said. "What's next?"

"I don't know." He drank some beer. "I watched her today. The way Hannah's bringing her up…it's everything she needs, really. Loving family, all the material things, a stable life. It's the way Hannah grew up, but it couldn't be more different from what I had as a boy. What do I have to give her?''

"You're her father, Liam. That's enough. If every father wondered what he had to give before he made a commitment to his child, there would be a lot fewer fathers around, believe me.''

"Hannah will get married again and whoever she marries will probably do a better job of being a father to Faith than I ever could.''

Brid looked at him. "So drop it then.''

"I should.''

"What's stopping you?''

He shrugged, but had no answer to her question. "I'd want to be a good father,'' he said after a moment. "Not just someone who sends a birthday card and presents at Christmas. But if I can't be the kind of father I'd like to have had myself, I might as well walk away.''

"Liam.'' Brid put her elbows on the table and looked into his eyes. "Let's back up a bit. You're on tour eight months out of the year, and when you're not touring you're recording. You live and breathe your music. Tell me how you'd find the time to be a good daddy to your daughter.''

He shook his head. He didn't know.

"You need to make a choice, Liam. Right now, the band is the most important thing in your life. If you choose to keep it that way, then I'd say let Hannah find a new father for her daughter, because there's no way you can fill the role. But if you don't, if you really want to be the kind of father you're talking about, then you need to have a long talk with Hannah.''

ALTHOUGH MARGARET HAD ADVISED Hannah to pay attention to her feelings, she'd still been furious when

Hannah opted out of dinner at Kelly's. But, as Hannah had pointed out, if her mother had consulted her before making the arrangements, she would have told Margaret that what she really wanted after the party was a quiet evening to herself. Which is exactly what she was having when Liam knocked on the front door.

"Liam." She raised a hand to her hair, which she'd scraped up into a scruffy ponytail after removing all her makeup. She'd also pulled on a pair of faded black leggings with a hole in the seam, an old red flannel shirt that had been her father's and fleecy gray socks. Her comfort clothes. "What…what's up?"

"I wanted to talk to you," he said.

She hesitated a moment, then motioned for him to come in. "Everybody's gone out to dinner. Faith included." She led him into the living room where he stood, arms folded across his chest, his expression hard to read.

"Have a seat." She moved the day's newspaper from the sofa, but he remained standing. He'd worn a tie with a gray cotton shirt to the party. The tie was gone now, the shirt opened at the neck, a leather jacket over it. It occurred to her that she couldn't remember seeing Liam in a tie and the thought of him putting one on for his daughter's birthday party tugged at her heart. She had a sudden urge to touch him.

"Want something to drink?" she asked instead. "Beer, wine, soda? I'm having chamomile tea, myself."

"A beer would be fine." He followed her into the kitchen, stood with his back against the counter, watching as she moved around.

"Did Faith enjoy her party?"

"She had a great time." Hannah opened the refrigerator. "Bud or Miller."

JANICE MACDONALD 101

"Either."

She opened a Miller. "You didn't stay to see her open her presents," she said as she handed him a bottle.

"I know...your mother coming into the kitchen threw me off track a bit. I'd been about to suggest we take Faith to the zoo. I've heard there's a great one in San Diego." He opened the beer, drank some. "I thought tomorrow, if you were free."

Hannah had set a glass down for him, but she returned it to the shelf when she saw him take a swig from the bottle. "Why, Liam? What's the point?"

"I'd like to spend some time with my daughter."

"*You'd* like it. What about Faith?"

"It's been a long time since I was a child, but I think I would have been thrilled at the chance for a day at the zoo."

"What do we tell her about who you are?"

"We don't have to tell her anything. Tell her I'm a friend from Ireland. What's wrong with that?"

Hannah microwaved a cup of tea. What *was* wrong with that? Faith would certainly enjoy a day at the zoo. She'd been clamoring to go ever since she'd seen the baby koalas on TV. The microwave pinged and she removed her cup.

"So you take her to the zoo—"

"*We* take her to the zoo."

"Okay, we take her." Her face felt hot. *We. Don't read anything into it.* "What then?"

"I don't know."

She looked at him.

"I *don't* know, Hannah. I can't give you a definite answer. I'm still sorting things out. I just know that I can't walk away and pretend she doesn't exist." He picked up a copy of *Cosmopolitan* that Rose had left on the table, glanced at the cover and set it down again. "I want to start paying toward Faith's support, no matter whether I'm involved in her life or not," he said. "We can set that up later."

She nodded, her mind still on the zoo. "I just don't think taking her out for the day is a good idea," she said. "Even if we don't tell her who you are, she'll be curious. Kids pick up vibes. It could be unsettling for her."

"It isn't my fault she doesn't know me," Liam said.

"I know that."

"Your mother didn't look happy to see me."

"She wasn't."

"She's lucky I didn't tell her exactly what I thought of her little ruse. I would have, except I didn't want to spoil Faith's birthday party."

"Thanks, I appreciate that."

"But I still deserve the chance to spend a little time with Faith. No matter how your family feels about me."

Hannah felt herself wavering.

"If it weren't for your mother's intervention, we might still be together."

She waited a moment before she spoke, disconcerted by the possibility that Liam might actually regret their divorce. Somehow, she'd always imagined him emotionally unscathed.

"There's not much point in that kind of speculation, Liam," she said finally. "We were young and we hardly knew each other before we got married. Add that to all the time you spend on the road, and it's pretty much a recipe for failure, regardless of what my family did."

"What's the situation with you and the pirate's dad? Are the two of you…?"

She shrugged, leaving the interpretation up to him. "Allan's a sweet guy."

Liam smiled.

"What?"

"Sweet guys are seldom the love of anyone's life."

Hannah eyed him for a moment. "You know that from personal experience?"

He grinned.

Flustered, she quickly drank the cup of lukewarm tea, dumped the bag in the trash and ran water into the mug. "Sometimes we settle for strength and stability over excitement and romance," she said, realizing that she sounded exactly like her aunt Helen. *Damn it, Liam. Go away, you're confusing me.* She turned to see him studying her. He held her glance until she looked away.

"Okay, I know that didn't come out right," she said. "I didn't mean 'settle.' What I'm trying to say is I'm happy with my life. I don't need a whole bunch of ups and downs, I'm perfectly content with…a more even pace."

"Except you'd rather be doing landscaping than teaching nursery school."

"Well, yes, that."

"And will Allan be a part of this even pace?"

"I don't know that yet. Maybe." A moment passed. "What about you?"

"No one. Is that what you're asking?"

She nodded. "Your singer?"

He laughed.

"What?"

"I don't know. For some reason, I thought you'd be the exception. Everyone suspects Brid and I have something going. The papers have had a field day with our supposed romance. We're the best of friends and that's it.''

''Oh.'' For some reason, the knowledge that there was no one in Liam's life gave her a little charge. They stood for a moment, faint sounds filtering into the silence between them. The hum of the refrigerator, a car driving by. She imagined herself with Liam and Faith driving down to San Diego for a day at the zoo. She'd pack a picnic. Maybe they'd take the coast route. And the zoo really was terrific. She could almost feel it, the sun warm on their backs as they made their way up the hill to the exhibits. Faith between them, holding their hands.

She searched for a reason to say no. And came up empty. Faith would be thrilled. But Faith wasn't really the issue. Faith had come along on a couple of dates before and had taken it all in stride. Her hesitation was for herself. Right now, standing here in the kitchen with Liam; watching his face, hearing his voice, his laugh. She could fall in love with him all over again. And she would if they spent any time at all together. And then, when it ended badly, as it almost inevitably would, she'd have to start the rebuilding all over again. Was it really worth the risk?

''What time tomorrow?'' she asked.

CHAPTER SEVEN

HANNAH AWAKENED around midnight to someone knocking on her bedroom door. She heard Rose call her name, the door opened a little and Rose stuck her head around it.

"You sleeping, sweetie?" she called.

"Not anymore." Hannah sat up in bed and flipped on the bedside lamp. "What's wrong?"

"Your mom." Rose sat down on the edge of the bed. She wore a leopard-skin print velour robe and her red hair was done up in a yellow banana clip. "I wanted to wait until she was asleep before I talked to you. Hannah..." Rose leaned a little closer, dropped her voice, clutched Hannah's arm. *"Your mother broke down at Kelly's tonight."*

Hannah looked at her aunt. Rose's hectic color and fruity breath suggested she'd had a few drinks; her breathless, exclamatory manner confirmed it. Rose had a way of conveying news that a glass or two of wine served to exaggerate. Sentences sprinkled with moments of prolonged eye contact as though she were waiting for the full import of whatever she'd said to sink in. Lots of touching. Deb did a wicked imitation of how a tipsy Rose could make the most banal pronouncement sound dramatic. *Hannah, the grass grows a little bit every day.* Deb would clutch Hannah's arm, stare into her eyes. *Every day, Hannah! Can you believe it?*

Still groggy from sleep, Hannah leaned her head back against the pillow. "What do you mean, she broke down?"

"I mean she broke down, Hannah." Rose engaged Hannah's eyes. "*Right in the middle of dinner.* She didn't even touch her filet. And she loves the way Kelly's does filets. They are *so* delicious." She licked her lips as though the taste still lingered. "Allan was wonderful with her, Hannah. *He is such a prince.* Why didn't you come? He was so disappointed."

"Yeah, I know, he called me. So tell me about Mom."

"Well, I ordered a carafe of burgundy." Rose smiled. "Allan took one sip of it and you'd have thought it was poison or something. *He's just used to better quality, Hannah.* You can tell that just by looking at him. Anyway, he orders this Chateau Neuf de something or other. Forty bucks a bottle. *I saw it on the wine list. Forty dollars!* I mean, it was good, but forty bucks for wine?"

"What about Mom, Rose?"

"That's what I was getting to. Well, we all had some of the wine Allan ordered, but then your mom also polished off the burgundy. *The whole carafe, Hannah.*"

"I know…" Hannah picked at a cuticle, to avoid eye contact with her aunt. "She's drinking too much. I'm going to have to talk to her."

"She is drinking way too much," Rose agreed. "*Way* too much. We were all talking so I didn't really notice how much she was drinking but then she started getting weepy. She thinks she's losing you and Faith, Hannah. And Deb, too, and she doesn't know what to do about it. *She was hysterical, Hannah.* Sobbing, mascara running down her face."

Hannah drew a deep breath. She had the clear sensation of a very large glass dome being placed over her head, a feeling she'd been getting quite often lately. "Deb's broken up with Dennis and moved back home," she said after a moment. "Why would Mom think she's losing her?"

"Because Deb's decided she's not moving back after all. She had a little tiff with your mom this morning and now she says she's going to move in with a girlfriend. *Hannah, your mother was so excited about having another grandbaby—*"

"Deb's not going to have the baby?"

Rose sighed. "That seems to be up in the air, too." She looked at Hannah for a moment. "You hungry?"

"Not particularly." She glanced at the clock by the bed. "It's after twelve, Rose."

"You know what I'd like? *Mashed potatoes.*"

"Mashed potatoes?"

"Mmm-mm. Yummy mashed potatoes. *With bacon bits, Hannah.*" Rose pulled back the quilt on Hannah's bed. "Come downstairs and talk to me while I make some."

"Rose…"

"I'll put sour cream in them."

"I don't want to eat mashed potatoes at midnight, I don't care what you put in them."

"Chives and cream cheese," Rose said in a wheedling voice. "Come on, Hannie, do it for your old auntie. What joy do I have in my life?"

"You've got plenty of joy." Hannah pulled on the red flannel shirt she'd worn the evening before over the knee-length T-shirt she slept in and stuffed her feet into a pair of terry-cloth mules. "Damn it, Rose," she protested as she followed her aunt out of the bedroom and down the stairs. "I promised myself I was going to stop this sort of thing."

"Instant or the real thing," Rose called from the pantry. "Ah hell, let's make it easy. Instant's okay when it's fixed up." She brought a box of Ore-Ida into the kitchen, held it at arm's length while she read the directions. "Stop what sort of thing?"

"This." Hannah pulled out a chair and sat down. "Do I want to be in the kitchen at midnight making stupid mashed potatoes? No, I want to be sleeping. So why am I here? Because you asked me and I couldn't say no. I'm like that with everyone and I'm sick of it."

"You have a gift, Hannah," Rose said, still squinting at the box. "You are kindhearted, loving and a good listener. The world would be a better place if there were more people like you." She took a gallon of milk from the refrigerator. "You think if I double the recipe, it'll be enough?"

"You're the only one eating," Hannah said. "So Mom's upset about Deb?" she prompted.

"Not as upset as she is about you and Liam."

"Maybe it's time she realized Deb and I are both grown women."

"She will always be your mother, Hannah," Rose said. "And she will always worry. It's what mothers do. God knows, I've tried to get her to do things with me, like that Single Sailors thing last week. She might have met a nice man with a boat, but it's always you girls…"

Wait until she hears Liam and I are taking Faith to the zoo tomorrow, Hannah thought. Her legs, bare below the nightshirt, were cold, and she scooted them up onto the chair, pulled the shirt down to cover them and wrapped her arms around her knees. "Liam and I are taking Faith to the zoo tomorrow," she told Rose. Later, she knew, she would ask herself what misguided impulse had prompted this disclosure. The best answer she could come up with right now was that she needed to talk about it to someone. Even Rose. She saw the dismay on her aunt's face, watched as Rose set down the measuring cup into which she'd been pouring potato flakes.

"No." Rose shook her head sadly at her niece. "Please tell me you're joking."

"I'm serious."

Rose clutched Hannah's arm. *"Don't do it, Hannah.* Please. For your mother, for yourself, for all of us. *Don't do it."*

Hannah rested her chin on her knees. "But I want to."

"But I want to," Rose mimicked in a whiney, child-like voice. She picked up the cup again, measured out the potatoes and put them in a bowl. "That's a very selfish attitude."

"How is it selfish?"

"For one thing, it's going to worry your mother to death."

"So that's why I shouldn't do it?"

"No, not just that…"

"What then?" She knew she should probably stop. It wasn't as though Rose was going to come up with some compelling reason that would make her change her mind, but something perverse was making her press on. "Give me one good reason why I shouldn't go to the zoo with Liam and our daughter."

"Because…" Rose microwaved a cup of milk, poured it over the potato flakes, then returned to the refrigerator. "What has fewer calories?" she called over her shoulder. "Butter or sour cream? Ah, the hell with it." She brought a tub of sour cream and a stick of butter over to the table and looked at Hannah. "Because none of us want to see you waste yourself with Liam. Sweetie, we'd all feel so much better if you and Allan—"

"Just got married, moved into his house on Riva Alto Canal and had a couple more kids?"

Rose grinned. "You are such a smart girl. Look, take it from your old aunt who's been married to two losers, there's nothing romantic about poverty. When the *va-va-va-voom* wears off with Liam, Allan's going to look a whole lot better. I'm telling you, he wouldn't hear of any of us paying anything toward dinner tonight. Can you believe that? And Kelly's isn't cheap. Just the broiled chicken is $16.95, which I think is ridiculous. *A piece of chicken,* Hannah. How much can—"

"I'm not marrying Allan, Rose."

"Well it's early yet. Allan's not going to rush you. 'I know it happened kind of quickly,' he told us, 'but I knew from the moment I first saw her.'"

"He knows I don't want to get married. He's a nice guy, but I'm not in love with him."

"Taste these." Rose shoved the bowl of potatoes at Hannah. "Tell me what they're missing."

"Rose…" Hannah pushed the bowl away. "I don't feel like tasting potatoes. I came down to talk about Mom."

"We're talking about her." Rose held a spoonful of mashed potatoes out to Hannah. "Come on, one little taste won't kill you. Butter? Salt?"

"Damn it." Hannah tasted the potatoes. "Butter."

"I thought so." Rose sliced a stick of butter in two and stirred one half into the potatoes. "Hannah, your mother has always relied on you. You're the dependable one, she's always said that. Well, except for the Liam Lapse. Deb was the one who caused her problems, but now Liam's back and, honest to God, Hannah, I see her drinking more now and I think he's the reason why."

Feeling beleaguered suddenly, Hannah stuck her elbows on the table, held her head in her hands. The whole thing with Liam was complicated enough without Margaret playing a central role in the drama. "What about Deb? Mom's always crying to me about how she doesn't understand why she and Deb can't get along. And Deb's pregnant, for God's sake. Why can't Mom just give me a break and focus on Deb for a while."

"Hannah." Rose looked at her niece. "Your mom isn't worried about Deb, because she knows Dennis isn't taking Deb and the baby and running off to Ireland where she'll never see them again." She pulled up a chair beside Hannah, sat down and took her hand. *"Worry over Liam killed your father."* Rose stared into her eyes. *"If you're not careful, your mother's going to drink herself into an early grave for the same reason."*

"BUT I DON'T WANT TO GET UP," Faith grumbled when Hannah woke her at eight-thirty the next morning. "I want to sleep some more."

"Okay." Hannah sat on the edge of Faith's bed. "Here's the deal. You can keep on sleeping, or you can go and see the koalas at the zoo."

"The koalas?" Faith rubbed her eyes. "Like the ones on TV?"

"Yep."

Faith grinned widely. "I've been wanting to see the koalas forever. Now I get to. I'm *sooo* happy."

"Well, good." Hannah selected a yellow sundress from Faith's closet, dug in the dresser drawer for a pair of matching socks. "When you're happy, I'm happy."

Which, she reflected, as she coaxed Faith into her

clothes, was exactly the sort of thing Margaret would say to her. *Not fair to put the responsibility for your own happiness on someone else's shoulders.* God, her neck was stiff with tension and the top of her head prickled. After the talk with Rose, she'd lain awake most of the night. Around four in the morning she decided that she couldn't assume all the responsibility for her mother's drinking. She was going to go to the zoo, because that's what *she* wanted to do.

Tonight she would talk to Margaret. Right now she wasn't in the mood for a confrontation.

A sweater for herself and a change of clothes for Faith bundled under her arm, she tiptoed down the stairs. The smell of coffee from the kitchen told her Margaret was already up and probably gearing for battle.

"Is Auntie Rose coming to see the koalas?" Faith asked.

"No, sweetie." As they made their way down the stairs, Hannah eased Faith's arms into a white cotton sweater. "Just you and me and…a friend of Mommy's."

"Jen?"

"No, a friend you haven't met." God, she couldn't look at her daughter's face. Maybe this wasn't such a good idea. "We'll talk about it in a little while, okay? Right now, I want you to go eat some cereal. I have to get dressed and make a quick phone call." She started back up the stairs. *Please don't tell Grandma where you're going,* she thought. *I'm not in the mood for a fight.*

Deb was not happy to be wakened by the telephone when Hannah reached her at a girlfriend's house. "Jeez, Hannah it's like the middle of the night."

"It's eight-forty-five in the morning. I've been up for two hours."

"Well, good for you," Deb said. "Some of us like to sleep in."

"So what's the deal with you and Mom?" Hannah asked her sister. "Rose said you guys had an argument and now you're not moving back home. And what's this about the baby?"

"Jeez." Debra sighed noisily. "Of course I'm keeping it. Mom said something that made me mad, I can't even remember what it was now. Probably something about Dennis, and she was talking to me like I was a little kid and it pissed me off, so I told her I was rethinking the baby. Plus, she'd been going on and on about Liam, the whole doom-and-gloom thing and I was bored with listening to it."

Hannah stared at her reflection in the mirror and wondered if it was just the morning light that made her look as though she'd been up for three nights straight. "Do me a favor, Deb." She shifted the phone to her other ear. "Don't give Mom more stuff to obsess about, okay? I don't think I can take it. Rose said Mom got really plastered last night because she was so upset about us."

"About *you,* Hannah," Deb corrected. "Listen, can we talk about this later? How about I drop by around ten? Maybe we could go have breakfast."

"I won't be here," Hannah said. "Liam and I are taking Faith to the zoo."

"Liam! You've got to be kidding. *Why?*"

Hannah took a deep breath. "Because I want to."

"And *you're* telling *me* not to give Mom stuff to obsess about?"

Five minutes later—Debra's snort of disgust still ringing in her ears—Hannah walked into the kitchen to face her mother. Margaret's nostrils pinched in cold fury as she glared at Hannah. Obviously either Rose or Faith had broken the news. After Faith finished her cereal and went upstairs to get her backpack, Margaret turned on Hannah.

"Everything I've ever done for you and Debra, I've done because I love you and want what's best for you. The two of you have always been my first priority. Always." Her voice broke. "I can't believe you're throwing it all in my face."

"I'm not throwing anything in your face, Mom. This isn't about you." Hannah reached into the refrigerator and tried to harden herself to the appeal in her mother's eyes. Suddenly the outing seemed more trouble than it was worth. She could take Faith to the zoo herself and avoid all the anguish. "This is a day at the zoo. Period."

Margaret snorted. "Day at the zoo! You might be fooling yourself, but you're not fooling me. It's that man screwing up your life again. Not to mention confusing your daughter."

"His daughter, too, and he has a name." Hannah dropped a stack of paper napkins into a wicker picnic basket. "It's Liam. And I wish you would just accept this, Mom, because all you're doing is making it difficult for everyone."

"*I'm* making it difficult?" Margaret leaned her back against the counter. "*I'm* making it difficult because I'm concerned about my daughter and granddaughter? Why don't you open your eyes, Hannah? It's not going to stop with this, I'll tell you that right now. You might as well just go and buy the damn tickets to Ireland."

Hannah looked at her mother, suddenly weary of the argument. "Mom, does it ever occur to you that all of this is *my* problem? Faith's *my* daughter? Liam was *my* husband. Faith's *our* daughter. I appreciate you're concerned for us, but damn it, I have a right to lead my life without having to factor your reaction into everything I do.''

"No." Margaret shook her head. "You're wrong, this isn't just *your* problem. You and Faith have lived in this house from the day she came home from the hospital. I was right here, in this kitchen, watching when she took her first step. Who picked her up from her first day at kindergarten? Who took her to swimming lessons? I could go on and on.''

"You did all those things because *you* wanted to do them, Mom. You begged me to let you pick her up from school. You think I wouldn't rather have done it myself?''

"Then you should have said something.''

"I know that now. Remember yesterday when you told me to start paying attention to my own feelings? Well, that's what I should have done. But I didn't, because you were always telling me how much you loved doing all these things and I decided it wasn't worth getting into an argument about it.'' She shook her head. "But I've learned my lesson. I'm going to start doing what *I* want to do. And I want to go to San Diego with Liam and Faith.''

"*Liam.*'' Margaret said the name like a curse. "You might have forgotten the state you were in when you were married to him, but I haven't.''

"How could I forget when you and everyone else reminds me of it on a daily basis? God, I am so sick of hearing about it. So I made a mistake. Big deal. Deb's made a few mistakes. Everybody makes mistakes in their lives.''

"But they learn from them and move on. All you're doing by seeing him again is compounding your mistake.''

"Liam deserves a chance to spend some time with his daughter," Hannah said. "It wasn't his fault—"

"You know what I'm sick of?" Margaret asked, her voice low and fierce. "I'm sick to death of hearing about poor Liam and his goddamned rights. Fine, do whatever you want, it's your life. If you're so besotted and foolish that you'll agree to whatever this idiot wants, there's not much I can do about it. I'll tell you this though, Faith's my granddaughter and if you think I'm going to let him steal her away, you'd better think again."

"Grandma!" Faith burst into the kitchen. "Look! I have five dollars and I'm going to buy you a present at the zoo."

"Oh, my goodness." With a visible effort to compose her expression, Margaret got down on her knees, wrapped her arms around Faith's waist and looked into her granddaughter's eyes. "That is *so* sweet of you. But you know the nicest present you could possibly give me?"

Faith smiled. "What?"

"Just be my little darling girl," she said, her voice breaking. "Grandma loves you very, very much. And you know what? When you come home tonight, Grandma will have a great big surprise for you."

HANNAH AND FAITH WERE WAITING outside the house when Liam pulled up in Miranda's Mercedes. Faith, in a yellow dress, was hopping on one foot and circling her arms like a windmill. Hannah wore a green sundress and looked as though she might have been crying. As he got out of the car and walked around to where they were standing, Liam realized his heart was pounding.

He smiled at Hannah, then squatted down so that he was eye level with his daughter. *His daughter.* Eyes exactly the same dark, almost-navy-blue as his own. Faith clutched her mother's legs and peered warily at him. "You must be George," he said.

"No." She shook her head.

"Fred?"

A glimmer of a smile suggested she was on to his joke. "Fred's a boy's name," she said.

"Ah, you're right. Let me think a bit. I know. You're Griselda."

She released her grip from Hannah's leg. "My name is Faith."

"Faith. That was going to be my next guess. Well, good morning, Faith." He held out his hand. "I'm Liam."

Her eyes briefly registered his hand, moved to his face. "Hi."

"Hi. Shall we shake?" Faith nodded slightly, and he took his daughter's small hand in his own. "Nice to meet you, Faith," he said.

She rewarded him with a broader smile. "Nice to meet you, too," she said.

He felt a little thrill of victory, glanced up and met Hannah's eyes. She was smiling, too. He looked back at Faith. "I don't know about you, but it seems awfully early to be up and around. I haven't even had breakfast. What about you?"

"I had cereal."

"Cereal." Liam pulled a face. "Are you all that keen on cereal, then?"

Faith looked up at her mother.

"He's asking if you like cereal," Hannah said.

"Not the kind we have now," Faith replied. "But Mommy said I had to eat it."

"And what kind is it you have now?" Liam asked.

"The kind that gets all soggy when the milk goes on it."

"There's nothing worse," Liam said. "Tell me though, what are your thoughts on doughnuts?"

"Doughnuts?" Faith grinned. "I love doughnuts, don't I, Mommy?"

"She's a huge doughnut fan," Hannah said.

"Could you eat two, do you think?"

"Three," Faith said.

"Three." He gave her a skeptical look. "Ah, come on."

"I can. If they're doughnut holes."

"Right then." He held out his hand again. "If you'll help me to my feet, I think we should go and find a place that sells doughnut holes."

They found a place as they headed south on Pacific Coast Highway toward San Diego. Faith had spotted a Dunkin' Donuts, and Liam made a show of slamming on the brakes and zooming up to the shop as though they were on a mission of great importance. Hannah had shot him a reproving look, but now as they sat across from each other at a plastic table by the window, watching Faith drop quarters into a video game, Hannah seemed relaxed and happy enough as she sipped her double nonfat latte, or whatever complicated thing she'd ordered, and he felt he could breathe a little easier. Only an hour into the day, but so far things were going well enough. He said so to Hannah and she smiled.

"Of course they are. You're buying her doughnuts and taking her to the zoo. What wouldn't be okay about that?"

"I suppose you're right." He drank some coffee from a paper cup. "You know, in my whole life, I doubt I've spent more than twelve hours with children. I never know what to say to them. I thought maybe she wouldn't like me.''

She eyed him over her coffee cup. ''Girls always like you, Liam.''

''Big ones though. And even that's not always true.''

''You're doing fine.''

''Is everything all right with you?''

''Meaning?''

''Earlier, I thought you might have been crying.''

''Yeah…'' She shrugged. ''My mother.''

''Let me guess. She's not happy about my seeing Faith?''

''To put it mildly.'' She picked at the edge of her napkin. ''We always seem to be fighting lately. I feel guilty for upsetting her and angry at the same time…'' She paused, bit her lip and seemed to struggle for a moment. ''My sister would just say to hell with her. She and Mom have never been that close. I don't know, maybe Mom just has a bad case of empty-nest syndrome, but I feel bad for her. Responsible.''

''Your sister's not at home anymore?''

''Well…'' She sighed. ''It's a long story. Mom's never quite known where she is with Deb, but I think she figured somehow that Faith and I would always be around. Now she's scared to death you're going to take us away.''

''The pirate's dad could do the same thing,'' he said. ''How would she feel about that?''

''She'd miss us,'' Hannah said. ''But…'' She hesitated. ''Allan's sort of won her over. Plus, she isn't afraid Allan will take us…Faith, I mean.'' Her face colored. ''He won't take Faith off to Ireland where my mom will never see her again.''

Liam watched Faith for a moment. Her ponytail had

worked its way out of the clasp and her shoulders tensed as she energetically steered the wheel on the video machine.

"It's strange really," he said, "all things considered. But I don't blame your mother for being concerned. I'm not sure how I'd feel if my daughter ended up with someone like me."

Hannah frowned across the table at him. "What?"

"Well, picture it yourself. Faith brings this boy home—"

"Years from now, of course."

"Of course. Years and years."

Hannah grinned. "Twenty at least."

"Let's say she's told you all about him, and you want to like him because she's so over-the-moon. And then you meet him and put him through the twenty questions rigmarole—"

"Like my dad did to you."

"Believe me, with your dad it was a lot more than twenty questions and he didn't like the answers to any of them. I wasn't close to being suitable. But you'll be that way with Faith, too. You'll want a boy who'll go on to college and become a doctor or something. Someone who comes from the same sort of family you do. Who doesn't eat his peas off a knife."

She laughed. "You never did that."

"Only because I could never get them to stay on."

And then they were both smiling, sitting there with a box of doughnut holes on the table between them, the smell of hot coffee in the air, watching their daughter shoot space aliens. Once, Faith turned to see them watching her, grinned, then went on with her game.

He looked down at their hands on the table. Hannah's nails were polished pink, and she wore a woven silver band on the middle finger of her right hand and something with a green stone on the index finger of her left hand. They'd both worn cheap gold rings when they were married. He would take his off before performances because it got in the way of the guitar strings. Hannah had clearly disbelieved his explanation though and looking back, it seemed that many of their fights had started around the same time every evening when he removed his ring.

"Liam…" She glanced up at him. "What you said yesterday about how we might still be together if my family had stayed out of our lives?"

He nodded. "Right."

"I was surprised, to say the least. Do you really think about it much?"

"I used to." His glance shifted back to Faith for a moment, then across the table to Hannah. "But I'd remind myself about the abortion and after a while…well, I came around to thinking that, all in all, it probably happened for the best. Like you said last night, we had a lot of strikes against us. In hindsight, I can see that you were in a pretty bad state. I think it says something about what a self-absorbed bastard I was that I couldn't recognize it myself."

"Self-absorbed? That's how you think of yourself?"

He shrugged. "Single-minded, intensely focused, tunnel vision. It all pretty much comes down to the same thing."

"You did used to get kind of wrapped up in the music. Especially when you were writing songs."

"Which was all the time." He laughed. "Remember when I nearly burned the kitchen down? What was it I'd done? Left a saucepan on the stove or something."

"A pot of chili. I came into the kitchen and there was

all this smoke billowing up and you hadn't even noticed.''

"Day-to-day survival sort of goes by the board when I'm really tuned in to what I'm doing," he said.

"Still?"

He nodded. "Music at the cost of everything else."

HANNAH KEPT REMINDING HERSELF of that as they drove down the coast to San Diego. Reminded herself every time she looked at Liam and pictured scenes starring the three of them. Seated around the dinner table, going on vacation together and, her favorite, grouped around a bassinet smiling at the newest addition to their family.

The fantasies both compelled and annoyed her. It wasn't as though she'd put her life on hold while she waited around for Liam to say he wanted them to try again. Besides, as she kept telling herself, this day wasn't about her and Liam. It was about Liam spending time with his daughter. Hannah was only along for the ride.

She'd tried to keep that thought in mind last night as she prepared for their trip to the zoo. After Liam had left, but before everyone else got home, she'd roasted chicken, made a green salad and Faith's favorite macaroni salad, defrosted a loaf of pesto cheese bread and baked a pan of chocolate brownies. Then shoved everything in the back of the refrigerator so Margaret wouldn't see it.

"So Faith…" Liam turned his head slightly to address his daughter. "I bet I know what you like best about the zoo."

"What?"

"Uh…" He furrowed his forehead, feigning deep

thought. "Wait, it's coming to me. I think it's…uh, right, I'm getting a picture of it. It's…the koalas."

"Hey." Faith kicked her foot at the back of his seat. "How d'you know that?"

"Because I know everything," he said.

"Everything?" Faith cackled. "Uh-uh."

"I do though. Ask me a question."

"Um. How many is nine hundred and forty-two million, million, million and six billion, million?"

Liam groaned. "Ah, Faith, how could you do it to me? That's the one question I don't have the answer to." He looked at Hannah. "You told her, didn't you? You told her to ask me that question."

"No, she didn't." Faith leaned forward in her seat to touch Hannah's shoulder. "You didn't tell me, did you, Mommy?"

"I never said a word," Hannah agreed.

"See! Mommy didn't tell me."

"But how do I know you and your mum aren't in cahoots?" Liam asked with a wink at Hannah. "How do I know you're not just sticking up for her?"

Hannah gave Faith's foot a little tug, resisted a sudden urge to reach over and give Liam a quick hug. She pictured it—her arm around his shoulders, the way he'd feel as she pulled him close. His quick look of surprise. They'd been studiously careful to avoid even the most casual physical contact. He'd apologized for accidentally grazing her arm as they left the doughnut shop. She'd leaned far back in her seat when he reached over to get his sunglasses from the glove compartment. A tacit agreement, it seemed, that this day was all about their daughter, not her parents.

The beach towns rolled by. Seal Beach, Huntington, Newport. In Laguna, as they stopped for a light, she watched three teenage girls in bikini tops and towels, wrapped sarong-style around their hips, saunter across the road, tossing glances over tanned shoulders. She'd only been a year or so older when she married Liam.

She shifted in her seat and brought her foot up under her, turning slightly so that she could see Liam without appearing to be watching him. His faded navy T-shirt had a small hole on the shoulder. His jeans were similarly worn, his feet thrust into a pair of battered brown sandals. Allan had an expensive and extensive casual wardrobe of color-coordinated shirts and pants. Once he'd complained that it had taken him two weeks to find exactly the right shade of cream shirt to go with a new pair of khakis. Everything was either too yellow or too beige, he'd told her. If she asked Liam what color shirt he was wearing, she knew without a doubt that he'd have absolutely no idea. The thought made her grin. A moment later, as though he'd read what she was thinking, he turned his head to smile at her. The physical impact was like a bolt through her body.

Blood rushing to her face, she turned to glance at the back seat where Faith had fallen asleep, her head bent awkwardly. Hannah unfastened her seat belt, kneeled up on the front seat and shifted her sleeping daughter to a more comfortable position. Back in her seat again, she sat with her knees close together, her eyes straight ahead, intensely aware of Liam's hands on the steering wheel; of his legs, his neck. They passed through Laguna, past massive Spanish-style homes that blocked all but brief glimpses of the ocean. Bougainvillea climbed white stucco walls, tumbled over wrought iron gates. Hands, legs, neck. Mouth. She shifted in her seat.

This day wasn't about her and Liam.

Her body hadn't quite got the message. Shoulders

touching as they'd stood at the kitchen window the day before. Mouth curved in a smile. Would he take her hand as they walked through the zoo? Kiss her when he dropped her off tonight?

Pay attention to what *you* want, Margaret had said.

CHAPTER EIGHT

SOMEWHERE BETWEEN the zebras and the monkeys, Liam made a decision. They'd been traipsing around for hours from exhibit to exhibit. Faith had liked the monkeys. She'd also liked the elephants, the zebras, the lions and the giraffes. And, of course, the koalas. Then it was a return visit to the lions, several trips to the petting zoo, a stop for the picnic lunch Hannah had packed and then a final ogle at the monkeys.

Faith's hand was warm and sticky in his as they trudged up the hill, past an enclosure of exotic birds. His shirt sticking to his back, Liam had looked down at her face, flushed with heat and exertion, her hair tangled and blowing, and known there was no longer any question of simply going back to Ireland and forgetting about her.

He wanted his daughter in his life.

Brid was wrong about it being either Faith or his music. There was room for both. In fact, by the time they'd packed up the food and headed over to the monkey exhibit, he'd worked out a plan that would have Faith spending part of every summer and every alternate Christmas with him in Ireland.

He stood with Faith and Hannah watching small gray monkeys dart from branch to branch. He would tell Hannah when they were back in Long Beach tonight. At the same time, they would also discuss when to tell Faith that he was her father. The thought excited him so much that it was all he could do not to rush them through the exhibits so that he could tell Hannah about his decision.

A daughter. He looked down at her. *My daughter.*

"Hey, Liam." Faith tugged at his hand. "Do you want an ice cream?"

"An ice cream?" He pretended to think about it. "Nah. What I'd really like is a nice big plate of brussels sprouts."

Faith's look said she was on to him. *"Uh-uh."*

"Sure, I love them. Great big green ones with lots of salt and pepper. I bet your mother likes them, too." He shot another look at Hannah. "Ask her."

"Mommy wants ice cream," Faith said. "Right, Mommy?"

"I think someone has already had more than enough sugar for one day," Hannah said. "How about an apple?"

"No." Faith's face crumpled. "I want an ice cream."

"I want an ice cream, too," Liam said.

Hannah looked at him long enough for him to understand that he'd made a strategic mistake. "On the other hand, an apple sounds good, too," he amended.

"Hey, Liam, you know what?" Faith smiled up at him. "Allan said when we go camping, we have to put bits of apple on the stick when we roast the marshmallows because if you eat too many marshmallows, your teeth will fall out."

Allan should go to hell, Liam thought. And, suddenly a cloud drifted across his horizon, colliding with all the sunny thoughts of the things he wanted to do with his daughter. Allan's role hadn't occurred to him. Allan— who would be there when he wasn't. Birthdays, outings, meals together. Liam couldn't stop Hannah from seeing Allan, or anyone else she wanted to see, but children's

attention spans were short. He might have made a hit
with Faith today, but in a week or so she'd hardly remember his name. She'd end up thinking of Allan as her
real father and himself as a sort of fun uncle she saw a
couple of times a year.

THEY RODE BACK to Long Beach in silence, Faith asleep
in the back seat. Hannah had dozed a couple of times,
woken to look at Liam, who seemed lost in his thoughts.
It was a little after eight when they pulled up outside the
house, the lights were on in the living room. The drapes
twitched once, then the room went dark. Hannah glanced
at Faith, still sleeping, then at Liam, his face shadowy
in the dim glow from a streetlight. She hoped to God
her mother and Rose weren't sitting at the kitchen table,
waiting for a debriefing.

"It's been a nice day," she said. "Faith obviously
enjoyed it. I did, too."

"So did I." Liam turned in his seat to look at her.
"How long do you think Faith will remember me?"

"After today? I don't know." She felt, rather than
saw, Liam's reaction and tried to soften the words.
"Faith had a great time, Liam, but she's only six."

"She'll forget me," Liam answered his own question.
"I'll be gone in a day or so, and she'll forget all about
me."

Again, Hannah tried to think of something to say that
would make him feel better. "I think you made an impression on her. I think she genuinely enjoyed being
with you."

"Until the pirate's dad takes her camping, or back to
the zoo, or whatever. And then what?"

She looked at him, unable to come up with an answer.

Or at least an answer that wouldn't hurt him. The truth was, he was right.

"I'll help you carry her inside," he said. "She'll be a dead weight."

Hannah got out, held the seat forward as Liam lifted Faith out of the car. Cradling his daughter in his arms, he followed Hannah up the driveway. As she unlocked the door, she felt her pulse speed up. From the kitchen, she heard a chair scrape.

"Okay," she whispered. "Let's take her straight upstairs."

He nodded. At the top of the stairs, Hannah pushed open Faith's bedroom door and stood aside for Liam to carry her in. Margaret called from the kitchen and Hannah tiptoed to the top of the stairs. "I'm up here, Mom. With Liam. We're putting Faith to bed."

When she returned to the doorway, Liam had removed Faith's sneakers and covered her with a folded blanket.

Seated on the bed beside their daughter, he turned around to look at Hannah. "She'll be out for the night, then?"

"Completely."

He smiled, his eyes taking in the room with its menagerie of stuffed animals and toys littered across the floor. "Well…" He stood. "I'd better be going. I've a radio interview in Los Angeles tomorrow early."

Outside Faith's room, they stood in silence for a moment, then Liam turned and walked down the stairs. Hannah followed him to the front door, opened it and stepped onto the porch, waiting for Liam to say whatever was on his mind. Her stomach suddenly felt tense with apprehension.

"I don't have this all worked out yet," Liam said. "But I want to be a father to Faith. A *real* father. I want to spend birthdays and Christmas with her, whether it's here or in Ireland. I want her to come to Ireland for her summer holidays. Before I leave, I want us to tell her I'm her father.''

Hannah couldn't speak. Ireland. He wanted to have Faith with him in Ireland. *Exactly what Margaret had predicted.* ''Maybe you're moving a little fast, Liam,'' she finally said. ''You just said you don't have it all worked out. Maybe we need to think things through a bit.''

''I want to be a part of her life. I want her to get to know me. I've already lost too much time.''

''I understand that. But this isn't simply about what *you* want. It's about what's best for Faith. You've spent one day with her. There's a whole lot more to being a father than a day at the zoo.''

''I'm sure there is,'' he said. ''Until now, unfortunately, I haven't had the chance to find that out.''

''Look, let me at least prepare her a little.''

''Prepare her for what? The shock of hearing I'm her father?'' He laughed. ''Oh right, I forgot. She thinks I'm in heaven, doesn't she? I suppose that could be a bit of a shock…''

''Liam, come on, I'm not the enemy here. I'm concerned about my daughter…our daughter. If we do tell her, I want to be absolutely sure it's the right thing to do.''

''You need to consult with your family first, is that it?''

''This isn't their decision, Liam. It's ours. Yours and mine.'' But even as she said the words, she recognized their fallacy. Expecting that her mother and the rest of the family would just quietly accept whatever she and Liam decided was unrealistic, to say the least. As if to underscore the point, the curtain in the living room twitched again.

"Let me ask you something." She studied his face for a moment, trying to read some indication of whether this was true commitment, or more of a spur-of-the-moment fantasy. "You're on the road most of the time. How can you devote any kind of quality time to her?"

"I told you I don't have all the details worked out."

"Maybe you need to do that before you make a decision like this."

"Really?" Liam asked. "And what then? If you approve, I can be her father? But if not, the pirate's dad gets the job? To hell with that." He turned as though to go, then stopped. "Your family decided once that I wasn't fit to be a father, they're not going to bloody well do it again. I'll be by tomorrow, about six. I want to see Faith before she goes to bed and then we'll talk."

HER HEART THUNDERING so hard she felt sick to her stomach, Hannah watched the Mercedes peel up Termino and out of sight. As she pushed open the front door, she heard footsteps in the hallway and then Margaret was peering anxiously into her face.

"Well?"

"Well what, Mom?"

"Well, how did it go?"

"It went fine." She pushed past her mother and headed for the stairs. All she wanted was to lie down on the bed and try to sort out her thoughts. Rose appeared from the kitchen. Rose and her mother were wearing matching purple fleecy robes trimmed with white piping. They'd seen them on sale at the May Company a month or so ago and, even though Margaret always sniffed that Rose had no taste when it came to clothes, both sisters liked the robes so much they'd each bought one. Rose had some sort of pale green mask on her face and her hair was pushed under a pink stretchy headband. Margaret's hair was pulled up into an elastic and she was holding a glass of white wine.

"Did he say anything?" Margaret asked.

Hannah stopped halfway up the stairs, looked down at her mother and aunt. "Anything about what?"

Rose grinned, sending bits of her mask fluttering to the floor. "Damn it, I need to get this stuff of my face." She looked up at Hannah. "Your mother's *terrified,* Hannah," Rose said. "She thinks he's going to take Faith back to Ireland,"

"Well, it's not exactly unheard-of, Rose." Margaret's voice was indignant. "Oprah had a show about parents who kidnap their own children. So don't act as though it's some outlandish thing I dreamed up."

"I tried to tell her." Rose addressed Hannah. "But Ms. Gloom-and-Doom always thinks the worst. I told her, no way does that guy want to be a daddy. He's a musician, for God's sake."

"Musicians *do* have families, Rose." Margaret looked at her sister as though she were talking to a slightly dim-witted child. "And he's Irish, no less. The Irish are big on family. Next thing you know, Hannah will be pregnant again—"

"And barefoot, Mom," Hannah said. "Don't forget about that. Barefoot, pregnant and living in a shanty."

"Don't be sarcastic," Margaret said. "I'm your mother. It wouldn't be natural if I didn't worry." She took a sip of wine. "So when does he plan on trying to see her again?"

Hannah watched her mother for a moment. "You

know what, Mom? I think you need to lay off the wine a bit. I'm worried about your drinking.''

AT SCHOOL the next morning, Jen threw a music magazine down on the table where Hannah was setting out little bottles of apple juice. "Rocky subscribes to it. Your boy's got quite a photo spread," she said. "Read the bit about the redhead."

Hannah's eyes moved from the three pictures of Liam and Brid arranged around a center article. Liam playing a guitar, his face pensive. Liam, head bowed over a yellow notepad, a pencil in his mouth. Writing Songs, the caption read. The largest picture showed Liam on a city street somewhere. He wore jeans and a black leather jacket and stood slouched, unsmiling, against the plate-glass window of what looked like a nightclub. Visible inside, a stage with a microphone and band posters on the wall.

Beside him, Brid, with her chin on his shoulder, arms wrapped around his waist. She looked tiny and insubstantial, lost inside a heavily zippered black jacket almost identical to Liam's and, incongruously, a filmy white dress that came almost to her ankles. Just Good Friends, the caption read.

Hannah looked at Jen, who shrugged. "So did you guys have a good time at the zoo yesterday?"

"Yeah." Unsettled now, Hannah forced herself to look away from the picture. *We're just good friends,* Liam had said. Not that his relationship with his singer mattered to her, anyway. "Actually, it was pretty much Faith's show," she said. "She had a great time."

The kids started filing in for their snacks, and Hannah got very involved with handing out bottles of juice, aware of Jen watching her thoughtfully.

"My mother's a psychiatrist," Morgan Montgomery announced as she took the juice from Hannah. "And she's going to an important conference in San Francisco."

"Great," Hannah said. Liam was also going to San Francisco. Maybe she should go, as well. Grab a quick session with Morgan Montgomery's mother and see if they could figure out why she kept having these totally unrealistic delusions about Liam falling in love with her and quitting the band to buy a tract home in Orange County so he could be a part of Faith's life without taking her off to Ireland.

"Are you going to see him again?" Jen asked after the kids had filed back out to the playground.

"Tonight."

Jen grinned. "Cool. And…?" She wagged her head from side to side. "Sparks?"

"It's not like that. He wants to see Faith."

"And that's it? There's nothing else going on?"

"He wants to be…" She held up the first two fingers of each hand. "Quote, part of Faith's life. That includes having her spend time with him in Ireland."

"God." Jen's smile faded. "What are you going to do?"

"I don't know yet. We're going to talk about it tonight."

"How did your mom take that?"

"She doesn't know yet."

Jen shook her head. "Poor Hannah. I don't know how you do it. If I lived with my mother, either I'd end up killing her or she'd kill me."

Hannah looked at Jen for a moment. "I think I need to move out." Her face felt hot. Having said the words, it was as if she'd opened a box and released something that couldn't be put back. "I need a place of my own. Me and Faith. It's time."

"Because of all this…" Jen waved her hand at the magazine with Liam's picture.

"That and…" An image of Margaret and Rose in their purple robes waiting for her to come home flashed across her brain. "Just everything."

"CAN YOU BE READY in twenty minutes, Liam?" Miranda Payton's blond head appeared around Liam's bedroom door.

"Sure." Liam stood and stretched. The sky outside the window was the usual ceramic blue, and he could hear voices from the pool beneath his window. It sounded like Pearse. He set down the notebook he'd been using to jot lines for a song. His usual working position—crouched over the pages with the guitar lodged under one arm and a pen in the other hand. Spread over the floor were the pictures of Faith that Hannah had given him. Next to them, an old picture of Hannah he'd kept in his wallet.

Miranda's glance moved around the room; lighted on his guitar, the notebook, on a shirt he'd thrown over the back of a chair, lingered on the unmade bed and finally came to rest on the pictures on the floor. Liam waited for her to say something, but the silence lengthened, and finally she just looked at him and smiled.

"I don't mind driving up to L.A. if you've got something to do," Liam said. In fact, he would rather go alone, but Miranda had offered and since he'd be using her car, he couldn't think of a way to refuse without seeming rude. "I think I've got the hang of California motorways now."

"Freeways, Liam." Miranda revealed her perfectly

white teeth. She was wearing black. Trousers, skintight shirt and leather jacket. "Listen, cutie, there's absolutely no way you can talk me out of going. I am *so* excited. I've never been inside a TV studio before."

"It's not that exciting, Miranda." Liam dug through his battered gig bag for the list of media interviews Joel, his manager, had lined up. An interview with a reporter at a coffee shop on Sunset; a visit with a radio DJ who seemed quite enthusiastic about the band and a taping for a TV chat show. Not one of the big ones, according to Joel, but any exposure was better than none. "A load of blah-blah-blah," Liam said with a grin at Miranda. "That's what it really comes down to."

Miranda watched him for a moment. "That's what *you* say, Liam. I think there's much more to it than that." She bent to pick up the pad he'd left on the floor. "What's this? A new song?"

"Yeah." He reached for the notepad. "Let's have it."

She pulled it away, out of his reach. "'Faith,'" she read. "'Faith, faith, faith. Hope. Hannah. Faith. Love.'"

"Miranda."

"Sorry."

"Forget it." He stuck the notepad in the bag. "I'll go and see if Brid's got herself together."

"Wait, Liam." She caught his arm. "I'm sorry, really."

"It's nothing. Drop it."

"Kind of personal, huh?"

"I said drop it, Miranda. It's nothing. Just words. *Blah-blah-blah.*"

"Music?" The landlord cocked his head slightly. "Yeah, I hear it. Thump, thump, thump. It's the kid next door. I've told him to keep it down, the walls are too thin for that sort of thing. Other neighbors complain, but—'' With a what-can-you-do-about-it shrug, he looked at Hannah. "What d'you think?"

Hannah tried for something diplomatic to say. The duplex wasn't quite what she'd envisioned. "I need to think about it," she said.

"Suit yourself," the landlord said. "For what you want to pay, you're not going to get a luxury condo at the beach."

True, but she'd hoped for something a little nicer. She followed him into a small hallway with scuffed hardwood floors. The faint smell of cigarette smoke and new paint filled her nose, and she tried to imagine bringing Faith home here. On either side of the hallway were two small bedrooms, painted stark white. Dusty, uncovered windows stared out like blank eyes onto the street. The largest room was half the size of the one Faith now slept in.

She felt her throat clog with tears. In a little over two weeks, she'd gone from being comfortably secure in the center of a warm and loving family to feeling suspicious, alone and slightly adrift.

"I've got three other people wanting to look at it," the landlord called. "No skin off my nose if it's not what you're looking for."

"Just give me a minute." She walked into the other bedroom and peered out the window. The view was uninspiring, but the window box could be filled with geranium cuttings. She turned from the window to look again at the room and thought about an ad for bed linens she'd seen in the latest *Redbook*.

The picture was exactly the way she'd like her bedroom to look. Shades of taupe, cream and off-white; muslin curtains fluttering in the breeze and a bed piled high with fluffy pillows and comforters. And—not shown in the ad, but materializing now in her brain— Liam on the bed, pillows propped behind his head. Wearing nothing but a faint smile as he watched her undress.

She slammed a door on the image. But took the place anyway.

THE TV HOST, Rachel something or other, was a skinny redhead with enormous black-rimmed glasses, crimson lips and the longest fingernails Liam had ever seen in his life. More like talons really.

He sat on a high stool on a set designed to look like a chic living room, listening to her describe his music as "a touch melancholy, but also joyous and uplifting." Rachel sat opposite him on another stool, legs in sheer black stockings crossed at the ankles, her expression intense.

Ten minutes into the interview, Rachel had started to get on his nerves, tossing out idiotic questions that had little to do with music. Brid would have answered some of them if she'd been there; idiotic questions didn't bother Brid. But Brid hadn't been in her room when he'd knocked that morning. Hadn't been home last night when he'd got back from San Diego and, from her undisturbed bed, it appeared she hadn't been home all night. Anxiety about her wasn't doing much to improve Liam's mood.

"You've been quoted in the European press as saying you tend to live life on the edge." The interviewer leaned closer. "What exactly did you mean by that?"

"I suppose that I'm bored when things get too predictable." He couldn't actually remember having made the remark, but it was the way he felt sometimes. "Excitement, intensity, that sort of thing, make me feel alive. I'd be miserable going off to the same job every day, for instance. Coming home to the same house every night.'' *So how can you expect to be part of Faith's life?* Rachel was waiting for him to say more. He shrugged as if to say that topic was closed.

Rachel consulted her notes for a moment, then reeled off highlights from the band's history. ''Your second release, 'Betrayed,' made the UK charts a few years back,'' she said. ''And you've got a new release set for later this year.'' A quick glance at her notes. ''August. And Wild Rovers fans in this country can catch you…''

''In Santa Barbara next week, San Luis Obispo the next day, then San José and San Francisco.''

''And then?''

''And then back to Ireland to do an album and another European tour later this year.''

Rachel smiled. ''It doesn't sound as though you'd have time to be bored.''

''It's the way I like it,'' he said. *I want to be a part of Faith's life.*

Rachel leaned forward on her stool. ''What would you have been, do you think, if you weren't a musician?''

Liam thought for a minute. ''I don't know.'' He shrugged. ''An ambulance driver.''

''Really?'' She smiled at him. ''And why is that?''

''Danger,'' Liam said, improvising because he really didn't know why the hell he'd given her that answer. ''Catastrophe. Physical risks. All that sort of thing. I thrive on it.''

''Ah.'' Rachel's smile grew knowing. ''A man who craves intensity and stimulation, who abhors the dullness and meaningless of a mundane existence.''

''If you say so,'' he said, glad now Brid wasn't here

listening to this rubbish. She'd have hooted him off the stool. Except that it wasn't *all* rubbish. He thought of the guests at Faith's party, grouped around the barbecue in their color-coordinated golf clothes. The joker in the apron and a chef's hat. He'd die before he put on an apron. But he didn't need an apron to be a father to his daughter.

Rachel had another look at her notes. She held his glance for a moment before she asked the question. "You've been linked romantically with your lead singer, Brid Kelly."

He made eye contact with her. "I have."

"But you both deny there's any truth to it."

Liam folded his arms across his chest. "Right."

"Right you're linked romantically, or right there's no truth to it."

"The latter," Liam said.

"And is there anyone in your life right now?"

"There are a lot of people in my life right now."

"A special someone?"

"I don't discuss my personal life," he said.

HANNAH HAD GIVEN the landlord a check for first and last month's rent and, on her way home, she stopped to pick up a few things she'd need for the new place. Her fantasies called for linens and dishes from the Pottery Barn and Williams-Sonoma, but her depleted checking account dictated Wal-Mart. Outside her mother's house, she turned off the ignition, leaned her head against the back of the seat and tried to think. If she packed a little every night when she got home from school, she could move this weekend. Jen had offered Rocky's truck and his help for the cost of a couple of six-packs and a pizza.

First though, she had to get through this evening.

Liam's visit and—before or after, she hadn't decided—
the little matter of telling Margaret that she and Faith
were moving out. Her brain couldn't, wouldn't, deal
with Faith spending her summer vacations in Ireland.
The prospect was so unimaginable, it was easier not to
think about it. Which was a little like trying to ignore
an elephant in the living room. With a sigh, she opened
the car door and started up the steps to the house.

Faith greeted her in the hallway.

"Grandma has a big surprise for you, Mommy."

CHAPTER NINE

"SHE DOES?" Hannah hauled Faith up into her arms, and grinned as her daughter's legs wrapped around her. "God, you're getting big," she groaned, setting her down. Grandma's big surprise for Faith yesterday had been an elaborate jungle gym, installed in the backyard while they were at the zoo. What Margaret's latest surprise might be she had no idea and didn't want to imagine. She nuzzled Faith's neck. "I have a surprise for you, too."

Faith pulled away to look at her. "You do?"

"Yep. Remember Liam? He went to the zoo with us yesterday? He's coming to see you tonight."

"He is?" Faith jumped up and down. "Yay. I like Liam. Hey, Grandma." She started up the stairs. "Guess who—"

"Faith." Hannah put her fingers to her lips. "Let's not say anything right this minute, okay?"

"How come?"

"Just because." *Great. This from a teacher at La Petite Ecole?* She drew a deep breath. "Where is everyone?"

"Grandma's upstairs working on your surprise and so is everyone else. I have to make you stay down here, because if you go up, you'll ruin everything. Wait here, okay?"

"Got it." Hannah dropped her car keys onto the small

wooden table by the front door, and leafed through the day's stack of mail. After she and Liam broke up, she used to make daily pilgrimages to this table, frantically searching through the mail for a letter from him. He'd never written. Or maybe he had, she thought now.

She sat on the bottom stair. A scent of baking apples wafted out from the kitchen, mingled with the Lemon Pledge polish her mother used. When her father was alive, the smoky vanilla smell of his pipe tobacco would drift through the house like a presence. Years from now, Lemon Pledge and pipe tobacco would still mean home. In her new place, she would use this organic polish she'd seen in Trader Joe's. Beeswax, or something. In *her* home.

More laughter from upstairs. On the wall above the hall table, a picture of herself at a year; ribbons in her hair and a frilled dress. Within the same frame, a picture of Faith plunging tiny hands into her first birthday cake. Other pictures ran gallery-style along either side of the wall.

Margaret had been obsessive about framing all school pictures, even the hated eighth-grade one. Zits and a mouthful of braces. Embarrassed and mortified by the picture, Hannah had removed it from the wall and hidden it at the bottom of her underwear drawer, praying her mother wouldn't notice it was missing. No such luck. The picture was back again the following day.

She looked at it now, thinking of all the dramas— major and minor—that had played out in this house. Now she was about to take her daughter to an anonymous place with no memories, no warm associations; a place where traces of other lives had been eradicated with a few gallons of semigloss.

"Hey, look who's finally here." Her mother appeared

at the top of the stairs. "Hannah's home," she called
out. Rose and Helen emerged from the spare bedroom;
behind them, Joe Graves, the guy from down the road,
his shirtsleeves rolled up to the elbow. They were all
smiling.

"I get to put the blindfold on Mommy." Faith jumped
up and down beside Hannah. "Okay?"

"Here, honey, use this." Rose pulled off the red ban-
danna she'd worn around her hair and tossed it to Faith.
It fluttered like a gaudy leaf and settled on the stairs.
Hannah, slightly bemused, watched Faith scamper up to
retrieve it.

"Okay, Mommy, bend down so I can tie this." Faith
said. "And don't peek."

"I'm not peeking." Hannah felt Faith's small hands
at the back of her head, tangling strands of hair into the
knot she was trying to tie. After several failed attempts,
Rose called out an offer of assistance, which Faith
stoutly declined. Finally, with the scarf so loose around
her face that she had to tense her neck to stop it falling
off, Hannah felt Faith grab her hand and they started up
the stairs. Eyes closed because she could see through the
bottom of the blindfold, she laughed as she tripped on a
runner. In her enthusiasm, Faith was practically dragging
her up the stairs. "Not so fast, sweetie," Hannah said,
still laughing. "I can't see where I'm going, remember?"

At the top of the stairs, they made their way hand in
hand down the carpeted hallway. She heard a door open.
Someone removed the blindfold.

"Ta-da!" Her mother and Rose said in unison. Hannah could only stare in silence at the completely unre-
cognizable spare *room*.

"Look, Buddy, she's made it pretty clear she doesn't want to talk to you," the bouncer from the club told Liam. "So why don't you do us all a favor and take a hike?"

"I will. After I've heard it from her." Liam stood in the litter-strewn alley outside the Hooligan, a club in downtown Long Beach where he'd finally tracked down Brid. Rock music drifted out on a wave of smoke filled air. The bouncer had a shaved head and a pierced left eyebrow. His shoulders filled the narrow doorway. "Let me talk to her, all right?" He made to push past the bouncer. "Five minutes, and I'm gone."

"I said beat it."

"Look, she's got problems—"

"No." The bouncer poked Liam in the chest. "You've got problems, buddy."

"She needs medical help, or she's going to die," Liam said.

"Yeah, well, we're all going to die one day," the bouncer said. "You, too. Sooner than later if you don't get the hell out of here."

Liam was considering his options when four girls in black leather strolled up. One of the girls had rings in her nose, purple hair and, it appeared, a suspicious ID. As the bouncer examined it, Liam slipped inside.

He saw Brid in the lap of a guy the size of a refrigerator. One arm wrapped around his neck, her long hair all over his face and shoulders, the other arm hanging loose at her side, fingers curled around an empty glass. Liam took the glass, set it on the table and tapped her on the shoulder. If she came with him without a fuss, he'd have just enough time to take her back to Huntington Beach before he went to see Hannah and Faith.

The blow to the side of his face knocked him off balance and he staggered slightly. Brid emerged from the guy's neck. "Come on." Liam grabbed her arm and pulled her to her feet. Then he felt a thud to the back of his head.

BY FIVE-FIFTY, ten minutes before Liam was supposed to arrive, the tension in the back of Hannah's neck was so bad that she took Margaret's Advil from the cabinet above the sink and downed two pills with a glass of water.

Behind her, Rose, in her black hot-date pantsuit, lots of gold jewelry and bloodred sling-back heels, was telling Margaret not to wait up for her tonight because she had a feeling she was going to get lucky. Margaret in gray sweats and a harried look was clearly trying to pretend she wasn't watching the clock. Earlier, Deb had sent Margaret into a spin by announcing that she was off to see Dennis and maybe patch things up. Right now that was overshadowed by the Liam vigil.

"Nearly six." Margaret removed a half gallon of vanilla ice cream from the fridge and began spooning it onto dishes of apple crisp cooling on the counter. "You're sure he's coming?"

"He said he'd be here at six, Mom." Hannah eyed the ice cream melting over the apples and wished that Margaret and Rose would go away so she could just gorge and not think about whether Liam was going to show or not show. God, her mouth was watering. She went to the sink and downed a glass of water. "It's exactly six now."

"Liam was always late," Margaret said. "I remember you standing at the living room window, waiting for him to drive up in that old van of his." She dropped the spoon in the sink and returned the ice cream to the freezer. "I did tell you Allan called, right?"

"Twice." Hannah wandered over to the window. When Liam got here, they could sit outside. On the patio. Out of earshot. She ran upstairs, mostly to get away from Margaret and the apple crisp, but also because she'd decided the pink-striped shirt she was wearing was too…June Cleaverish. In her bedroom she stood at her dresser mirror frozen with indecision. Blue denim? White sleeveless? Cotton sweater? God, her hair looked ridiculous. She turned to check her backside in the mirror. Images of pencil-thin *Cosmo* models in designer jeans danced through her head, mouthing Liam's name as they laughed at her big butt. She thrust her arms in the blue denim, ran back downstairs.

"You changed your shirt," Margaret observed as Hannah reappeared in the kitchen. "What was wrong with what you were wearing?"

"I've decided to start living life on the edge, Mom. I want to be wild and crazy. I thought I'd start with this shirt."

"Don't be sarcastic." Margaret refilled her wineglass. "Maybe *I* need to get out of this house. I'm getting a little tired of your attitude lately, you and Deb. I don't know what I've done to make you girls so hostile. I really thought you'd be happy with our little surprise."

"I'm sorry, Mom. Really. It was a lovely surprise. I'm just…" She felt tears brimming and turned away so Margaret wouldn't see. While she'd been at school, Margaret and Rose had painted and papered the guest room. All her books had been neatly arranged in newly installed floor-to-ceiling bookshelves and, on the new computer station, in front of a new and ergonomically correct chair, was the latest Macintosh system. She'd wanted to cry then, too. The geometric-patterned wall-paper and sleek, contemporary chrome and glass fur-nishings were unlike anything she would have chosen for herself. And she was fine with her old computer which, she didn't have the heart to point out, wasn't compatible with the new Mac. Fine also with the cozy space she'd created in her own room. Brick-and-board bookshelves, a scarred old desk that had been her grand-father's and a rocker draped with afghans. Her place to retreat from the world.

With Margaret, Rose, Helen and Faith all eagerly awaiting her reaction, she'd just stared, dumbfounded, finally managing to stammer out a thank-you. They were all smiling and happy with this incredible gift they'd given her. A gift that had probably cost more than a year's rent on her new apartment.

"I know how much you wanted a place where you can keep all your books and papers," Margaret was say-ing now. "And we decided that right now was as good a time as any."

"It was either that or a trip to Acapulco," Rose said. "Which I personally would have preferred."

"Well, that's you, Rose," Margaret said. "Hannah's not the frivolous type. What about the wallpaper? I picked out the pattern. Helen wanted to go with that textured paint she has in her bedroom. Personally I don't care for it."

"Ralph Lauren," Rose said. "Twenty-five bucks a gallon."

"Ridiculous," Margaret said. "You're paying for the name. Maybe you should call Liam, Hanny. Maybe he's just held up by…something.

"He'll be here," Hannah said with far less conviction than she'd had ten minutes ago. Margaret was right,

Liam *was* always late. If he didn't arrive in the next half hour, she was going to put Faith to bed. *I want to be a part of her life.* She felt a hot surge of anger.

"Hannah, have some apple crisp," Margaret said. "It's not fattening, I used honey instead of sugar and the ice cream's low-fat."

"I don't want any, Mom." Hannah remained at the window.

"She's thinking about her weight," Rose said.

"No, she just likes that cherry filling better," Margaret said. "Rose kept insisting it was apple you liked, sweetie, but I knew you'd rather have cherry. Ever since you were a little girl, you've loved cherry pie filling. It's Deb who likes apple. Hannah, it's ten after. You really should call Liam."

"For God's sake, Mom—"

"Don't snap at me again," Margaret said. "I'm getting a little tired of it. This is a different side to you, Hannah, and I can't say I like it very much."

"Well, time for me to go," Rose said. "Wish me luck. This guy is *loaded.* By the way, Hannie, the miniblinds were my idea. How d'you like them?"

"They're great." Hannah turned to look at Rose. "Terrific." Her head was killing her. She looked at the clock. Six-twenty. Where was Liam?

"BUT I WANT TO STAY UP and see Liam." Faith sat in the tub, splashing water with her foot. "Please, Mommy. I want to show him the picture I made."

"I know, baby, but it's after seven and you've got school in the morning."

"Quit calling me baby," Faith protested. "I'm not a baby."

Despite herself, Hannah smiled at Faith's indignation. "But you're my baby."

Faith frowned, not entirely appeased. "Okay, but just don't call me that." She grabbed the red plastic bucket that contained all her bath toys, and held it under the surface of the water. "Will you call him and tell him to come tomorrow?"

"We'll see. Come on, before you turn into a prune." Trying for a calm she didn't feel, Hannah lifted Faith out of the tub and toweled her dry. After she'd tucked her daughter into bed, she used the phone in her own room to dial Miranda Payton's number. No answer.

Damn him. She stared at her reflection in the mirror; picked at a zit on her chin, brushed her hair, sat down on the edge of the bed, got up again. At the window, looking out at the dark of the backyard, she rehearsed what she'd say to him when he finally showed up. Then it occurred to her that he probably wasn't going to show up. She dialed Miranda Payton's number again. A guy answered. Irish accent, but it wasn't Liam.

"Haven't seen him," he said. "Hang on, I'll see if anyone else knows."

"Thanks." Hannah loosened her grip on the receiver. *It's not me you're hurting,* she imagined herself telling Liam. *Personally, I don't give a damn what you do. But I won't let you hurt Faith.* She could hear music and laughter and then the guy came back on the line.

"Someone said he went to a bar somewhere to look for Brid," the guy said. "I didn't get the name of it, but if you hang on I'll find out."

"Thanks, I don't need it."

"Shall I tell him who called?"

"No." Her hand shaking, Hannah replaced the receiver. God, she couldn't deal with this. *In a bar with*

Brid. While his daughter was waiting to show him the picture she'd drawn for him. She stood in the middle of the room trying to think. Why was she surprised? Had she expected anything more?

"Hannah," her mother called from the bottom of the stairs. "How about some tea?"

Hannah squeezed her eyes shut. Obviously Liam wasn't going to make it, so she might as well move on to the next item of the evening and break the news about the apartment. "I'll be down in a minute," she called.

Margaret was on the couch in the living room. She'd lit a fire and changed into her purple robe. The TV was on with the sound off and Judge Judy was admonishing a guy with a huge beer belly. Even voiceless, Judge Judy struck Hannah as formidable. *If you were stupid enough to be taken in by him,* she could imagine Judge Judy snapping at her, *you deserve what you got.*

"So Liam didn't show up," Margaret said.

"Sure he did, Mom," Hannah said, irritated at her mother's I-told-you-so tone. "He's sitting here on the couch. You can't see him?"

"Come on, Hanny." Margaret's glance drifted over to Judge Judy for a moment, then she patted Hannah's knee. "You're upset."

"I'm not."

"Yes, you are." Margaret reached for a glass of red wine on the coffee table. "I'm your mother, I think I can tell when my daughter's upset. I can see it in your face."

"I'm only upset because you keep telling me I'm upset, damn it." Hannah sat down on the couch, and picked at a worn spot on the upholstery. Okay, that wasn't entirely true. When she looked up, her mother was watching her. "I thought you were drinking tea."

"I was." Margaret smiled. "Now I'm having a glass of wine."

"I think you're drinking too much, Mom. Rose thinks so, too."

"Oh, Rose should talk. She isn't exactly averse to a glass or two herself."

"I'm talking about you, Mom."

"Have I ever complained about a hangover? Ever not been able to get up in the morning? Ever got a DUI?" Margaret brought her feet up on the sofa, and tucked her robe around them. "Don't worry about me, Hannah. Worry about yourself. Worry about what Liam is doing to you. I knew he'd let you down. If you'd asked me before you invited him over, I would have told you."

"Mom." Hannah caught her mother's hand. "Sit down. I need to talk to you."

"What is it? Bad news? You're not preg… Rose said she thought you'd put on a few pounds, but…" She stood. "Let me get the pie first. Do you want a piece?"

"Damn it, just sit down, okay?" She waited until Margaret sat down again. "I'm not pregnant. We're going to move out. Me and Faith. I rented a duplex on Tenth Street."

Her mother's face froze. There was a moment of silence while she appeared to absorb the blow. Then, her expression stricken, she reached into the pocket of her robe and pulled out a tissue. She dabbed it at her nose. Moments passed.

"Tenth Street," she finally said. "God."

Hannah frowned, puzzled. "What?"

"*What?* Tenth Street, that's what. I mean anything above Fourth is…I can't believe you're going let my granddaughter live on Tenth. I swear to God, this wouldn't have happened before Liam came back on the

An Important Message
from the Editors

Dear Reader,

Because you've chosen to read one of our fine romance novels, we'd like to say "thank you!" And, as a special way to thank you, we've selected two books from our Home and Family series — a wonderful combination of Harlequin Superromance and Silhouette Special Edition books — plus an exciting Mystery Gift, to send you absolutely FREE! You'll get one book from each of the 2 series in this collection, with absolutely no obligation.

Please enjoy them with our compliments...

Pam Powers

P.S. And because we value our customers, we've attached something extra inside...

Peel off Seal and Place Inside...

The Home and Family Collection....

As a special Editor's "Thank You" gift, you'll receive one FREE book from each of the below series:

HARLEQUIN SUPERROMANCE®:
Longer romance novels featuring realistic, believable characters in a wide range of emotionally involving stories.

SILHOUETTE SPECIAL EDITION®:
Stories which capture the intensity of life, love and family.

Your **2 FREE BOOKS** have a combined cover price of $10.00 in the U.S. and $12.00 in Canada, but they're yours **FREE!**

Don't forget to detach your FREE BOOKMARK. And remember...just for accepting the Editor's Free Gift Offer, we'll send you 2 books and a gift, ABSOLUTELY FREE!

The Editor's "Thank You" Free Gifts Include:

- 1 Harlequin Superromance® book!
- 1 Silhouette Special Edition® book!
- An exciting mystery gift!

PLACE FREE GIFT SEAL HERE

Yes I have placed my Editor's "Thank You" seal in the space provided above. Please send me 2 FREE books and a fabulous Mystery Gift. I understand I am under no obligation to purchase any books, as explained on the back and on the opposite page.

387 HDL DU3F   **187 HDL DU3P**

FIRST NAME   LAST NAME

ADDRESS

APT.#   CITY

STATE/PROV.   ZIP/POSTAL CODE   (H-HF-05/03)

Thank You!

The Harlequin Reader Service® — Here's how it works:

Accepting your 2 free books and gift places you under no obligation to buy anything. You may keep the books and gift and return the shipping statement marked "cancel." If you do not cancel, about a month later we'll send you 4 additional books from the Home and Family Collection, which includes 2 Harlequin Superromance books and 2 Silhouette Special Edition books, and bill you just $16.92 in the U.S., or $19.46 in Canada, plus 25¢ shipping and handling per book. Tha total saving of 10% off the cover price! You may cancel at any time, but if you choose to continue, every month we'll s you 4 more books from the Home and Family collection, which you may either purchase at the discount price or returr us and cancel your subscription.

*Terms and prices subject to change without notice. Sales tax applicable in N.Y. Canadian residents will be charged applicable provincial taxes and GST.

scene. There's no way you would have rented anything on Tenth Street. God—''

"Mom. Stop, okay? You're driving me nuts." The street numbers increased as they moved away from the ocean, and she'd forgotten about her mother's dictum that the only decent place to live in Long Beach was below Fourth. Preferably below Second. Tenth wasn't even on Margaret's geographic compass.

"What about Faith? What if she wants to play outside?"

"The neighborhood is perfectly safe, Mom. Or I wouldn't have rented the place."

"I knew this would happen," Margaret said. "I told Rose. I said, 'Just wait, he'll fill her head with all these ideas and the next thing you know she'll be moving out.'"

"Mom, this has nothing to do with Liam. I want my own place. I want Faith to have her own home. It's just time."

"He's moving in with you, isn't he?"

Hannah took a deep breath. Her mother's lower lip was trembling. Guilt battled with irritation. And won. She put her arm around Margaret's shoulders. "Come on, Mom. I know this is hard for you. I know you love having Faith around, but you'll still be a part of her life. Our lives."

Margaret brought the tissue from her sleeve and dabbed at her eyes again. A tear splashed onto the lap of her purple robe. "I can't imagine getting up in the morning and not seeing her little face when I come down to breakfast."

"Mom." Tears prickled in Hannah's nose. She caught Margaret's hand, held it for a moment. "Please try to understand. This isn't easy for me either…"

''So this means it's all over with Allan?'' Margaret asked.

''This has nothing to do with Allan. I've just decided I want my own place.''

''I know what it is,'' Margaret said. ''You're still angry at me for what I said to Liam, and this is your way of punishing me.''

''I'm not punishing you. This isn't about you.'' But she wasn't sure. *Was* she moving out to punish Margaret for lying to Liam? And, in doing so, was she also punishing Faith? Maybe even herself?

Margaret picked up her empty wineglass from the table and carried it into the kitchen. The phone rang once. Heart thundering, Hannah glanced around for the receiver that was always getting lost under sofa cushions. By the time she'd found it, the line was dead. She went into the kitchen. Margaret was refilling her wineglass.

''Who was on the phone?'' she asked her mother.

''Some guy for Rose,'' Margaret said.

''I thought it might be Liam.''

''Some guy for Rose,'' Margaret repeated, her back to Hannah. ''Next thing I know, she'll be moving out, too. Then Deb, although at least Deb's always likely to come back the next day. So *is* Liam moving in?''

''Damn it.'' Hannah glared at her mother. Anger, like a bucket of red paint, obliterated all other emotions. ''Do you want to know a big reason I'm moving out?''

''All I know is you never mentioned moving out before you-know-who showed up on the scene.''

Hannah gritted her teeth. Margaret *was* going to drive her crazy. Any minute now she'd start gibbering. She paced the room, trying to calm down. ''I want you to listen to me, okay? Just listen. This has nothing to do with Liam. Nothing to do with Allan. Nothing to do with Prince Charles, nothing—"

"Prince Charles? What does he have to do with—"

"Listen to me, Mom. Just listen. I'm trying to tell you this has nothing to do with a guy. I'm not pregnant. I'm not getting married. No one's moving in with me. I just want a life of my own."

"Well, you have a life of your own now."

"No, I don't. I have a life under a microscope. Everything I do is endlessly discussed—"

"Discussed?" Her mother's expression turned indignant. "If you think we sit around discussing you, you're wrong. Like I said to Rose, Hannah's life is her business."

"Mom, that's exactly what I'm talking about…" What was the point? She peered into her mother's face. "Be happy for me, okay? Think of all the extra time you'll have not cooking and picking up after me and Faith."

Margaret managed a brave little smile. "You're my life, honey, you and Deb and Faith. Whatever I do, I do willingly because I love you."

THE NEXT DAY WAS a school holiday, and Hannah came home from her run to find Faith in the kitchen crouched next to a wicker basket.

"A late birthday present from me and Max," Rose told Hannah. "My new sweetie. His dog had eight puppies. This little guy was the last one left."

"My whole life, I've always wanted a puppy exactly like this." Faith held the tiny caramel color puppy up to her face, squealing as it licked her nose.

Rose laughed. "Your whole life, huh? Wow, *my*

whole life, I've been looking for Prince Charming." She looked at Hannah. "Cute, isn't he? The puppy, I mean."

Hannah cupped her hand behind her neck where a massive knot of tension had not been relieved by the run. The rental agreement she'd signed clearly stated no pets. She looked at Faith, stretched out on the floor, flat on her stomach in deep eye-to-eye communion with the puppy, and walked over to check the cork bulletin board on the wall where telephone messages were pinned.

Allan had called. Liam hadn't. Not that she'd expected him to. Except she had. And he hadn't. No apology for disappointing his daughter. Nothing. She glanced at Allan's message. "Just wanted to tell you I miss you," it read. Rose was watching her, so she opened the refrigerator and hid her face among the cartons of yogurt and cottage cheese.

"What did you have for breakfast?" she called to her daughter.

"Ice cream," Faith said.

"Ice cream?" Hannah glanced over her shoulder at Faith. "For breakfast?"

"My specialty," Rose said. "That and boiling water, but water's iffy. I tried to talk her into a jelly doughnut, but she wanted Ben and Jerry's."

"Liam bought me doughnut holes," Faith said. "And I ate three."

"No kidding," Rose said. "I bet you really like Liam, huh?"

"Uh-huh. He's nice. He put me on his shoulders."

"Wow, that sounds like *fun*," Rose said. "So are you guys going to do some more fun things with him?"

"Maybe if Mommy calls him. I did a picture for him."

"Faith." Hannah emerged from the refrigerator and

glared at Rose. Then she addressed her daughter. "Go upstairs and get all your clothes out of the hamper and bring them down so I can start a wash." She waited until Faith was out of earshot. "Don't pump her for information," she said. "If you want to know something, ask me."

"Oh, lighten up," Rose said. "What's the big deal? Liam's some sacred topic no one can discuss? Your mother's the same way. I mention Liam's name and she screams at me that it's none of my business. *Excuse me?* Aren't we all family here?"

Hannah put the kettle on for tea. One thing had just become a whole lot easier. If Liam still had any ideas about being part of Faith's life and taking her off to Ireland, he could damn well forget them.

"Hey, Mommy." Faith ran into the room, a pile of laundry in her arms. "Guess what I'm going to call my puppy?"

Hannah stared at the dog, her mind blank.

"Spot?" Rose asked.

Faith frowned. "But he hasn't got any spots."

"I'm going to call him Raisin. You know why, Mommy?"

"You okay, hon?" Rose interrupted. "You're not upset about…" She nodded in the direction of Faith, now on her back, the puppy extended above her at full arm's length. "I just thought since we all felt so bad when Turpin passed on, it was time for a replacement. And Faith's been wanting a puppy forever."

"Forever," Faith echoed. "And now I've got one. And his name is Raisin because he's got eyes like little raisins. Hey, Grandma," she called as Hannah's mother appeared in the doorway. "I've got a puppy."

"A puppy." Margaret shook her head slightly as

though she couldn't quite comprehend the situation. She looked from Hannah to Rose. "Where did he come from?"

"Me," Rose said, then she laughed. "Well, not me literally."

"No, Rose, I didn't think you meant literally," Margaret said. "Well, I just hope this apartment Hannah rented allows animals."

"Apartment?" Rose looked at Hannah. "You're moving out."

"Mom." Hannah gave her mother a warning look. Faith had been asleep when she'd gone on her run, so she'd decided to tell her later. That was before she'd learned about the puppy. The phone rang. Hannah watched her mother answer it. She could feel Rose staring at her, obviously dying to ask about the apartment. Margaret hung up and came to sit at the table.

"Well, how about this for a piece of news?" She looked at Hannah. "That was Helen. She's watching the local news." She lowered her voice and leaned across the table. "Liam was in some kind of brawl last night. The cops had to break it up."

CHAPTER TEN

LIAM SAT in a marina coffee shop eating a concoction of scrambled eggs, chili peppers and avocado. He'd walked over to the marina from Miranda's house and brought a notebook with him, thinking about a song he wanted to write. He'd half finished it, then run out of inspiration. Another half-finished song to add to the pile. His life was full of half-finished things.

A waitress in white shorts and a blue shirt smiled at him and held a coffeepot above his cup. He glanced up at her, nodded and waited for the inevitable remark.

"Walked into a door, huh?"

"Right," Liam said. Since the fight the night before, he'd heard a dozen variations of the comment. "It was in my way," he said. The waitress smiled and he watched her move on to the next table.

The incident last night had turned out to be more of an embarrassment than anything else. He'd blacked out briefly but was fully conscious by the time the cops arrived. If the cop hadn't recognized him and Brid from a publicity photo, the whole thing would have been just another bar scuffle. As it was, he'd been treated to a lecture from the cop and warned to stay out of trouble. The bar owner hadn't pressed charges, but he'd obviously tipped off the media because the following morning, Miranda had woken him to say there was a reporter on the phone. He hadn't taken the call.

He ate a forkful of eggs, and speared a piece of avocado. He'd eaten more avocado since he'd been in California than he had his whole life. He pushed his plate aside and watched a gull make a dive for a bit of orange peel garnish.

At the zoo, Faith had charmed him out of some change to buy birdseed. She'd held out her palm for the birds to feed, then retracted it, squealing whenever a bird swooped down. He'd watched Hannah watching their daughter and told himself he wanted a life like that. Sunshine and family outings. And then he'd returned to Miranda's to hear that Brid hadn't come home and it was as though he'd stepped out of one world and back into another. Now, thinking of Faith and Hannah again, it seemed he had a foot in each world.

You have to make a choice, Brid had said.

He finished his food, glanced at the check the waitress had dropped off and put some bills on the table under his plate. His thoughts still on his daughter and her mother, he made his way back to Miranda's. Past a waterside bar, past a bagel shop and past a Realtor where the pictures pasted in the window showed million dollar properties with red-tiled roofs and ocean views.

At a pay phone, he dug in his jeans for Hannah's phone number. He listened to a phone ring three times, and then her mother answered.

"Don't hang up again, Mrs. Riley," he said, expecting to hear the click of a disconnection. "It's Liam. May I talk to Hannah, please."

"She doesn't want to talk to you," Margaret Riley said.

"She can tell me that to my face," Liam said.

"She's not in," Margaret said.

He leaned his back against the wall. From where he

stood, he could see the boats rocking in the slips. A middle-aged man in white shorts and a blue shirt wheeled a wooden cart down one of the gangways. "When do you expect her back?" he asked.

"I've no idea."

"Look, I don't want to cause a scene, Mrs. Riley," he said, "but this is the third time you've given me the runaround. I intend to speak to Hannah one way or another, if I have to camp out on your front doorstep."

"Why are you doing this?" Margaret Riley asked. "Why are you trying to push your way back into Hannah's life? She doesn't need it, neither does Faith. If you had any feelings for either of them, you'd leave them both alone."

"If you'll excuse my saying so, Mrs. Riley, that's my business. And Hannah's."

"Hannah's my daughter," she said.

"And Faith's my daughter."

She laughed, a humorless bark. "You can throw the term around, Liam, but you're not her father in the real sense of the word—"

"Because I was robbed of the chance to be."

"Robbed." She gave another laugh. "Look, if you're expecting an apology, you're going to be disappointed. If you were honest with yourself, you'd admit you weren't prepared for the responsibilities of taking care of a wife or child. And you're still not. My daughter sat at home waiting for you last night, while you were out getting arrested for a bar brawl."

Liam thought of the day Margaret Riley had told him about Hannah's abortion. She hadn't asked him in— they'd stood at the front door talking. Her teeth had been chattering and she had worn a gray cardigan that had a bulge in the sleeve just above her wrist. A tissue, it turned out, with which she dabbed at her nose continuously. He'd been reminded of his Auntie Maude; always a hanky·up her sleeve ready to swipe snotty little noses. And always candy in her apron pocket. One of the few good memories of his childhood. Margaret had been so distraught on the porch that day that he'd had an irrational urge to assure her everything would be all right.

"You were a bad influence on her," she was saying now. "Do you have any idea at all what a fragile emotional state she was in? If her family hadn't stepped in, I hate to think what might have happened."

Liam shifted the phone to his other ear. Now, as he had back then, he wanted to hate her, but felt mostly sympathy. What did he know about the whole loving family bit? After his ma walked out, he'd been like an odd bit of luggage, carted around from place to place, no one quite sure where he belonged, or in any hurry to claim him. No big loss either if he went missing and never turned up again. For Hannah, things couldn't have been more different.

"Look…" he started. "That's in the past, there's nothing to be gained in going over and over—"

"It was all over the news about your bar brawl." Margaret went on as if he hadn't spoken. "Hannah was shocked, of course, although why it would surprise her I don't know. It goes with your lifestyle, as far as I can see."

"*Is* Hannah there?"

"Ever since you came back into the picture, nothing we do is right for her. She fights with me, she criticizes my sisters. We've bent over backward to make her happy and what does she do? Last night, she announces that she's moving out."

Liam said nothing, but the news surprised him. He'd

had the impression that Hannah and Faith were quite happy living in the family home. He tried to remember whether Hannah had said anything about moving during their trip to the zoo. He remembered her red eyes that morning.

"It's her life, of course, which is what I'm always telling her," Margaret said. "Far be it from me to interfere. It's just her reason for moving out that upsets me. She denies it, but I know it's because she's got this idea that you were wronged and now she doesn't trust any of us, so she's uprooting herself and my granddaughter…" Her voice cracked. "Look, I'm begging you, please leave her alone."

"I WANT TO MAKE Rocky something really incredible for dinner," Jen told Hannah as they walked down the aisles of the Trader Joe's on Pacific Coast Highway, checking out the bags of gourmet pasta and imported mustard. She held up a plastic bag for Hannah's inspection. "Look. Squid pasta. See, it's shaped like little squiddy things."

"But it's black." Hannah pointed out. "You think he'd go for black food?"

"Yeah, good point." Jen set the pasta back on the shelf. "They had this really cute heart-shaped pasta for Valentine's Day and I knocked myself out making a great alfredo sauce to go with it. He wouldn't touch it." She shifted her basket to the other arm. "So what's the word on Liam?"

"Nothing… Well, I called the place he was staying in Huntington Beach and the woman who answered said he was out somewhere, so I guess they don't have him locked up in jail."

"But he hasn't tried to call?"

"Nope."

"Maybe he did and your mom didn't give you the message."

"No, I don't think she'd do that. She'd figure I would find out somehow."

"So how does Faith feel about moving?" Jen asked.

"She isn't happy. She doesn't understand why we have to move if we can't take the dog, and now my sister and aunts are giving me these lectures about being selfish." Earlier that morning, as she'd left the house to drop Faith off at her friend Tiffany's, Deb had asked Faith for a few minutes to "talk to Mommy about private stuff," then angrily accused Hannah of putting her obsession with Liam in front of Faith's happiness. And then Rose, who was thinking of moving in with her boyfriend, had begged Hannah to reconsider moving because it would leave Margaret alone. "I'm suddenly the monster," Hannah told Jen.

"Screw them," Jen said. "It's your life. Faith can go visit the dog at your mom's house. Don't let it get to you. What time do you have to pick up Faith?"

"Not till six."

"Want to have lunch?"

"Actually, I think I'm going to track down Liam." She dug in her purse for her billfold, fished out a five-dollar bill for the parmesan cheese and pasta she'd picked up. "Not because I give a damn if I ever see him again, but we need to have a little chat about his intentions regarding Faith."

Ten minutes later, as she drove slowly along the street of expensive waterfront homes where Miranda Payton lived, Hannah tried to talk herself into actually parking the car, getting out, knocking on the door and asking Miranda if she could talk to Liam.

The problem was, she didn't want to do it. Didn't

want to see the beauteous Miranda, with her cleavage and hundred-watt smile. Didn't want to look like some desperate groupie stalking Liam. Didn't want to hear his justification for choosing Brid over Faith. Didn't want to be so damned obsessed with Liam Tully that she'd allowed him to invade her every waking thought and pretty much take over her dreams, too.

Faith. I'm doing this for Faith.

Outside Miranda's house, she peered through the tangle of bougainvillea to the front door. She lost her nerve and drove around the block again, past the house and back onto Pacific Coast Highway. At the next light, she pulled into the left-hand lane, made a U-turn and returned to Huntington Harbor. Miranda lived on a cul-de-sac. She drove past the house, parked two doors away outside a mansion with green-and-white awnings and a bubbling fountain in the front yard.

The engine idling, she tried to talk herself out of confronting Liam. Since he hadn't called, or come to see her, his talk about wanting to be part of Faith's life was apparently just that—talk. One option was to simply accept it. Deal with it by not dealing with it. As she'd pointed out to Liam, Faith would quickly forget him. Why stir things up?

A Mercedes convertible drew up behind her and parked at the curb. Through the rearview mirror, Hannah watched a tall blonde in white jeans and a black bikini top get out, then disappear into the tropical foliage.

Hannah pulled down the mirror, and stared at her reflection. God, why did she have to look so damn *wholesome?* If they were casting her in a movie, she would be the girlfriend from Iowa. She dug into her purse for lipstick. She couldn't let him just leave. Nothing had been resolved. If Liam walked out of her life again, it wouldn't be until they'd cleared up a few things.

As she pulled up outside Miranda's, the front door opened and Liam walked out. He wore baggy khaki shorts and a black T-shirt. *Liam*. Blue eyes, wind-tussled hair.

Once he'd been her life. Now he wasn't. Her life would go on without him in it. But God, no one had ever made her heart beat as hard as it was doing right now. Her face felt hot as she stretched across the passenger seat to look at him through the open window.

"We need to talk," she said.

ONE HAND ON THE ROOF of Hannah's little red Toyota, Liam leaned into the car. Her yellow shorts and sleeveless white shirt were all summery sunshine, but her face was tense; her fingers were locked in a death grip around the steering wheel. He met her eyes for a moment and then, on an impulse, climbed in and slammed the door.

"Drive somewhere," he said.

She didn't move. "You have a black eye."

"I hadn't noticed, but thanks for pointing it out. How's Faith?"

Her jaw tightened. "Faith's fine."

"I'm sorry I didn't make it over to see her last night."

"Really." She flashed a tight smile. "Well, that was easy, huh? You're sorry and now everything's fine."

"Hannah, look…I couldn't help—"

"Of course you could. You had a choice. You could spend the night hanging around bars tracking down your singer, or you could be with Faith. Faith lost out."

He looked at her. "I'm sorry, Hannah. I mean that. I'm sorry if my apology isn't enough. I'm sorry that I disappointed Faith. I'm sorry. What do you want me to do?"

"What do I want you to do?" She stared at him. "What do *I* want you to do? Well, let's see. For starters I want you to think about what you really mean when you say you want to be part of your daughter's life."

"Hannah, look—"

"No, you look. Being a father isn't something you just do when it suits *you,* Liam. It's a full-time commitment, one you're obviously not ready to make. You might be her biological father, but you know nothing about what it really means to be a father. So, to answer your questions, what I want you to do is stay the hell out of Faith's life."

Liam felt her anger like a blow to the chest. Her eyes blazing, body tensed, clearly ready to pounce on the next word from his mouth. It struck him that he'd never actually been the recipient of Hannah's anger. She'd been upset with him before, but she'd tended to withdraw rather than fight back. In the past, he'd never been quite sure where he stood with her. This time he had no doubt.

"Can we continue this somewhere else?" he asked.

"I have nothing else to say."

"Well, I do and I'd like a chance to say it. But not here."

"Where?"

"I don't know." He saw the massive oak front door to Miranda's house swing open. Miranda's blond head emerged briefly, then disappeared. "Anywhere. Someplace where there aren't multimillion-dollar houses and other testimonials to conspicuous consumption."

She put the car in drive and pulled slowly away from the curb.

"I'm a hypocrite," he said. "If it weren't for Miranda's multimillion-dollar place, we'd all be kipping in some fleabag.''

"One of your many character flaws,'' she said, but there was less heat in her voice.

"A veritable walking flaw,'' he said. "That's me.''

"Does your eye hurt?''

"The pain is excruciating.'' He buckled the seat belt. "What about the beach?''

Without a word, she drove out of the complex and north onto Pacific Coast Highway. He watched the jumble of signs and billboards, Hannah's anger beating a steady tattoo in his brain. A medical office advertised flu shots, the tanning parlor next door had an introductory offer. Doughnut shops and taco stands, yacht brokers and surfing shacks. The breeze through the rolled-down windows tossed Hannah's hair around, filled the car with the flowery scent he used to dream about. Her thighs and knees beneath her yellow shorts were completely smooth and lightly tanned. *You know nothing about what it means to be a father.*

"Seal Beach is the closest,'' she said.

"Fine.'' They drove down a street lined with small shops. Main Street the sign read. There had been a Main Street in one of the towns he'd lived in as a kid. Some place in Armagh, the sort of abandoned-looking crossroads with its strip of narrow, paint-peeled houses that only looked picturesque if you didn't wake up every morning in one of them. Two bars where his stepdad had spent most of his waking hours, a church in which no one he knew had ever set foot and a newsagent's where his ma bought packs of Players before she took a notion that she wanted to start her life over in Liverpool free of small boys and other encumbrances.

"Now for the difficult part,'' Hannah said as she

pulled onto the ocean front. "Finding somewhere to park."

"Over there." He pointed to a white van that was pulling out and watched Hannah's arms as she maneuvered the car into the empty space. Tanned like her legs.

"There," she said after she'd got the car squeezed in between a dune buggy and a Mercedes convertible. "Pretty good parallel-parking job if I do say so myself." She turned off the ignition, removed the keys and moved around to face him. "So?"

"Let's go for a walk." He got out of the car, came around to her side and pulled open the door. Hannah swung her legs around and sat there for a moment, looking up at him. He could hear gulls screeching behind him, the loud roar of the waves. Wind blew his hair, billowed the back of his shirt. A car passed and he instinctively stepped closer to Hannah. He'd worn an old pair of tan shorts that belonged to Pearse and he felt the warm air on his legs and then the brush of Hannah's skin against his own. He saw the contact register in her eyes and everything seemed to stop for a moment. And then he leaned into the car and kissed her. When she didn't immediately pull away, he kissed her again and his brain all but ceased to function.

"Damn you," she said a moment later. "I'm still furious at you."

"Go ahead with it then." She looked as dazed as he felt. "Hit me if it makes you feel any better."

She caught his face in her hands. "Shut up."

They kissed again, so hard that he felt her teeth against his lips. Another car zoomed past, inches from where he stood halfway into the car, Hannah almost reclining across the seats. He drew back to look at her.

"I changed my mind about the walk," he said. "I have a better idea."

HANNAH SAT UP, ran her fingers through her hair. Liam walked back around the car, opened the passenger door and got in. Dazed, she turned in the seat to look at him. No point now in telling herself this was all about Faith. It wasn't. She knew it and he knew it. Everything had suddenly changed. Later, her mind would kick in—the analysis, the second-guessing, the regrets. Right now, bodies ruled.

"I've got a guitar I want you to give Faith." He touched her knee, cut his eyes up to her face. "I left it in the tour bus. If I remember rightly, it's only a minute or so from here, on a lot behind Fiddler's Green. We can talk there."

She started the car. As good an excuse as any to find a place where they could rip off each other's clothes in private. With Liam giving directions, she drove. Her brain was a haze of jumbled thoughts and flashing warnings; her body felt liquid, every nerve loudly proclaiming that without immediate satisfaction, they would all gang up on her and drive her insane with lust.

Five minutes later, she stood behind Liam on the steps of the tour bus, waiting while he unlocked the door. Inside, it was dark and cool and smelled faintly of stale beer and cigarette smoke. A strip of sunlight glimmered from beneath the dark fabric covering the windows, faintly illuminated a small living area furnished with a couple of couches. The green digital numerals of a microwave glowed 4:13 p.m.

She heard the muffled roar of traffic on Pacific Coast Highway, the sound of her own breathing. Liam put his hands on her shoulders and kissed her again, and it was like drowning. No one had ever kissed her like Liam. No mouth had ever felt like Liam's. Everything about him seemed familiar—the wiry frame of his body, now hard against her own, the shape of his shoulders under her hands. Familiar and yet so dreamlike and insubstantial she wanted to preserve it somehow before it slipped away.

He took her hand, and led her to the couch, where they sat down and kissed again. She wanted him to keep on kissing her—if he kissed her until tomorrow, it wouldn't be enough. When they eventually parted, he reached past her to switch on a light and took a small guitar from a box beside the couch.

"This is for Faith," he said. "There's a note on the back to her."

Hannah took the guitar, and tried to emerge from the sexual fog. He'd printed Faith's name in big block letters, each letter outlined and shaded in a different color. With her finger, Hannah traced the *F*. Imagined him carefully lettering his daughter's name.

"Pearse walked in on me as I was doing that," Liam said. "Gave me a hard time about it, called me Daddy Liam. I threatened to knock his teeth out."

She set the guitar down. Why would that bother him? It wasn't something she wanted to dwell on right now.

"Brid got herself in a bit of trouble last night," Liam said after a moment. "That's what the scuffle was all about. I'd gone to find her and the idiot she was with didn't appreciate my showing up. She's finally admitted she needs help. We've got her back at Casa Pacifica until she's well enough to go on the road again."

Hannah said nothing. From the couch where she sat, she could see the pictures pinned to a bulletin board on the wall opposite. Brid in black lace, holding a guitar.

One of Liam, onstage. Newspaper clippings, a schedule of performances. She folded her hands in her lap. Liam sat close enough that she could feel the heat of his body. The strip of light from beneath the curtains fell in a bar across her thighs, disappeared, then reappeared just below the frayed edge of Liam's shorts.

Without a word, he drew her onto his lap, and they kissed until she was almost lying across him; her brain gone to mush, her body moving in rhythm to the thrust of his tongue in her mouth. They kept kissing. He pressed the flat of his palm against her crotch, held it there. She groaned and moved against it.

"What's this all about then, Hannah?"

She caught his hand, held it still. "Well, I've got you figured out, Tully. The guitar was just a transparent attempt to get me into this den of iniquity."

He nuzzled his face in her neck. "You saw right through me."

"Of course." Even stilled, the pressure of his palm was driving her crazy. She squeezed it between her thighs. "You think I'm some little bimbo groupie?"

"Aren't you?" He freed his hand, and made to push her off his lap. "Off with you then. I'm only interested in ladies of easy virtue."

"There's something contradictory about ladies and easy virtue," she said, "but at the moment I'm not thinking too clearly."

"Well, I can straighten one thing out." He grinned, his teeth white in the murky light. "This should clear up any thoughts you might have that this is just about Faith." He kissed her neck, her throat. Stopped to look at her again. "Despite your little lecture, I do want to be part of her life. I've never been as serious about anything before. But Faith isn't the whole picture. I can't think of her without you.''

Hannah's arm was still around his neck, her legs across his lap. She thought about what he'd said. Weighed whether to say what was really on her mind, then decided that, if nothing else, they should be honest with each other.

''If we take Faith out of the picture, Liam, I think what we have together pretty much boils down to sex.''

His grin broadened. ''And that's a bad thing?''

''It depends. If it's the foundation of a relationship, we're off to a shaky start. We've been there. What did we know about each other when we got married? Nothing. And we had nothing in common…except sex.''

''I bet if we'd taken up stamp collecting, we'd still be married today.''

She punched his shoulder.

''Or lawn bowling. Except we'd have probably caused a scandal each time I threw you down on the green and had my way with you.''

''Seriously though. We created Faith, and now here we are again…''

''And it's still all about sex?''

She squirmed around to look at him. ''Tell me how it's anything else.''

He undid the top button of her blouse, and watched her face as he undid the rest of the buttons. Kept watching as he pulled off her shirt and tossed it on the floor. Didn't take his eyes away as he snapped open the clasp of her bra.

''If you're trying to convince me otherwise,'' she said as he lowered his mouth to her breasts, ''you're not doing a very good job.''

He said nothing, just circled his tongue around her

nipples until she lost herself again in the feel of his hands, his mouth, his tongue. She didn't need his confirmation. It *was* all about sex. Always had been, always would be. Which was fine. Maybe every woman needed a guy like Liam. Purely for sex, because you couldn't count on him for much else. And then, he slid out from under her and stripped off her shorts and panties.

CHAPTER ELEVEN

THE SHORTS CAUGHT around her foot. He unsnagged them, lifted her legs and swept all her clothes to the floor. The couch was some sort of fake leather and it felt cool and a little damp under her bare skin. Liam stood above her for a moment, watching her. A little self-conscious and grateful for the dim light, she shifted slightly and clasped her hands behind her head. Still in his khaki shorts and T-shirt, Liam trailed his fingers down over her stomach, then kneeled between her legs.

"The last time I saw you naked, we had a fight." He kissed the inside of her thighs, and parted them with his hands. "Do you remember? We were living in that place in San José?"

"The place with the fire escape outside. There was a woman downstairs who…" She stopped, her breath uneven as she felt his tongue move inside her. A sound escaped from her throat, loud and surprised to her ears. Liam glanced up at her, caught her ankles and draped her legs around his shoulders. For an instant, she saw it all through the eyes of a detached observer. A couch in a dimly lit tour bus. Liam's dark head between her thighs. Her own pale body: breasts, stomach, bare feet on either side of his neck. An afternoon tryst. A little tawdry maybe, an experience she'd be unlikely to reveal to anyone, but more exciting somehow because of that.

Briefly she wondered about other women who may have lain on this couch with Liam.

And then she stopped thinking altogether. With his tongue inside her, she lost herself in heat and sensation. Her unchecked cries filled the air; her hips rose higher and higher. Building, building, her body arching spasmodically. A vibration had started somewhere inside her, a done of bees growing louder and louder. "Oh yes, yes…" Every nerve in her body was screaming now, the hum filling her brain.

"Liam, I'm…I think I'm going to… Oh yes, yes…" She collapsed against the couch. In an instant, Liam was out of his clothes and driving into her, his breathing harsh, his mouth against her neck.

When he came, moments later, he toppled off her, pulling her with him from the narrow couch to the floor. They both started laughing. Bodies, slick with sweat, legs still entwined, wedged between the couch and a low coffee table, they laughed and laughed and kissed some more.

"God, Hannah, I love you," he said. "I've never stopped loving you."

BUT EXACTLY WHAT they were going to do about it was another matter, Liam reflected as Hannah drove him back to Miranda's. Hannah had chosen to ignore his declaration. Had probably put it down to the sort of postcoital ardor that would cool almost as soon as the clothes went back on. She hadn't expressed similar feelings for him, and he hadn't asked. Now he felt let down and morose.

They'd had their fling—he could almost hear Hannah thinking—now he could make her life a whole lot simpler by getting back on the bus and riding off. Which was probably the best thing he could do for everyone in the long run, himself included.

But he wanted his daughter and he wanted his ex-wife. A few days ago, Brid had asked him whether he missed being close to someone. He'd responded with a joke. Either he hadn't really known the answer, or he hadn't recognized his own needs. Now he did.

Except that his daughter didn't know him, and her mother didn't love him.

"Beverly, that was the name of the woman downstairs," Hannah said suddenly. She turned to look at him. "That place in San José with the fire escape. Beverly lived in the apartment below ours. Beverly Mc-something or other."

Liam roused himself from his gloomy musings. "I don't remember a woman downstairs," he said.

"Really?" Hannah gave him a skeptical look. "You don't remember how we used to sleep outside on the fire escape because it was so hot in the apartment? One night, you had no clothes on and you said it didn't matter because no one could see you and then the next day Beverly said you had a cute butt. You don't remember that?"

He shook his head. Not only did he not remember, he didn't care. What the hell did any of that matter?

"That's what the fight was about." Hannah stopped for a light, turned again to look at him. "Beverly was always coming on to you. You have to remember her. Long blond hair, big boobs?"

Liam shook his head. "As I recall, we fought because I wanted you to sleep naked and you insisted on covering yourself up with this frilly little cotton nightie you had. Rosebuds around the neck."

"You remember that nightgown?"

"It's what you always wore."

"Oh God." She shook her head. "I guess I was kind of on the modest side. Prudish. Self-conscious. I don't know."

"I could never understand why."

She smiled.

"I'm serious."

"Oh come on, Liam. How could I not be? There were always women fawning all over you. Fantastic-looking women. They'd stare at me, and I knew they were thinking, 'God, what's he doing with her?' And then all the nights you didn't come home till three and I could smell cigarettes and perfume…"

"Proof, of course, that I was running around."

"Well, it didn't exactly take a huge stretch of imagination."

"Apparently not." He waited a moment. "If you thought I was running around, why didn't you say something?"

"Because…" She hesitated and shot him a glance as though to gauge his possible reaction. "It sounds crazy now, I know, but I was scared to have my suspicions confirmed. So I just kept them to myself."

"You thought I was running around, but you didn't say anything because you thought I'd leave you?"

"Pretty much."

"I'm sure the logic must be there somewhere, but I've got to say I don't see it."

"I told you it seems crazy now, but I loved you. It was easier not knowing for sure."

Loved you.

He'd hardly heard anything after that. A pulse throbbed in his temple. A grim need to get all the bad news over with made him push on. "Listen, Hannah," he said as she pulled up to the curb outside Miranda's house. "What would I need to do to make it work between us again?"

She parked at the curb and turned in her seat to look at him. Waited a moment before she answered. "I don't think it could ever work again, Liam," she said softly.

Her words seemed to hang there for a moment; the air in the car filled with them, echoing in his head. "And you've got all the reasons ready to trot out, I'm sure," he finally said. "You don't trust me. Our lives are too different. We have nothing in common. I'm always on the road."

"Are you arguing with that?" Hannah's tone was incredulous. "Can you really see yourself in a suburban tract home, going to PTA meetings and washing the car on Saturdays?"

"That's only one version of life," he said. "There are others."

"It's pretty much my version though. It's what I've always known. What I want for myself. What I think is best for raising my daughter."

"Our daughter."

"Sorry."

"What if I said I want to give that kind of life a try?"

"I'd say you'd need to give it a lot more thought."

"I could give up the touring," he said impulsively. "Get a job...I don't know, teaching music, or something."

She slowly shook her head. "It's not you, Liam. You'd never be happy. What about the band? What about Brid? The other musicians? You can't just walk away. You said yourself that everything comes second to your music. What about the commitments you've made?"

"Everything's on hold for the next week while Brid's in rehab."

"So fatherhood would be something to keep you occupied in the meantime?"

Her words hit him like shards, puncturing the balloon of optimism he'd been trying to get off the ground. "Give me a break, Hannah, will you? I know to you this is a bloody joke—"

"No, Liam, it's not a joke to me." Spots of color on her face now, Hannah's anger matched his own. "It's pretty damn serious. You're telling me you want to be a father to Faith, you want us to have a relationship again. I don't think it's a joke at all. I'm not about to have my life, or Faith's, turned upside down for something you decide on a whim."

"It's more than a whim," he said.

"How do I know that?"

He didn't answer immediately. And then he said, "Give me a week. Starting tomorrow, a week to be with you and Faith. We'll take her to school, do things together. Get to know each other. At the end of the week, we'll see what happens. If you're right and it turns out to be just a whim, I'll be on my way and you won't hear from me again. If it isn't, we tell Faith who I am and take it from there."

"If you're doing this to test whether there's any possibility for us, Liam, I can tell you right now, you're wasting your time. It'll never work."

"A week. It's not asking much."

She said nothing. They were sitting outside Miranda's, the car windows open. The air seemed glittery and golden, the way it did in California; he could smell flowers, orange blossom maybe, although in Miranda's neighborhood he hadn't spotted many orange trees. It

wouldn't be a bad life. A house by the beach maybe—
if he ignored all he'd heard about the price of homes in
California. What he'd do for a living, what he'd do about
the band and the commitments they had for the next year
were matters he'd have to think about.

His arm was over the back of the seat and he touched
his fingers lightly to Hannah's shoulder. Felt her skin,
warm and smooth. They'd work something out. If she'd
just believe in him, they'd work something out.

"Okay, a week," she finally said. "A week so that
you can spend time with your daughter."

He grinned, almost light-headed with relief. "We'll
pick Faith up from school."

"*Okay,*" she said slowly. "But this *is* about Faith. A
chance for you to get to know her. It's not about us.
Forget what happened this afternoon. There is no us."

"Right, Hannah, if you say so."

"I do."

AND JUST TO ELIMINATE any doubts about the "us"
thing, Hannah went to dinner at Delmonico's with Allan
that night. Actually, Allan, along with Margaret, Rose,
Deb, Helen, Faith and Douglas. Technically, it was
Rose's Mystery Casserole Tuesday, but Allan had managed to convince everyone to join him and Hannah for
dinner instead. Allan was clearly family.

They all sat around the window table eating bread
sticks and drinking red wine while they waited for the
food to arrive. In the middle of the adults, Douglas and
Faith were coloring on paper placemats printed with out-
lines of Italy and pictures of pasta bowls to designate
key cities.

Allan had his arm across the back of Hannah's seat.
Every so often, his fingers brushed her shoulders. *Just*

as Liam's had. Five minutes after they'd sat down, Hannah was wishing she'd stayed home. Maybe she had told Liam there was no "us," but she wanted to think about Liam making love to her. About Liam telling her he loved her. About Liam telling her he wanted to try again. She wanted to think about it, but more than that, she wanted to tell someone about it. To spill it all out, the excitement, the doubt and confusion, the fact that she absolutely couldn't go more than five minutes without thinking about Liam.

It'll never work. That's what she'd told him. So why did the need to see him again feel like a physical ache? She *hurt* to see him. Her chest, her stomach, her head. But it *wouldn't* work. Wouldn't, couldn't, and yet a stubborn little spark of hope refused to be doused. Maybe, just maybe. God, she had to talk to someone. But who?

"I think that would work, don't you, Hannah?" Margaret asked.

Hannah gave her mother a blank look.

Allan squeezed her shoulder. "Daydreaming, kiddo?"

Hannah gritted her teeth. *Kiddo.* Why was she here?

"Allan was saying it would be fun if we all went out on his boat tomorrow night," Margaret said. "If I pick up Faith from school, you can go straight to the boat when you get off work."

"Should we pack a picnic?" Helen asked Allan. "I have a wonderful chicken terrine recipe…"

"No, don't bother about it," he said. "Tomorrow's Wet Wednesday at the yacht club. They have a big barbecue after the race. The kids will love it."

"So, Allan?" Rose's voice was elaborately casual. "Do you actually belong to the yacht club?"

He smiled. "My family's belonged for as long as I

can remember. My father and grandfather, too. We've always enjoyed sailing.''

"Big boat?" Rose wanted to know.

Allan shrugged. "A fifty-foot Columbia."

"Wow," Rose's mouth and eyes opened wide. "That's *big*, huh? Listen, is it okay if I bring Max?" She winked at Allan. "He's my significant other."

"Significant other du jour," Deb nudged her aunt.

"Does anyone have an Excedrin?" Hannah asked.

"Excedrin or Advil?" Helen dug a bottle of each from her bag and set them on the table.

Allan brought his mouth close to Hannah's ear. "What you need is a back rub."

Hannah smiled. And gulped down two Excedrin with a glass of water. God, life would be so much easier if she could feel something for Allan. She *wanted* to feel something for Allan. If only because the man had the patience to sit through a dinner with her family. By now, Liam would be restless; shooting her looks intended to convey that if he didn't leave in five minutes, the top of his head would explode. She entertained herself by imagining that she'd just announced her plans to bring Liam along on the little sailing trip.

Liam, who had made love to her on the couch of a darkened tour bus that afternoon. Liam, who had told her he loved her. "I've always loved you," he'd said. *It'll never work.*

"So let's see how many people do we have coming?" Allan asked. He started around the table with Hannah. "You and Faith—"

"I can't make it," Hannah said. "Neither can Faith."

All eyes turned to her, and she knew she'd made a strategic mistake.

"Oh no." Helen made a little mewl of disappointment. "What a pity."

"How come?" Rose asked.

Margaret drank some wine and looked at her daughter. Hannah turned away.

"But I want to go on a boat," Faith said. "Why can't I go?"

"We'll talk about it later, sweetie," Hannah said. "I've already made other plans," she told the others. "But you guys go, it sounds like fun."

"Can Douglas come on our other plans?" Faith asked.

"So what other plans have you made?" Rose asked. "Sound mysterious."

Deb looked across the table at Hannah. "Liam?" she mouthed.

"*I* want to go on the boat," Faith wailed. "No fair, I don't want to have other plans. I want to go on the boat."

"Somebody is getting a little cranky," Margaret said. "Maybe Grandma needs to take you home."

"Faith." Hannah addressed her daughter who was decimating a bread stick. "Put the bread down and wipe your hands."

"Where were you this afternoon, Hannah?" Helen asked as the waiter arrived, plates of steaming food held aloft on a large silver tray. "I wanted you to see this darling little outfit I got for Faith at Nordstrom's. I brought it over to show you, but your mother said you were with Jen."

"The funny thing is I thought I saw Jen in Albertson's," Margaret said. "She was buying a pork roast. I remember thinking, that's weird, I thought Jen didn't eat meat. Anyway, it was just after four."

Hannah watched Rose sprinkle parmesan cheese on her linguini. Just after four. Around the same time she was making love to Liam. Maybe, she could tell Margaret. Maybe she could make her mother understand how confused and mixed-up she felt about Liam. Maybe she could describe to her mother how you just sort of go on with your life, not unhappy, but not really happy either, although you don't do anything to change it. And then you fall in love and it seems selfish and irresponsible, but it makes you happy and you just want to go on being happy.

Except that she wasn't in love. *She wasn't in love.*

"You remind me of someone." Rose eyed Allan through narrowed azure-blue lids that exactly matched the nylon jogging suit she wore. "That guy who used to play Marlo Thomas's boyfriend on *That Girl.* What was his name?"

"That Girl." Debra hooted. "Jeez, Aunt Rose, how long ago was that?"

"I don't like this spaghetti, Mommy," Faith said.

"So why can't you go sailing tomorrow?" As she glanced over at Hannah, Margaret splashed red wine on the sleeve of her white blouse. "Damn." She dunked the corner of a napkin in her water glass and dabbed at the spot. "Can you change your plans, honey? I love it when both of my girls are together and we do things as a family. We don't do that so much anymore."

"Mommy. I *hate* this spaghetti," Faith said. "I want SpaghettiOs."

"What do you have that's so important tomorrow, anyway?" Margaret asked Hannah.

"Omigod," Deb said. "You'll never believe who just walked in."

"I HAVEN'T BEEN HERE for years," Miranda Payton told Liam as he held open the door of Delmonico's for her. "Frankly, I find the food a little old-fashioned, but it's kind of fun in a quaint, old-world way."

Liam breathed in the aromas of tomato and garlic and glanced around the small foyer. A bench along one wall and half a dozen folding chairs were all packed with people, indicating a wait was likely. Miranda was undaunted. All peach-colored silk and flowing blond hair, she swept past tables of diners, trailing cigarette smoke and calling loudly for the manager. Heads swiveled in the booths lining the walls. A large party over by the window all turned as one.

And then Liam saw Faith.

She seemed to appear from nowhere, her hair tied up with red ribbons, bread crumbs around her mouth. She beamed broadly, clearly pleased to have spotted him.

"I don't like my spaghetti," she told him. "If you want it, you can have it. Mommy's got lasagna and my grandma has...I forget what she has, but I don't like that, either. Can we go to the zoo again?"

Liam grinned at his daughter, surprised by the sudden and sharp upward turn his mood had taken. He had a mad urge to lift her onto his shoulders and gallop around the restaurant proclaiming to everyone that this was his daughter.

"Well, let's talk about this a bit." He caught her hand and led her to one side, out of the path of an oncoming waiter. He crouched so that they were eye-to-eye. Behind him, he heard Miranda complaining loudly about inferior service. And then her voice suddenly stopped and he sensed her putting two and two together. Faith was watching him, waiting for him to speak. "Tell me," he said, trying to rally his thoughts, "what exactly is it you don't like about spaghetti?"

"I only like the kind that's in little circles," Faith said.

Liam peered past Faith's shoulder, trying to spot Hannah. "What about little squares?"

"They don't make little squares," Faith said.

"She's talking about SpaghettiOs," Miranda said. "God, revolting stuff. My mother's housekeeper used to try to feed it to me."

Faith looked uncertain. "I like SpaghettiOs."

"So do I," Liam said, having no idea what they were. "There's nothing like SpaghettiOs. In fact, you know what I think we should do? I think we should go and find your mum and buy three hundred tins of SpaghettiOs and eat them until SpaghettiOs come out of our ears."

Faith giggled. "You're funny," she said. "They don't come out of your ears."

"Well, they might if it was a really, really big bunch." Liam pulled himself to his feet, and glanced over at Miranda. "I hate to leave you in the lurch, but I'm on a mission, all right?"

Miranda's face darkened. "For God's sake, Liam."

He shot a look at her over Faith's head, a look intended to convey that if she chose to make a scene about this, she'd be sorry. Then he addressed Faith.

"Let's go and talk to your mummy."

He took his daughter's hand. It was soft, warm and sticky, just as it had been at the zoo on Sunday. Did all six-year-old girls have warm, sticky little hands? His own felt cold as Faith walked him over to the table where Hannah sat with her party of fifty. Or at least that's how many seemed to be gawking up at him over their dinner plates and brimming wineglasses. Fifty, maybe a hundred. Not one of them looking happy to see him. His feet were also cold and his heart was doing overtime; pounding in rhythm with the pulsing beat of his right eyelid. Miranda, still in tow, was asked by a waiter to extinguish her cigarette. Her response was a pithy and anatomically impossible suggestion, clearly audible over the Puccini on the sound system. Liam tightened his grip on Faith's hand and considered making a dash for it, yelling over his shoulder for Hannah to join them. A foot or so from the table, he made eye contact with Hannah, who looked nervous and tense, hardly surprising really—he felt pretty nervous and tense himself. God, who *were* all these people with her? He recognized her mother. Margaret's face was flushed, her expression strained. *Sorry, Margaret, I know you told me to stay away from her, but I ended up making love to her instead.* And there was the pirate's dad. And the pirate, not in costume tonight, though. The pirate's dad had his arm around Hannah's shoulder. Liam pictured himself taking the pirate's dad out. One quick blow to that chiseled jaw would do it.

"And here's Liam," Faith said, drawing his name out like a sidekick on a television show announcing the big star. "He said we're going to buy a whole big bunch of SpaghettiOs and eat them until they come out of our ears. Okay, Mommy? We can give my spaghetti to Raisin." She looked up at Liam. "Raisin can't come with me to our new apartment because you can't have dogs there."

"Then we'll have to look for a place where you *can* have a dog," he said.

Hannah shot him a look, whispered something to the pirate's dad and eased her way out of the booth. Her face flushed, she nodded at the door, and he followed her, Faith's hand still in his. A moment later, they were outside the restaurant. Tall, skinny palm trees in the center median waved their frondy top knots at the dark blue sky and the night air felt cool and damp. That was one thing that had always surprised him about California. Even the hottest days cooled off rapidly when the sun went down. Hannah was looking at him as though she expected an explanation.

''The week isn't supposed to start until tomorrow,'' she finally said.

CHAPTER TWELVE

LIAM SHRUGGED. "I didn't know you were going to be here."

"Can we get SpaghettiOs?" Faith asked.

"Faith doesn't like the spaghetti at that place," Liam said. "I told her we'd get the stuff she likes."

"Faith has a plate of untouched spaghetti inside the restaurant," Hannah said. "Until she takes a bite, she really doesn't know whether she likes it or not."

"But I don't," Faith wailed. "I only like SpaghettiOs."

"She only likes SpaghettiOs," Liam said.

Hannah gave him a long look. An eyes-narrowed, hands-on-hips long look.

"I'm just telling you what she likes," he said. "And it's not the stuff in there."

"I like SpaghettiOs." Faith released his hand, hopscotched along the sidewalk. "SpaghettiOs, SpaghettiOs," she sang. "I only like SpaghettiOs."

"You heard her," Liam said. "She only likes SpaghettiOs."

"If you say that one more time, I'm going to hit you," Hannah said.

He watched her face. She was trying hard not to smile. So was he. Both of them, standing there with the waving palm trees and Faith singing about SpaghettiOs. He broke first and grinned at Hannah.

"You are impossible, Tully."

"SpaghettiOs?"

She raised a hand as though to swipe at his face.

Ten minutes later they were pushing a cart down the aisle of a supermarket. He watched Faith briefly disappear around the corner of Aisle 15—pasta, tomato sauce, olives—reappear, then take off again. "Shouldn't she sit in the cart?" he asked Hannah.

She gave him a scornful look. "Faith would be very insulted if she heard you say that. She hasn't sat in a cart since she was three."

He shrugged. "What do I know?"

"We have very strict rules about how far she can stray. No more than one aisle over from where I am, and she has to come back as soon as she hears me. Or else."

"Or else what?"

"Just *or else*. It's something parents say to kids."

"I'll remember that," Liam said.

Hannah gave him a look he couldn't read. She considered his interest in Faith a whim—he had little doubt about that—and was surprised by anything he said that suggested otherwise. Suddenly the week he'd asked for seemed so ridiculously inadequate that he felt himself sinking into the state Brid called his Misery Mode. "Snap out of it," she'd tell him when he'd succumb to the moody gloom, or as Pearse put it, the Celtic Crud. "You're a misery to look at and a bloody misery to be around."

"So where are we going to cook this gourmet feast?" Hannah reached for a can of SpaghettiOs. "I'm pretty sure you don't want to do it at my mother's house."

"I don't care," he said, although the idea of sitting in the family kitchen with the aunts and Margaret shooting him dagger looks wasn't loaded with appeal. "Sooner or later Margaret's going to have to get used to me being around."

"Let's make it later rather than sooner, okay? She's in this emotionally fragile state right now. My sister's pregnant and—"

"And I'm just one more problem she doesn't need, is that it?"

"Liam…"

"I'm sorry." He'd regretted the words as soon as he'd said them. "This is about us, not your mother. And the last thing I want is a fight." He thought for a moment. "The tour bus has a hot plate," he said. "We could cook there."

Hannah smiled, a doubtful smile that spoke volumes. "Nix the tour bus?"

"After this afternoon, it has…certain associations that don't exactly go with cooking SpaghettiOs for Faith."

He smiled, too—the gloom sent packing by the certainty that Hannah, despite her cool demeanor, had been as bowled over by their afternoon together as he had. "You don't think I'd try to ravage you over a plate of SpaghettiOs."

"The thought crossed my mind."

He tried to look injured. "I do have *some* moral principles."

She raised a brow. "No kidding?"

"Absolutely. They're good on toast with grated cheese."

"Did I mention you were impossible?"

He kissed her neck. "Did I mention you were fantastic today?"

"Did I mention that you're wasting your time if you think there's going to be a repeat performance?"

He put his arm around her shoulder, and brought his face around to kiss the side of her mouth. "I don't believe you."

"Wait and see."

"Want to bet?"

"No, thank you," she said primly. "I don't gamble." She glanced at him. "Not that it matters to me at all, but…"

"No, I'm not sleeping with her."

She steered the trolley into his leg. "You didn't *know* that's what I was going to ask."

"Weren't you?"

She grinned. "Maybe."

Faith reappeared, peeked into the basket. "I don't see any SpaghettiOs."

Liam took the can Hannah had been holding and dropped it in the cart. He looked at Faith. "What d'you think? Five more? Ten? Six hundred?"

"Six hundred," Faith said.

"What if we split the difference and make it two?"

"Two's good, too." She grinned. "Hey, I made a joke. Two's good, too," she chanted as she ran down the aisle.

"So did we establish a place?" Hannah asked

"What about your new home?"

"There's no furniture there yet," she said.

"Electricity? Gas?"

"The utilities haven't been turned on."

"Have you got the key?"

"Yes."

"Good. I've got an idea."

FAITH SAT CROSS-LEGGED on a blanket, a paper napkin tucked under her chin, shoveling SpaghettiOs, heated on a Sterno burner, into her mouth. Half a dozen candles set on paper plates around the room made flickering shadows on the walls.

"I like this place, Mommy," Faith said. "It's like camping, only better." She looked at Hannah. "But you don't get to pee in the woods."

"Faith." Hannah protested.

"When we go camping with Allan and Douglas, Mommy says we get to pee in the woods."

"Faith, I really don't think Liam cares about that," Hannah said.

"Yes, I do." Liam, studiously ignoring Hannah, smiled at Faith. "I want to hear all about it."

"She said we have to take flashlights so we don't trip over something," Faith went on, clearly encouraged by Liam's interest. "And Allan's going to cook marshmallows."

Hannah caught Liam's eye, held his glance for a moment. "Allan invited us to Yosemite this summer," she said. "Faith and I will have our own little tent, Allan and Douglas will have theirs." She saw a smile flicker across Liam's face; she knew he knew she was telling him that she wouldn't be sleeping with Allan.

"More SpaghettiOs?" she asked Liam, who was making a valiant effort to finish the food already piled on his plate.

"That's all right," Liam said politely. "I've had plenty. Help yourself."

"You have them, Liam," Faith said. "I want to see them come out of your ears."

"Yeah, Liam." Hannah said as she emptied the pan onto his plate. "Let's see them come out of your ears."

She tried unsuccessfully to keep a straight face. This was fun. Doing things with Faith was always fun; Liam gave it a new dimension. There is no us, she'd told him. But didn't they kind of feel like a cozy little threesome right now? Sitting here in an empty apartment eating canned spaghetti they'd bought because it was their daughter's favorite?

But a relationship was more than a picnic in an empty apartment. It took dedication, commitment, mutual respect. And as she watched Liam and Faith clown around together—Faith urging Liam to "eat, eat, eat"—she marched out all the reasons their marriage hadn't worked the first time and wouldn't work if they tried it again. Marched them out, paraded them for inspection, then tried to shoot them down. And just when she was just on the verge of deciding their relationship might actually work, a parade of nameless, beautiful women trooped through her brain, reminding her of the all-consuming jealousy and insecurity she'd felt before.

"Mummy's not paying attention," Liam told Faith. "Which is a pity, because she missed one of the best tricks of the evening." He winked at his daughter. "Right?"

"Right," Faith said. "You missed it, Mommy."

"What did I miss?" Hannah asked.

Faith gave Liam an uncertain look. "What did she miss?"

"Ah, come on, Faith. You know." He crooked his finger and she came over to him. With one hand, he brushed her hair aside, and whispered something in her ear. "Now tell your mum what she missed."

"You missed seeing SpaghettiOs coming out of Liam's ears," Faith said. "It was a really good trick, too."

She smiled at Liam. "You have talents I never even suspected."

He met her eyes. "All I need is a chance to demonstrate them."

Hannah looked away, then busied herself with picking up paper plates. Faith started telling Liam about the time that Douglas laughed so much that milk came out of his nose. Liam sat with his chin in his hand, his expression thoughtful as he interrupted Faith's description with questions. "Just a minute now, Faith," he'd ask solemnly. "Was this *skim* milk? Did it come out of *both* nostrils, or just one?"

For all Liam's concerns about not knowing how to behave around small children, Hannah reflected, he was succeeding incredibly well with his daughter—who was clearly enchanted by him.

"Douglas and Grandma and Auntie Rose and everyone get to go for a ride on Allan's boat tomorrow." Faith had moved on from the milk incident. "But Mommy said we can't go because we have other plans."

"But I think you're going to like those other plans." Hannah looked from Liam to Faith. "Guess who's going to pick you up from school?"

"Grandma?"

"Guess again." Hannah felt a vague sense of trepidation. As she'd left the restaurant with Faith, she'd caught a glimpse of her mother's apprehensive expression. Now she was going to have break the news to Margaret that Liam would be picking up her granddaughter from school.

"If it's not Grandma..." Faith looked from Hannah to Liam. "Then it's..." She pointed her finger at Hannah. "Mommy."

"And me," Liam said.

Faith grinned. "*Liam.* Cool. Then we can all go out on Allan's boat."

"Actually, I've got a better idea," Liam said. "I know a great big boat we can go on."

"As big as Allan's?"

"Bigger."

"Is it your boat?"

"No, but I have a special arrangement with the captain."

"Cool," Faith said again. And then she got up from the cushion she'd been sitting on and moved next to Liam. "Hey, Liam." She looked up at him. "You know something?"

"What?"

"I like you."

Hannah watched Liam's face. He was sitting cross-legged on the floor, his back against the wall. For a moment, he didn't speak and then he put his arm around his daughter and kissed the top of her head.

"That's good," he said. "Because I like you, too. A lot."

"And I love Raisin," she said. "He's the best dog in the whole world."

"But can he play a guitar?" Liam asked.

Faith eyed him for a moment. "He's a dog, silly."

Hannah remembered the guitar Liam had given her that afternoon. She'd left it in the car, thinking that she'd wait until Liam was there before she gave it to Faith. While Liam was telling Faith that he'd like to teach her to play, Hannah slipped outside. Liam smiled as she came back in, holding the guitar. "Liam has a present for you," she said.

He crooked his finger at Faith. "C'mon over here. I'll teach you to play it, then you can teach Raisin."

This struck Faith as so funny she dissolved in giggles and ended up spilling her glass of ginger ale down the front of her shirt. The lesson was postponed while Hannah stripped off the wet top. Belatedly she realized that she didn't have a replacement.

"Here. Wrap this around her." Liam pulled off his shirt, and handed it to Hannah. "Clean this morning."

Faith giggled even harder, rolling around on the floor now, hyped-up and overtired. Laughing and flinging her arms as she leaped around the room. A sprite, completely unselfconscious, clad only in a pair of red shorts.

"*I* don't have a shirt and *you* don't have a shirt," she told Liam between peals of laughter. "*You* don't have a shirt and *I* don't have a shirt. *Mommy* has a shirt, but *you* don't have a shirt. *I* don't have a shirt…"

Hannah met Liam's eyes. "She'll wind down in a minute."

"Hey, Hannah." He touched her foot with his own. "I love you."

"IT'S A SHAME she can't have her dog with her here," Liam said after Faith had finally fallen asleep on the living room floor on an improvised bed of blankets and cushions brought in from the car. "Have you spoken to the landlord? Maybe he'd reconsider."

"The lease was pretty clear about no animals," Hannah said.

"Let's find a different place," he said. "She should have a dog."

Hannah heard the word *let's*. She allowed herself a moment to consider what it implied. Togetherness, shared responsibility. She picked up a circle of spaghetti that had escaped her earlier cleanup. "This apartment is what *I* can afford, Liam. There aren't many places in my price range that allow pets."

"I'll contribute, I told you that." He glanced around

the empty, shadow-filled room. "Look, give me the landlord's number, I'll have a talk with him tomorrow. If I can't get him to change his mind, we'll find something else."

We. She felt her heart beat a little faster. It had appeal, this shared responsibility thing. Sharing, instead of assuming it all herself. Hannah couldn't remember a time when she hadn't felt weighted down by responsibility. "Let me talk to her," she'd tell Margaret. "I'll handle it," she'd say to Rose or Helen. "Don't worry about it," she'd assure Deb. "I'll sort it out."

And now Liam was saying, *Hey, take a break. I can handle it.* And it would be so easy to allow that to happen. Easy and comforting…and dangerous.

She studied him as he lay stretched out on his back now, his hands pillowed behind his head. She averted her eyes from his bare chest and his flat stomach. Averted her eyes, but found herself mentally stripping off his faded jeans. Sex is sex is sex, she reminded herself. Don't confuse it with real commitment.

"When I was about Faith's age, maybe a bit older, this dog followed me home from school." Liam smiled, as though remembering. "Black-and-white, he was. A little bit of everything. Bloody great feet and a tail that never stopped. My stepdad caught me opening a tin of beef and gravy for it to eat. Thrashed me and sent the dog packing."

"God, that's awful. What a jerk." Hannah pictured him as the small boy he'd been—dark hair maybe overdue for a trim and their daughter's blue eyes—and felt as retroactively protective as if it had been Faith he was telling her about. "What did you do?"

He grinned. "I went looking for the dog and found it

waiting outside a bar in town. Knew its place apparently—the owner came out a few minutes later.''

''I think that's the first thing you've ever told me about your childhood,'' she said. ''I remember when I used to ask you, you'd just change the subject.''

''Not much to tell,'' he said, still on his back, hands locked behind his head. ''My ma couldn't take care of me and none of the aunties and uncles were clamoring for the job either. I got shipped around a bit, which is no doubt why I'm the sterling character I am today.''

''But your mother...'' She found herself struggling with the concept of a mother just abandoning a child. ''Do you ever hear from her?''

''Two or three years ago, she rang. Out of the blue. I didn't even recognize her voice. She'd been living in England and had hardly any trace of an Irish accent. Just wondering about me, she said.''

''That was it?''

''That was it. I might have been an acquaintance whose number she'd just rediscovered.''

''I wonder what she'd think about being a grandmother.''

''I've no idea.''

Faith shifted in her sleep, and Hannah glanced over at her. One of the candles flickered wildly, then went out. She watched as Liam got up to relight it then stretched back on the floor again. ''Do you think you'll tell her about Faith?''

''I hadn't thought about it until now,'' he said. ''But I might. It would be good for Faith to know she has family besides yours. Give her a look at the two extremes.''

''It's funny to think Faith has another grandmother somewhere.'' Hannah sat cross-legged, shoulders pressed against the wall. "Margaret's so involved in Faith's life, I don't know how she'd deal with a competing grandmother."

"In the long run it doesn't matter," Liam said. "She's our daughter. The grandparents are just supporting players."

"Tell that to Margaret," Hannah said.

"She'll find out for herself soon enough." He sat up, looked at Faith and rolled over to smooth the blanket covering her back. "If I were the vengeful type, I'd take a lot of pleasure in the fact that your mother's lies are about to come back to haunt her."

Hannah felt uneasy suddenly. His face gave nothing away, but she had a gnawing sense that if she dug a little deeper, she would discover something she'd rather not know. Unspoken resentment? Had he, just now, inadvertently shown his cards? Was it truly Faith and Hannah he wanted? Or the opportunity to turn the tables on Margaret? As the silence lengthened, she tried to mentally formulate a question, but it sounded paranoid, even to her ears, Still she couldn't shake the thought.

"Stop it." Liam shifted across the floor to sit beside her. He took her hand, brought it to his mouth, then set it down again. "Stop telling yourself this won't work."

She turned her head to look at him. The room was dark except for the flickering candles. From the makeshift bed, Faith made soft whimpering noises in her sleep. Hannah started to speak and Liam shook his head.

"I need you to believe in me, Hannah." Again he took her hand, held it on his knee. "Once upon a time," he said softly, "there was this wee little boy who wanted to make his ma happy because she was having a pretty rotten time of it, crying a lot and always sad. So he decided he'd have a bang-up dinner ready for her when she came home from work. Chops and roast potatoes and an apple tart for afters.''

Hannah smiled and he put his arm around her shoulders and drew her close. Swept by a wave of tenderness, she felt a sudden insatiable need to know more of these vignettes about his life, all the things that he'd never shared with her when they were married.

"Do you have any pictures from when you were a little boy?" she asked.

"A few, not many." He squeezed her shoulder. "But you're interrupting my story."

"Sorry."

"Right, well where was I?"

"Cooking dinner."

"Ah yes, well that was a bit of a problem since the lad couldn't cook at all."

She grinned. "Still can't."

"I'll ignore that. Anyway, not only couldn't he cook, he was also a bit short of cash. Hadn't a penny, actually. But he was a resourceful sort, so he went down to the grocer's on the corner and asked would they let him pay for the food by helping out around the shop, doing a few errands. Well, they laughed in his face." He paused. "And that night his ma stuck her head in the gas cooker."

"Oh, Liam…" She'd been half smiling, anticipating the happy ending and what he'd said was so awful, she was stunned into silence. "I don't know what to say."

He ruffled her hair. "Don't go getting maudlin. They got her in time. But wouldn't it have been a far happier story if the shopkeeper had trusted the kid?"

"Yeah, but trust isn't always so easy."

"So I'm discovering."

"Liam—"

"You've got reason enough to be skeptical, Hannah, but I swear to God I never ran around on you while we were married and I know without a doubt that if we try again, we can make it work. But you have to believe."

He kissed her then and she could taste the sweet tomato of the SpaghettiOs. Her back slid down the wall as they kept kissing. When he let her go, her mouth felt warm and numb.

A moment passed and he pulled himself to his feet. "Well, enough of that. It's late." He glanced down at his sleeping daughter. "I'll carry her out to the car."

Hannah watched him bend and gently scoop Faith up in his arms. She blew out the candles, locked the front door and followed them to the car.

"So, we're on for tomorrow?" he asked after he'd strapped Faith into the back seat of the car. "What time does she get out of school?"

"Two-thirty. We can walk down there from the house."

"The house on Termino? Your mother's house?"

She nodded. "I'll let her know."

"Break the bad news, huh?"

"Come on…"

"After the boat, we could all have dinner somewhere." He grinned. "To counteract the SpaghettiOs."

"So who is it you know with a big boat?"

"Actually, I was stretching it a bit." His smile widened. "Isn't the *Queen Mary* docked in Long Beach? Pearse was telling me they've got these little water taxis that you can ride over on and I've heard there are all sorts of things to do on board. Don't tell Faith though. It'll be fun to see her face when she sees it. And," he added, "it *is* a wee bit bigger than Allan's boat."

She shook her head at him, then reached up to kiss him on the mouth. "I don't know about you, Tully."

And then they were both grinning, arms wrapped around each other. He leaned back against the car, drawing her to him. Beyond his shoulder, the small white wooden bungalows up and down the street glowed in the night sky and in that moment, it seemed absolutely possible that they'd be together forever. It was all she could do not to tell him that.

"How did it go?" he asked a moment later. "Our first day?"

"It went great, Liam." She wanted to say, *I love you Liam. I love you and I believe in you and I know it can work.* Instead she said, "Really great."

HE'D KISSED HER AGAIN after she dropped him at Miranda's; a soft tender kiss that left her feeling dreamy, floating on a fragile bubble of optimism. The feeling was still there ten minutes later as she turned onto Termino and pulled up outside her house. Her mother's house, Hannah thought.

She leaned her head back against the seat. This time next week, her home would be the apartment on Tenth where she and Liam and their daughter had just spent the evening. Images ran through her brain. Faith laughing openmouthed at one of Liam's jokes, paper plate of SpaghettiOs on the floor beside her. Faith, shirtless, dancing across the floor. Liam's face as he said, "I love you."

She did want it to work.
I want you to believe in me.
It would work.

CHAPTER THIRTEEN

THE OPTIMISM WAS STILL there the next morning. Bright and buoyant as a child's balloon, it bobbed gaily as Hannah got Faith off to school and was still afloat by noon when she called Margaret from school to suggest they meet for coffee at Babette's Feast.

Hannah was already sitting at one of the green wrought-iron tables on the outdoor patio when Margaret arrived.

"This is nice." Margaret smiled appreciatively, her eyes hidden by the knockoff Armani sunglasses she'd bought last week at the Long Beach Farmer's Market. "I'm very lucky, you know that? We both are."

Hannah grinned. "You lost five pounds this morning, too?"

Margaret leaned forward. "*Did* you?"

"*No.*" She spotted the black-aproned waiter bringing their cappuccinos in white cups the size of soup bowls. "But I ordered a chocolate Napoleon for us anyway. So why are we lucky?"

"Having daughters." Margaret sat back in her chair as the waiter set down the food. "Daughters are nice to have," she said after he left. "My friends with sons are always complaining how they never remember birthdays, but you and Deb…well Deb's forgotten a few of my birthdays—but you never have and that means a lot to me, sweetie. Not to get syrupy on you, but I really treasure our relationship.''

''So do I, Mom.'' Given the strain of past few days, she felt a stab of hypocrisy. Was *treasure* overstating it? ''I mean we've always gotten along,'' she amended, almost thinking aloud, ''and I feel sad about the way things have been with us lately. That's one of the things I wanted to talk to you about.''

Margaret stuck a fork under the Napoleon's flaky crust. ''How many Weight Watchers points, do you think?''

''Screw Weight Watchers,'' Hannah said. ''This is a celebration.''

Margaret looked at Hannah over the rim of her sunglasses.

''That's the other thing I wanted to talk to you about.'' She smiled. ''I'm in love, Mom.'' *There, she'd said it.* Suddenly she couldn't stop smiling. The balloon bobbed brightly, liquid sunshine flowed through her, filling her with this incredible incandescent happiness. ''God, I'm so in love I could stand on the table and yell it out.''

Margaret's expression had congealed slightly. ''Do I need to ask?''

''Liam, of course.'' Even saying his name aloud felt terrific. ''Be happy for us, okay?'' The balloon had dipped ever so slightly. ''I want you to get to know him.'' She watched a sparrow hop across the patio's flagstone tiles. ''He's going to be a part of our lives. Mine, Faith's and yours. You need to understand that and accept it.''

Margaret put her elbows on the table, and studied her daughter's face. ''Would you be happy if you saw Faith running out into the traffic?''

"Oh, for God's sake…I am not a six-year-old child running into the traffic." The balloon had taken a precipitous drop, but she could send it aloft again. She broke off a piece of the Napoleon and ate it, choosing her words carefully. "Look, I have a great idea. In this morning's *Press Telegram* there was an article about this program at Western Memorial. It's in the neonatal intensive care unit," she went on, warming to the subject. "Premature babies respond well to the human touch—being cuddled and hugged—but the nursing staff don't have the time to sit and rock them so that's where this program comes in. It's called Cuddlers and every volunteer is assigned to a baby. I think it would be perfect for you."

Margaret said nothing. Arms folded across her chest, she stared at Hannah through her dark glasses while the sparrows chirped and twittered around them and the sun threw shadows across the table.

"What, Mom?"

"Don't patronize me, Hannah."

"How am I patronizing you?" Hannah heard her voice rise. "This is a wonderful thing. The babies get what they need, and the volunteers know they're providing a much-needed service."

"Kind of like giving an orphaned lamb to a sheep, knowing that the sheep will nurse anything put in front of it."

Deflated, Hannah just shook her head. "I thought—"

"You thought that if you found something else to keep me busy, you'd be free to run off with Liam."

"No, that's not it at all." She mashed a crumb with her finger. "I mean I do think it would be a good thing if you had some other interests, but—"

"You just don't get it, do you? You really think that

I'm only having sleepless nights because I have nothing
better to do with my life.'' She pushed aside her coffee,
clearly angry. ''Give poor old Mom something mean-
ingful to do. I can just hear you and Deb—''

''Mom...'' Hannah frowned at her. Margaret's raised
voice had drawn curious glances from the occupants of
nearby tables. ''Keep it down, huh?''

''I don't care. I'm furious that you can be so blind
and stupid about this man. Who was that woman with
him in Delmonico's last night?''

''Miranda. He's staying at her place.'' Hannah felt her
face go hot. ''I mean the band's staying at her place.
She's married, Mom.''

Margaret lowered her sunglasses and eyed Hannah
over the rims.

''What?''

''I've seen Liam twice since he got back, and each
time he's been with a different woman.''

''Brid is his singer and I just explained who Miranda
is.''

''Why does he need them traipsing around with him?
Why does he need to bring his singer to his daughter's
birthday party? Why does he go out to dinner with this
Miranda? How come no one else in the band went
along?''

Hannah felt her mood take a steep plunge. Margaret's
voice had risen a notch with each question. She'd obviously been stewing over Liam's questionable fidelity
for some time. Then she remembered Liam's words. *I
need you to believe in me.* ''I don't care what it looks
like to you, Mom, he's not sleeping with Miranda or
Brid. He loves me, he wants us to be a family.''

''How do you *know* he's not sleeping with these other
women?''

"He told me."

Light glinted off the lenses of Margaret's glasses. "Oh of course, why didn't I think of that. So what happens next? He goes off on his tours and you stay home and play house? Or are you going with him? And where does Faith fit into the picture?"

"We haven't talked about it. I'm just trying to tell you how I feel." A sparrow had hopped onto the table and was regarding her with bright black eyes. "Can you at least *try* to understand?"

"I'm sorry, but I don't think I can." Margaret folded her arms across her chest. "I just don't trust what's happening, period. I don't believe Liam's serious about this daddy thing. I don't believe he's thinking about what's best for you or Faith. He's a womanizer, Hannie, just like your father."

"Mom, you don't even know him. You've never even tried to get to know him."

"I don't need to. I lived with your father for enough years. I know the type. They love to have women around them. Oh sure, they've always got some excuse, but bottom line, they like women."

Hannah thought of Beryl, her father's longtime secretary who'd accompanied him on business trips. Of the young widow down the road who was always calling on him to fix something or other; of Margaret's various woman friends who seemed to inevitably end up on the couch talking to her father whenever they dropped by. All innocent on the surface, just like Miranda and Brid.

"Hannah, your father cheated on me until the day he dropped dead. I'd catch him in some lie, and he'd confess and swear it would never happen again. But it always did. That's the way some men are. And I'm telling you, a good-looking guy like Liam is not about to trot home faithfully every night, especially when there are kids running around and dishes in the sink.''

''Liam's going with me to pick Faith up from school today.'' Hannah decided to ignore Margaret's gloomy forecast. She forced a smile. ''He's pretty excited about it. So is Faith. We're going to take her to the *Queen Mary*.''

''He's playing at being a parent, Hannah. And you want to buy into it. You're believing what you want to believe. We all do it at times. Unfortunately, it tends to blind us to the true situation.''

''Well…'' Hannah fished in her purse for her billfold. ''I'm ready…''

Margaret shook her head, then reached across the table to touch Hannah's hand. ''Look at me, sweetie. You've got to put Faith first in this situation, and I don't think that's what you're doing. What kind of a life is Liam going to provide for her? Forget all this starry-eyed nonsense about being in love with him. It's your daughter you need to think about.''

''WELL, IS SHE A GIRLIE GIRL?'' Miranda asked Liam as they walked the aisles of Ikea looking for children's furniture. ''Or a tomboy?''

Liam smiled as he thought about the question. It was the day after the SpaghettiOs evening. He thought of the small but growing collection of things he knew about his daughter. ''She loves animals, especially koalas, but also monkeys and giraffes. She doesn't like brussels sprouts or the spaghetti at Delmonico's, but she's very partial to—''

''SpaghettiOs,'' Miranda interrupted. ''I think you owe it to her to break her of that little quirk. I can't believe you and Anna—''

"Hannah." Miranda had apparently developed a mental block about Hannah's name. Just an hour earlier, she'd referred to her as Hillary.

"Hannah then," Miranda said. "I still can't believe the two of you actually ate that revolting stuff just because a six-year-old child happens to like it."

"This isn't just any six-year-old child, Miranda. This is a six-year-old child with very discerning taste. I personally believe she's just ahead of the gustatory curve. A year from now, all those fancy restaurants you go to will be serving SpaghettiOs."

"You're impossible." Miranda drew up at a white bedroom dresser, pulled open a drawer, closed it. "Cheaply made." She moved to a vanity table, and ducked to glance at her reflection in the child's eye-level mirror. "God, do I need a facial. I think I overindulged last night. Unlike some people," she said, "who drank ginger ale."

"Nothing wrong with ginger ale," Liam said. He would have preferred a Guinness last night, but had no problem at all sharing a ginger ale with his daughter. "Tasted quite good, in fact."

"That's because you're besotted." Miranda sat down on the lower mattress of a bunk bed, and looked up at Liam. "If your daughter wanted chocolate-covered grasshoppers washed down with cherry Kool-Aid, you'd go along with it."

"Faith would never waste a good grasshopper with chocolate," Liam said. "They're much better with strawberry jam. I'd go along with the cherry Kool-Aid, though."

"Pearse told me this morning he's worried." Miranda picked up a lamp with a frilled shade, examined the underside. "He thinks you have no idea of what you're getting yourself into. He said between Brid's problems and this thing with the kid, he's concerned about the band.'' She set the lamp down, and looked at Liam. ''Just relaying his thoughts.''

Liam rubbed his hand across the back of his neck. The children's furnishing department of an Ikea store in suburban Orange County didn't seem like the place to tell Miranda what she could do with her relayed thoughts, but she'd said one thing he couldn't let pass.

''The *kid* happens to be my daughter. Her name is Faith.'' He walked over to a grouping of furniture made of some sort of fabricated material. Probably laminated plywood, he thought. But the pieces were painted in bright primary colors. A red bed; dresser drawers in yellow, green and blue. A small yellow chair set in front of a blue desk. He could see Faith sitting there. He just wasn't sure what Hannah would think of it. She should be here with him, but he'd wanted to surprise her and Faith. He'd pictured them this evening, walking into Faith's room all set up with the new furniture.

''Liam.'' Miranda touched his arm. ''Don't be mad at me.''

Liam ignored her and looked around for a salesclerk. Faith would also need sheets and blankets. No doubt Hannah had plenty of her own, but he wanted to do this for Faith.

''You've put so much into the band, all of you,'' Miranda said. ''Brid, Pearse, Mick. You can't blame them for not wanting it to fall apart.''

''It's not going to fall apart.'' Liam took a credit card from his wallet, and checked his watch. ''Pearse knows I'd never let that happen.''

''He said he's never seen you like this. I'll be honest with you, Liam, Pearse and I had a long talk last night.

Maybe we'd had one too many piña coladas, but Pearse said he thinks this girl—''

"Girl?"

"Amy is it? No, Hannah, that's right. Why can't I seem to remember her name? Pearse thinks she's a bad influence. All she wants to do is come between you and the band and she won't be satisfied until she's got you trapped in Irvine or somewhere with two more kids and a mortgage."

"Right then," Liam said after he'd signed the credit card receipt. "I'm ready."

"Liam." Miranda caught his arm. "I care about you, I really do. You are making such a huge mistake. At least take a little time to cool off before you make a decision." She smiled at him, all perfect teeth and glossy hair. "Puerto Vallarta is lovely. I could make reservations for us."

As HE HEADED ACROSS the manicured grounds of Casa Pacifica looking for Brid, it occurred to Liam that anyone who hadn't seen the discreet sign noting a physician was on twenty-four-hour call could be forgiven for thinking that he or she had wandered into an exclusive hotel instead of a rehab center.

He found Brid lying on a lawn chair; eyes closed, her bare shoulders turning almost the same shade of pink as her bikini top. Liam tweaked her toe and she opened her eyes and smiled.

"Well, there's a sight for sore eyes." She sat up, and held out her arms to him. "Howya, Liam."

"Not so bad." He sat down on the grass. "And yourself?"

"Getting fat as a cow," she said.

"You've still a long way to go."

"Not with the way they're feeding me here."

"Just keep doing as you're told," he said. "I need you back on the stage beside me."

She studied him for a long moment. "What's wrong, Liam?"

"Pearse thinks the band's about to break up. He blames me."

Brid shook her head. "Blames you for what?"

"Breaking up the band. He told Miranda that Hannah won't be satisfied until I'm wearing a ring."

"*Miranda.*" Brid rolled her eyes. "A head case if ever I saw one. Pearse was probably trying to get into her knickers. No doubt he was feeling his drink and just letting off a bit of steam."

"You don't think it then? That I'd let the band be broken up?"

"Daft cod," Brid said. "You'd give up breathing first."

Liam grinned.

She gave him another long look. "But I think it says something that you had to hear me confirm it. Six weeks ago, you'd have laughed your head off if Pearse had said something like that."

"Six weeks ago Pearse wouldn't have said something like that."

"How are things with your daughter?"

"Grand." He smiled. "Fantastic."

"And it's killing you to think of how it'll be when we're back on the road again."

"It is."

"But you wouldn't be happy with any other kind of life."

"I know."

"Remember when I asked if you ever feel like putting down roots?"

He shook his head. "No, but I can imagine what I said."

"Something about taking aspirin and lying down until the feeling went away." She pulled a towel off the back of the chaise longue, wrapped it around her shoulders. "Maybe you should do that now, Liam."

HANNAH WAS CUTTING PAPER flowers from colored construction paper and trying not to let Margaret's parting advice completely ruin her mood when Allan stopped in her classroom just before two to pick up Douglas for a doctor's appointment. In a Zen-like trance—anything to block Margaret's voice in her head—she'd already cut out a pile of pink paper roses. Bouquets of yellow daffodils and purple tulips blossomed in colorful profusion across her desktop.

Allan picked up a paper rose, and studied it. "I really enjoyed meeting your family last night. Your mother's quite a character. They all are."

"Yeah, well…" Her face felt warm. "They like you, too, Allan."

"Unfortunately, you don't feel the same way."

"That's not true," she protested. "You're a terrific guy. I'm just—"

"You're just not in love with me." He folded his arms across his chest. "How were the SpaghettiOs?"

"Faith liked them."

Allan grimaced. "God."

"I know." She traced the edge of a rose with her finger. "I'm sorry about walking out on you. It was rude, I know."

He waved away her apology. "It bothered your

mother more than it bothered me. Not that I wanted to see you go, but I looked at you looking at that guy and I recognized I was fighting a losing battle.'' He perched on the edge of her desk, picked up a framed picture of Faith, studied it, and set it down again. "Listen, if I'm out of line, just tell me. I'm talking to you as an attorney who's done some family practice law, Hannah, not as a guy who would like to marry you.''

"Allan...''

"Sorry, strike that last part.'' He paused. "Liam is Faith's biological father, right? There's no doubt about that?''

She blinked. "Of course.''

"Okay, I just needed to know. And when the two of you were divorced, there were custody arrangements?''

"No. My mother told Liam I'd had an abortion.'' She saw Jen poke her head around the door and mouth the word *later* when she saw Allan. Hannah peered up at the clock on the wall. Nearly time to pick up Faith. "What's this all about?''

He looked at her as though debating how to answer. "I'm concerned for you.''

Hannah sighed, exasperated. "Join the club. God, I wish to hell everyone would stop being concerned about me and get on with their own lives.''

Allan looked offended. "This is just a case of a friend helping a friend,'' he said. "You've given me some great advice on Douglas. I'm just returning the favor.''

"I'm sorry.'' She touched his arm. "I'm a little weary of discussing Liam. I went through it this morning with my mom.''

"How serious is Liam about having a role in Faith's life?''

"Very.''

"Do you realize he has a good case for a lawsuit?" He waited a moment. "I'm not an expert on this, but I'm sure he could probably bring civil litigation against your mother. He could also sue for joint custody of Faith. I'm assuming he intends to go back to Ireland?"

She nodded. "Look, you're making it sound a lot more adversarial than it is. Liam's already told me he'd like to have Faith visit him in Ireland. I'm hoping it doesn't come to that, but if it does we'll deal with it."

"You'd allow him to take her to Ireland?"

"He's her father, Allan."

"So you're sure that whatever happens, that the two of you can work it all out?"

"I think we can."

He gave her a skeptical look.

"What?"

"What if you're wrong? What if he meets someone else when he goes back to Ireland? Marries her even. He'd still be Faith's father. Still have all the same rights to have her with him. Do you want another woman bringing up your child?"

"Of course not."

"Then I'd suggest you protect yourself. And Faith. If you want my advice, you'll launch a prepreemptive strike and file suit to stop him from trying to take Faith to Ireland."

"That's your advice, is it?"

"Absolutely."

"And it has nothing at all to do with anything my mom said to you at dinner last night, right?"

Before he could answer, the secretary stuck her head around the door to say that the nurse from Faith's school was on the phone. Faith had a stomachache and a fever of 101 and could someone come and pick her up?

LIAM WAS JUST LEAVING Miranda's when Hannah called to say the trip to the *Queen Mary* was off and that she'd already picked Faith up from school. "I don't think it's anything serious," Hannah said. "Too many Spaghet-tiOs last night, maybe."

Liam, staring through the plate-glass windows of Mir-anda's sunroom and out at the shimmering blue water, felt suddenly bereft, as though the whole reason for the day had just vanished. The feeling frightened him. Maybe Brid was right. Maybe he should lie down until these images of himself in an apron barbecuing on the back patio with Faith and Hannah looking on went away. He realized Hannah had said something.

"Sorry?"

"I asked if you'd like to come by for dinner tonight," she said.

"Your house?"

"My mother's. I want you to get to know each other a little better. She's convinced that you're a scheming womanizer and that I don't know what the hell I'm do-ing."

He laughed, but without much humor. "Are you as confused about all this as I am?" he asked.

"Yeah," she said. "I probably am."

"Everyone giving you advice? Making predictions?"

"Yep. You?"

"Advice and gloomy prophecies. The consensus be-ing that I've no idea what I'm getting into."

"Hey, Liam," she said. "Have faith."

SO WHILE THE BAND—without him and Brid—was doing a scaled-down gig at an Irish bar up in Pasadena, here he was sitting at the dinner table with Hannah's mother, her aunts and her sister, who were all clearly on their best behavior but not exactly welcoming him into the fold.

In an agony of indecision, he'd arrived with a box of chocolates for Margaret and flowers for Hannah. When Margaret took the chocolates, she'd said something about being on a diet and he realized he should have bought flowers for her, too, and maybe he should have picked up something for the aunts and the sister. Five minutes into the meal he was almost wishing he'd never come.

But truthfully he was glad to be here. Hannah sat next to him, her hand on his knee, and Faith, all better now, kept jabbing him with her small pointed elbow as she wielded her knife and fork. Every so often, she'd turn to grin at him and phrases like ''worthwhile sacrifice'' would drift through his brain as he imagined giving up music to have her in his life.

And although you could bounce a penny off Margaret's stiff expression, Hannah's sister Debra seemed friendly enough, as did Aunt Rose, who kept winking at him across the table and finding ways to bring him into the conversation, which, at the moment, was all about the price of houses in California—a topic Californians seemed to spend a great deal of time discussing.

''So anyway, Liam,'' Rose was saying. ''This guy I used to go with was also from Ireland and he said it's the same thing there. Germans buying up the west. Tearing down the thatched cottages and building these great big mansions on the water.'' She frowned, and scratched the back of her elaborately piled-up red hair. ''Or was it the south. Where's Clare?''

''West,'' he said.

''Cute guy,'' Rose said. ''Declan. Well, not cute ex- actly—he had a face like a potato—but I loved his accent." She winked. "Tore all my defenses down, if you know what I mean."

Hannah shot him a sideways glance and squeezed his knee.

Debra grinned. "We don't know what you mean by defenses, Aunt Rose. Actually, we didn't know you had any."

Helen cleared her throat. "Do you own property, Liam?" she asked.

"I do," he said. Hannah's hand was still on his knee. "In Galway."

"Gahlweh," Faith mimicked, and shifted around in her chair to look at him. "You talk funny, Liam."

"Faith." Hannah and Margaret said in unison.

"I didn't know you had a house," Hannah said.

"I bought it a couple of years ago."

"A big house?" Rose wanted to know.

"Big enough," he said. "Too big for me, really. A family of five could fit comfortably in it." After that, everyone went silent. He looked down at the lasagna on his plate. Hannah had made it herself—apologizing in advance because she wasn't much of a cook. He felt Faith's elbow again, heard the chink of cutlery against plates.

Tried to imagine his life this way, sitting down to supper every night with all this family. He and Hannah would get their own place of course, but where? Even with last year's success, he wasn't making the kind of money to afford California real estate.

Margaret drank some wine. She set her glass down and looked at him from across the table. "I remember Hannah telling me once that you never wanted to be tied down to one place. She said you were going to buy a gypsy caravan and roam around the country, just the two of you."

"I don't remember saying that," Hannah protested.

"What's a gypsy caravan?" Faith asked.

"Kind of like a Winnebago, honey," Rose said. "Except that horses pull it instead of an engine."

"Cool," Faith said. "I like horses."

"I used to ask Hannah what she would do if you had children." Margaret addressed Liam. "And she just laughed and said exposure was good for kids."

Rose laughed. "Exposure to what?"

Helen cleared her throat again.

"I really don't remember that." Hannah turned to look at him. "Do you remember that, Liam? The gypsy thing?"

"Actually, I do," he said. "I'd always wanted a caravan. I still wouldn't mind one, come to that." He drank some wine, angry at his response. How bloody brilliant was that? If he was trying to make an impression, that was just the thing to say. No wonder Hannah's family wasn't pushing for him and Hannah to make another trip to the altar.

Margaret directed a frosty smile at him. "Have you ever considered what you'll be doing…twenty or so years from now?" She bent her head slightly to spear a slice of tomato on her fork, and eyed him from across the table. "When you're getting older, looking toward retirement?"

"Liam's thirty-five, Mom," Hannah protested. "Who thinks about retirement at that age? I certainly don't. Neither does Deb." She looked at her sister. "Right?"

"Only that I damn sure don't want to be still waiting tables at Claim Jumper when I'm fifty," Deb said.

"Find a rich husband," Rose said. "That's my phi-

losophy. 'Course, *you'd* have to find a rich wife, Liam.''
She laughed. ''Unless...oh shut up, Rose.''

Helen gave her sister an arch glance. ''Good idea,
Rose.''

''To answer your question, Margaret,'' Liam said.
''No, I haven't thought that far ahead.''

Margaret's gaze was fixed on Faith. ''Well, Liam, if
you're...contemplating a family, I would suggest that
the future is something to which you *should* give some
thought.''

CHAPTER FOURTEEN

"SOMETHING TELLS ME I didn't exactly win over your mother tonight," Liam told Hannah as they stood in the kitchen washing dishes. "I should have lied and said, 'Yes, I've given it a lot of thought and I've decided brain surgery is the life for me with maybe a bit of investment banking as a sideline.' Would that have made her happy, do you think?"

Hannah drained the Chianti left in her glass. Faith was in bed, the others were in the living room watching *Survivor*. It seemed an appropriate choice, she thought wryly.

"Your goal in life isn't to make my mom happy."

"That's a good thing," he said, "or I'd be failing miserably."

Hannah draped the damp tea towel over the bar on the front of the stove. During lunch break at school, she'd skimmed through the *Los Angeles Times*. Actually, she'd been idly browsing the classifieds for herself, wondering about more fulfilling occupations than coaching the Taylor Beckers of the world to ace kindergarten exams.

A private academy in Studio City wanted a music teacher. She'd read the ad, reread it, then turned to the next page and gone on reading. But she couldn't stop thinking about it. Before she'd left to pick up Faith, she clipped the ad and stuck it in her purse. Now, her heart kicking up, she looked at Liam.

"I have something to show you." Her purse was upstairs in her room. She motioned for him to follow her. Inside her room, she closed the door and fished around in her purse.

Liam sat down on the edge of the bed. "Won't this raise a few eyebrows downstairs?"

She looked at him. "I'll keep both feet on the floor."

As he read the clipping she handed him, she watched his face and realized that she was holding her breath. The exchange with Allan had played in her head all afternoon. He'd raised a question she hadn't allowed herself to contemplate. The thought of Liam taking Faith to Ireland was only bearable if she pictured herself as part of the trio. But Faith in Ireland with Liam and...God, Brid—or an Irish version of Miranda Payton—helping raise Faith was more than she could bear.

He looked up at her. "This would do the trick, would it?"

She waited a moment, thinking about how to answer him. "It would be a stable and secure job," she finally said. "The money's not bad. You'd still be working in the music industry and you'd be here in California."

He held out his hand to her, and she sat down on the bed beside him. The room was warm and a little stuffy. The light through the pink floral lampshade by the bed glowed a rosy gold. Liam's eyes looked very blue. He put his arm around her shoulder, turned his head to kiss her. She could hear the TV downstairs. She knew Margaret had probably heard their feet on the stairs, in fact, had probably *listened* for the sound of their feet on the stairs. The kiss lasted as they fell against the bed, Liam on top of her, his erection hard against her groin. And then he sat up suddenly, as though a thought had just occurred to him. He leaned against the headboard.

"What about all the other stuff?" he asked.

"What other stuff?"

"My insatiable need to chase skirts for instance."

She picked at her fingernail. "I've thought a lot about that. Not you chasing skirts, I mean. Just the whole scene when we were married. I was so damn insecure that I managed to work myself into this constant frenzy of suspicion. I'm a lot more secure these days."

"Which isn't exactly a ringing endorsement of my fidelity."

"Maybe I had no real reason not to trust you when we were married. My mom said something today about believing what we want to believe. Maybe I almost wanted to believe you were running around because I was so damn sure you'd leave me eventually, I was just kind of preparing myself for the inevitable." She put her arm around his shoulder, and kissed the side of his mouth. "Plus, I could just tell myself you were a no-good jerk."

Smiling now, he studied the ad again. "We could live in Los Angeles. Buy his and her convertibles. A house with a swimming pool."

"On a music teacher's salary." She grinned. "Dream on."

"Something I've always been good at."

"Dreaming?" She got up from the bed, and locked her fingers behind her neck. "This is a huge decision for you. An incredible sacrifice—"

"It *is* a big decision, I'll grant you that. I don't see it as a sacrifice though. Not if I had you and Faith."

Hannah sat down on the bed beside him again. Something was stopping her from abandoning all resistance and saying, *Yes let's do it. Let's be a family again.* It was as though Liam were on the other side of a river and she couldn't quite bring herself to swim across the water that separated them. He was smiling, his hand extended. She wanted to be with him, but she couldn't quite do it.

"At least I can look into it." Liam glanced at the ad again. "I'll ring them tomorrow." He took her hand. "We're still on for the *Queen Mary,* right?"

"Yep." *The zoo, the* Queen Mary, *pretend camping in an unfurnished apartment. If they could just go on doing fun things, deferring reality, instead of dealing with dull stuff like jobs and security, life would be a whole lot easier.*

"IS LIAM YOUR BOYFRIEND, Mommy?" Faith asked the next morning as Hannah was pouring cereal into a bowl.

"Well, not exactly," Hannah hedged. "How come you're asking that?"

"Auntie Rose said he was your boyfriend."

Hannah poured milk into a bowl of Cheerios, and set it in front of Faith. "Don't forget to feed your hamster before you leave." Evasion by distraction, she thought. Not exactly the preferred La Petite Ecole method, but Faith was her daughter, not her student.

"I thought Allan was your boyfriend." Faith dug into the Cheerios. "Can people have two boyfriends?"

"Two boyfriends?" Rose shuffled into the kitchen. "Sure, honey, if you can manage it, more power to you."

Hannah frowned at Rose. She'd gone to bed after Liam left, then stayed awake half the night wondering whether it had been a mistake to tell him about the job. What if he took it and wasn't happy? What if he ended up hating her for forcing him into something he'd never really wanted? What if Faith wasn't happy having him around? She felt surly and distracted; her head ached with indecision.

"I like Allan, Mommy," Faith said. "Want to know why?"

"Huh?" She looked at her daughter who had left the table and was sitting cross-legged on the floor, the puppy in her lap lapping milk from Faith's cereal bowl. *"Faith."* Hannah grabbed the bowl, and set it in the sink. "The puppy has his own bowl to eat from."

"I like Allan because he has a little boy for me to play with," Faith said.

"And a big house on Riva Alto Canal," Rose said.

"Rose." Hannah glared at her aunt. "Shut the hell up."

"Oooh, Mommy said a bad word," Faith said.

"Mommy's not in a good mood this morning," Rose observed.

No, she wasn't, Hannah thought as she went upstairs to get ready for school. And her mood wasn't improved when she stopped to get a notebook she'd left in the study and found a downloaded page entitled: Getting Custody of Your Grandchildren.

Her face burning, Hannah read through the material.

According to the U.S. Census Bureau, in 1997, 3.9 million children lived in homes maintained by their grandparents, up 76 percent from 2.2 million in 1970. In a majority of the cases, grandparents were the primary caregivers. Despite this fact, it is not always easy for grandparents to get custody of their grandchildren. Courts are reluctant to award custody to anyone other than the parents.

The law varies from state to state, but in general, grandparents cannot petition the court for custody if the family is intact—i.e. both parents are at home with the children. Grandparents may, however, intervene in a custody dispute. In some states, grandparents may also ask for custody if the child has been living with them for an extended period of time (e.g., six months, one year).

Margaret had underlined the last two lines.

Hannah barged into her mother's room. Empty, the bed made up. She ran downstairs to the kitchen. Rose was pouring chocolate syrup onto a slice of toast. Faith was grinning, her mouth rimmed with chocolate.

"Hey, Mommy," she said as Hannah stormed in. "Look what me and Auntie Rose invented." She held out the bread. "Want to try some?"

"No, I don't, thank you." Ignoring Faith's wail of dismay, she grabbed the toast and stuffed it down the garbage disposal. "You know better than to eat chocolate on toast for breakfast," she told her daughter. "Even if the adults around here don't."

"Uh-oh," Rose said in mock terror. "I'd better get out of here."

"Rose." Hands on her hips, Hannah addressed her aunt. "Where's Mom?"

"She left early. Something about an appointment downtown."

THE *QUEEN MARY* WAS NOT turning out to be one of his better ideas, Liam thought as he watched Hannah run down the promenade deck after a sulky Faith, who had told her mother that she wanted to ride a real boat that went somewhere, not a stupid boat that just stayed in one place. She wanted to ride in a boat like Allan's boat. She liked Allan. She was bored. She wanted someone to play with. She wanted to call Douglas.

Liam looked out at the blue water. White boats glided back and forth. Sailboats, power boats churning up a wake, darting red water taxis, a streamlined white vessel that went over to Catalina. He'd suggested earlier, in light of Faith's unhappiness with the *Queen Mary,* that they take the boat over to Avalon, stay the night and return the next day. Faith had brightened at this, but Hannah frowned and reminded him that she had a job to go to.

She'd been tense from the moment he'd arrived at the house on Termino. He didn't know what was wrong. She hadn't offered an explanation, and he hadn't asked.

He turned from the water, and watched Hannah walk toward him, holding Faith's hand. Hannah was saying something to Faith that he couldn't catch, looking down at her as she spoke. Faith nodded a couple of times, her expression still petulant.

"What do you have to say to Liam?" Hannah asked as they reached the window where he stood.

Liam felt a surge of anger. Hannah could force Faith to apologize to Allan, or to any of her other boyfriends; he didn't want his daughter apologizing to him because she'd behaved like a six-year-old. He ruffled Faith's hair. "That's all right, listen, I've got an idea—"

"No, it's not all right, Liam." Hannah looked at her daughter. "Faith?"

Faith kicked at the wooden deck with the toe of her red sandal. "Sorry."

"Sorry, who?" Hannah asked.

"Sorry, Liam."

Liam flinched. Sorry, *Liam*. His daughter had called him Liam. He looked around, almost blindly, wanting to strike out at something. She'd called him by his name before, but this time it felt like a wound reopened. Hannah realized her mistake and touched his arm. He pulled away. "Let's get out of here," he said.

In silence they made their way to the elevator and off the boat. With no direction in mind, he started down a footpath that cut through a grassy verge along the edge of the water. He felt the wind in his face, saw the sunlight off the water. Something had gone wrong and he didn't know what to say to fix it. More to the point, he didn't know what had caused it to go wrong in the first place.

"Can we go in there?" Faith pointed across the water to a circular blue building painted with sea creatures. "I want to go in there and see the porpoise."

"That's not the aquarium," Hannah said. She glanced at Liam. "I don't know why Long Beach painted the convention center to look like an aquarium. The aquarium's down there." She nodded in the direction of a structure further across the bay. "People are always getting it confused."

"I want to go to the aquarium," Faith said.

"Not today," Hannah said.

"When?" Faith tugged at Hannah's hand. "When can we go to the aquarium?"

Anxious to turn the day around, Liam opened his mouth to suggest they go right now, then thought better of it. They all kept walking, past large rocks and boulders set along the water's edge. He stopped to look at a couple of boys with fishing poles sitting on the rocks. On some lower rocks, a couple of girls, maybe a little older than Faith, were jumping from one boulder to the next. Hannah and Faith had stopped, too, and stood beside him. He watched Faith watching the girls and edging a little closer. One of the girls jumped to a rock at the water level. The other one clambered down, arms waving to steady herself. Their laughter carried in the breeze.

"I need to go to the restroom." Hannah glanced over her shoulder in the direction of a low stucco building, then she caught Faith's hand. "Let's go."

"I don't need to go." Faith was still watching the girls.

"I'll watch her," Liam said.

Hannah took off across the grass. The girls on the rocks were both down at the water's edge, bending to look at a small tide pool in the hollowed surface of a rock. Faith looked at Liam.

"I want to go down there."

"Go ahead," he said. "I'll go with you." He took her hand and they climbed down three boulders. One of the girls waved to Faith.

"I know that girl," Faith said. "Her name's Yolanda. Can I go down where she is?"

Both girls were smiling up at Faith, calling for her to see the shells they'd found. Faith was clearly impatient to be with them. Liam checked his shoulder to see if Hannah had started back, but couldn't spot her. When he turned back in the direction of the rocks and water, Faith was on the boulder immediately below the one where he stood and had started to maneuver her way down, arms outstretched, to the next one.

"Hold on, Faith," he called as he scrambled down after her. "I'll give you a hand."

"Faith," one of the girls called out. "You have to see this shell, it is so cool."

"Faith," Hannah shouted from the top of the bluff. "Come on, let's go."

"She's fine, Hannah," Liam called over his shoulder. "I'm watching her."

Down at the water's edge, the rocks were green and shiny with seaweed. The girls held out dripping hands to show Faith what they'd found. Liam lowered himself onto one of the rocks. Faith was smiling now, a different child from the sullen one on the deck of the *Queen Mary*. He felt his mood lift as he watched her, wind blowing her hair about her face, billowing the back of her denim shirt. The trio had moved a few yards along the lower tier of rocks when he heard Hannah's voice behind him. He turned to see her climbing down the rocks to where he sat. Faith had also looked up to see her mother.

"Mommy. I have to show you this really neat thing." Her hands cupped, Faith made her way across the seaweed-covered rocks, her brow furrowed in concentration. "It is *so* cool, you'll be amazed."

Liam grinned and saw that Hannah was smiling, too. He put his arm around her shoulder, and pulled her to him. Infused with a sudden burst of happiness, he couldn't keep the smile off his face. He kissed the side of her mouth.

"Faith asked me this morning if you were my boyfriend," she said.

He felt himself tense slightly. "And what did you tell her?"

Whatever answer she might have given was frozen by the splash of noise and confusion at the water's edge. In an instant Liam was down there, lifting his shaking, shivering daughter from the bay.

AT TEN THAT SAME NIGHT, Hannah sat in her bedroom talking on the phone to Liam. "Look, quit blaming yourself, okay? It wasn't your fault. We were both there with her, watching her. It was just an accident."

"I keep telling myself I should never have let her go down there in the first place."

"Kids play there all the time, Liam. Deb and I used to spend hours on those same rocks and I was younger than Faith. I even fell into the water a couple of times. It's no big deal. I mean you could see that for yourself. She'd almost forgotten about it by the time we got her home. She's fine. In bed and sound asleep."

"Right…well. You know her best."

She switched the receiver to her other ear. Liam wasn't convinced. She could hear it in his voice. Faith's tumble into the water had been the low point in an afternoon that never really got off the ground.

Mostly it was her fault. All day, she'd been unable to shake the stunned disbelief that her mother had, at the very least, considered the possibility of getting custody of Faith. She'd tried, unsuccessfully, to reach Margaret later in the afternoon when Hannah got home from school. Margaret was out. She hadn't returned by the time Liam stopped by to pick up Hannah and Faith.

In a masterpiece of bad timing, Margaret *had* been home when they'd carried Faith, wet and shivering, into the house. Without a word of explanation, Hannah had taken Faith upstairs. After Liam left and Faith was in bed, she'd felt too exhausted to confront Margaret. Liam's call came just as she'd drifted off to sleep.

"I called about the job," he said, after the silence between them had become uncomfortable. "They asked me to send a résumé." He laughed. "I've never written a bloody résumé in my life."

"I can help you with that," she said, sounding in her own ears exactly as her Aunt Helen had years ago when Hannah protested that she really didn't have the background to apply for a position at La Petite Ecole.

"Help me with what?" Liam asked. "I've played in bands. Other people's and now my own. How do you turn that into a résumé?"

"Well, the position *is* for a music teacher," Hannah pointed out without much enthusiasm. Maybe they were trying to do the impossible. Square pegs in round holes, that sort of thing. She felt tired and discouraged. "Listen, we can talk about it tomorrow." She yawned. "Right now I'm so bushed, I can't even think."

"Yeah…" Liam said. "Right."

She waited a moment. "You're not happy, are you?"

He sighed. "I'm so bloody confused about everything, Hannah. I don't know if I'm pushing you into something you don't really want. I don't know if I'm pushing myself into something I don't really want. I don't know if what we're doing is right for Faith. I just don't know."

"Liam…" A deep wave of tenderness for him made her throat close. If all of this was hard for her, how much harder must it be for him? Regardless of what happened, she would always have Faith in her life. Liam didn't have that certainty. "I love you," she said, surprising herself.

"That helps," he said after a moment. "A lot."

"Well, I do." Despite her own doubts and fears, it suddenly seemed vital that she reassure him. "I love that you care enough about Faith that you're willing to make this huge sacrifice to be with her. I love the way you are with her and I love you, Liam…" She stopped, self-consciousness halting the stream of words.

"Go on," he said. "I'm feeling better by the second."

"I feel as though I'm seeing a side to you I never

knew when we were married. It's as though I didn't know you then. I mean, I still don't really…''

"And when you find out that I have this thing for women in black corsets, leather boots and whips…''

"Humor is a distancing mechanism," she said. "I learned the term from my Aunt Rose. She got a B+ in Intro to Psychology. Humor stops you from dealing with things you don't want to deal with.''

"Read any good books lately?''

"*Avoidance* is another term Aunt Rose told me about.''

"Is that right?''

"Yep. That's one thing that hasn't changed about you, Liam. It still kills you to talk about feelings, doesn't it?''

"Yeah," he said softly. "I've never been good at that. Never had much of a chance to be good at it, come to that. But don't let that stop you from saying things like you just did. In fact, do me a big favor, would you, and say it again.''

Hannah rolled over on her stomach, phone melded to her ear, smile spreading across her face. "I love you," she said.

"Ditto," he said. "We'll work it all out, won't we?''

"Yeah." Still smiling. Believing, at least for now. "And tomorrow? What's on the agenda?''

"Want to pick Faith up from school?''

"What time?''

"Come by about two. We'll walk down there.''

"How about if I make it earlier? Half-past twelve or so?''

"I'll still be in school. Why?''

"Oh, I don't know. An hour or so up in your bedroom has a lot of appeal.''

"Did I ever tell you you were bad news?''

"You might have mentioned it a few hundred times."

"Well you are," she said. "But I love you anyway."

She was still smiling as she walked downstairs, suddenly ravenous, to get something to eat. Halfway down, she caught the aroma of baking from the kitchen, heard her mother's voice and then Faith's saying something she couldn't quite catch. *What was Faith doing up at this hour?* Faith spoke again and then Hannah heard Rose's voice.

"...your mommy and Liam were *kissing* when you fell into the water?"

"They were sitting on the rocks and Liam had his arm around Mommy and I saw him kiss her," Faith said. "And then my foot slipped and I fell into the water."

Anger like a red haze in her brain, Hannah stood transfixed. Her mother was talking now, asking Faith whether she had ever seen Mommy and Liam kiss before. And then Faith was saying that Allan was her mommy's boyfriend, that she liked Allan because she could play with Douglas. Her heart beating so hard she thought it might actually burst in her chest, Hannah sat down on the stairs.

"So what about your mommy's new apartment?" Margaret asked. "Did you like going there with Mommy and Liam?"

"It doesn't have any furniture," Faith said. "So we had to sit on the floor and have candles. And then I spilled ginger ale on my shirt and Liam took his shirt off and then Mommy took mine off—"

"Mommy or Liam?" Margaret asked.

Something seemed to detonate in Hannah's head. She burst into the kitchen, plucked Faith and the blanket covering her up from the chair she'd been sitting on and left the room in a blur of movement; aware—as if in a dream—of Margaret's startled expression, of Rose darting aside to avoid being plowed down, of Faith's warm, wriggling body under the blanket as she was carried up the stairs, protesting that the chocolate chip cookies weren't ready and Grandma had promised she could have two.

In blind fury, Hannah set Faith down on the bed. She looked at her daughter and tried to bring her voice under control. "Listen, sweetie…" Her voice and body were shaking. "We're going on a kind of adventure, okay?" She went to Faith's dresser drawer, pulled out socks and underwear, dumped them on the rocker, opened another draw and gathered pants and shirts.

"But I want a cookie." Faith's voice turned tearful. "I don't like you, Mommy. You're being mean."

"Hannah," Margaret said from the doorway. "I think you need to calm down a little, okay? You're frightening your daughter."

Faith started crying, little whimpering sounds.

Her back to Margaret, Hannah clutched a pile of Faith's clothes. Her teeth were chattering, her body trembled. Behind her, Margaret was telling Faith not to cry. Mommy was just upset about something, Margaret was saying. Mommy would be fine. They'd all be fine. Still shaking, Hannah went to the closet and started to pull down Faith's overnight bag. A little red suitcase Helen had bought last Christmas. She tugged it out from under a couple of boxes, a jerky movement that sent it tumbling to the floor. One of the clasps had rusted and the case burst open, spilling assorted drawings and schoolwork Faith had brought home. In the few moments it took to stack them into an empty shoe box, reason trickled back in. Maybe this wasn't the way to handle the situation. Faith, already upset, would be confused.

Frightened. She had no idea why her mother and grand-mother were fighting. Hannah took a deep breath, and tried to compose her face as she looked at her daughter.

"Hey, you know what?" She studied her watch, noting in her peripheral vision that Margaret was no longer in the doorway. "It is *late*. Really late. After midnight, in fact." Faith regarded her wide-eyed, not entirely convinced things were back to normal. "How about a bedtime story?" Hannah asked her daughter.

"What about our adventure?"

"Let's put the adventure off until tomorrow," she said. "What d'you say? It's kind of late for an adventure tonight."

"Can I have a cookie?" Faith asked.

Hannah pretended to consider. "It's very late, but if you brush your teeth really well afterward, I guess you can have one."

She tucked her daughter into bed, kissed her forehead and went down to the kitchen to get a cookie. From the living room, she could hear the TV, but no voices. She got the cookie, poured milk into a glass and carried it upstairs. Faith was already asleep. Carefully she closed Faith's door, set the milk and cookies on the hall table and walked across the hallway to Margaret's bedroom.

CHAPTER FIFTEEN

MARGARET, IN HER PURPLE ROBE, was sitting up in bed, a *New Yorker* spread across her knees, her bifocals down low on her nose. One side of her face lit by the bedside lamp, she listened without a word as Hannah demanded an explanation for the downloaded information. Demanded an explanation *and* an apology for grilling Faith.

"You have seriously overstepped your boundaries, Mom. You have absolutely no right—"

"No, as far you're concerned, I have no rights, do I? It's all about Liam's rights. To hell with the fact that I'm her grandmother. To hell with the fact that Faith has been a part of my life from the moment she first came into the world. I *watched* her come into the world. And now suddenly, it's all Liam this and Liam that." The *New Yorker* slid to the floor and she leaned over to pick it up. "I'm sick to death of it. If this was a responsible guy with a normal job and the means to provide my granddaughter with a decent home, it would be one thing. Maybe I wouldn't be happy about it, but I could accept it. But no, it's some damn foreign musician who has decided he wants to be a daddy and suddenly you've abandoned any shred of common sense. Well, I'm sorry, but if you're expecting an apology from me, you're not going to get it. And I'll tell you one thing. Faith would never have fallen into the water if I'd been watching her."

After that, Margaret burst into tears. By then it was after one and since there seemed to be no way to resolve things, Hannah left and went into her room. She dropped fully dressed across the bed, but she didn't fall asleep. She thought about the things she'd said to Liam, the things Margaret had said to her. Thought about how to make everything all right again. Around four in the morning, she went down to the kitchen and poured herself a glass of wine from Margaret's jug. But still she couldn't derail her brain. It kept running down the same track, colliding inevitably with Liam's rights as a father and her mother's rights as a grandmother who'd helped raise her granddaughter. Liam's happiness if he gave up his music, her own happiness and, overshadowing everything else, Faith's happiness.

When the room began to fill with hazy morning light, she gave up on sleep altogether, pulled on her robe and began to make coffee. Some time later, Margaret came down, dressed in a burgundy blazer and gray slacks. When Hannah told her mother that she and Liam would be picking up Faith from school, Margaret gave a brittle smile, picked up her purse and walked out.

For the first time in the four years she'd worked at La Petite Ecole, Hannah called in sick that morning. After taking Faith to school, she spent the morning packing clothes from her room and Faith's into cardboard boxes. Debra dropped by about ten. She'd just returned from a visit to the obstetrician.

"When you had Faith, did you feel like a grown-up right away, or did you still feel like a kid?" she asked Hannah.

Hannah, on her knees trying to decide what to throw in a sack for Goodwill and what to pack, sat back on her heels to look at her sister. Her head felt like cotton from not sleeping, and she suspected Debra was more interested in spilling out her own feelings than listening to hers, so she took the easy way out. "Is that how you feel? Like a kid still?"

"Kind of. I mean, here I am back home again with Mom fussing over me, nagging me about eating right, and I'm thinking, God, I'm going to have this kid who is actually going to need *me*."

Hannah looked at her sister. Debra's face was flushed. She wore a baggy black T-shirt and gray leggings that ended just below her knees. Flopped on Hannah's bed, a black baseball cap pulled low on her head, she looked less like a mother-to-be than someone who had just wandered out of a college class.

"I mean, don't you ever kind of resent Faith?" Debra asked. "Like, if you didn't have her you'd be free to do all these other things, travel, bum around…I don't know, it just seems like this huge responsibility."

"It *is* a huge responsibility."

"But did you think about that before you had Faith? Or did you just kind of…get pregnant?"

"I don't know, Deb." Hannah shook her head. She wasn't up to philosophical discussion on motherhood. "I guess I didn't give it a whole lot of thought."

"Yeah…" Debra turned onto her side, face propped on her elbow. "Mom said the only thing you really cared about was Liam—"

"Mom said that, huh?" Hannah felt a return of last night's red rage. "Well, Mom can damn well go to hell."

"Hannah." Deb regarded her with a faint smile. "What are you getting so mad about? I mean, sure you love Faith now and you're a good mother and everything, but you were kind of like the way I feel right now.

It's like you weren't really a grown-up. You were just a kid who was obsessed with this guy and then you had a kid yourself. You were lucky Mom and everyone could help you out.''

Hannah managed to finish packing the box she was filling with Faith's underwear and nightclothes. She excused herself to Deb, went into the bathroom and stood under the shower for thirty minutes. Afterward, as she dried her hair, she stared at her face through a clear spot in the fogged-up mirror. Her mouth looked strained, her eyes puffy. If only she could have flat-out denied Deb's assertion...

SHE WAS DOWN at the mailbox, picking up the day's assortment of catalogs and grocery store fliers when Liam pulled up thirty minutes early. The mail in hand, she watched him reach for something on the seat, then open the passenger door of the Mercedes. He walked to where she stood, a smile on his face and a bunch of pink roses in his hand. Despite everything, her heart sped up with no regard to the turmoil churning in her brain.

"Any million-dollar checks for me there?" Liam asked, with a nod at the mail she was holding. "Checks, fan mail?"

"Hi." She smiled. "No mail for you." His white T-shirt read: What's The Craic! Find Out In The *Irish Post*.

"All things considered—" she flicked his chest "—not the best thing to wear to your daughter's school."

He frowned, peered down at his shirt. "What?"

"Craic?"

He grinned. "It doesn't mean crack, it means fun. It's Gaelic. The *Post* publishes a calendar of what clubs are playing where." He shrugged. "I see your point though. Kids could read it wrong."

"Yep."

"God." He sighed. "I've a lot to learn, haven't I?"

"Hey…" She glanced at the roses in his hand, up at his face, the smile gone now. "You're doing fine, don't worry about it."

He handed her the roses. "Do you know what pink means?"

She shook her head. "Do you?"

He grinned. "No idea."

"You're early. We still have about ten minutes before we pick her up."

"Alert the media," he said. "The first time in my life I've ever been early."

"I'll take these into the house." Roses in hand, she started up the path, aware of Liam following her. She walked through the back door into the kitchen, felt him watching her as she bent to get a vase from one of the lower shelves. She carried the container over to the sink, ran water into it and began to arrange the roses. Liam came up behind her and put his arms around her waist. Dug his chin into her shoulder.

"Talk to me," he said. "What's wrong?"

She stayed very still, suddenly on the verge of tears. "Oh…stuff."

"Stuff." His chin was still on her shoulder, his hands locked over her stomach. "Bloody awful that stuff, isn't it?"

"Yeah."

"What variety of stuff?"

"Everything." She exhaled. "My mom's talking about wanting custody of Faith."

He said nothing for a moment. Then he took her hand,

led her over to the table and they both sat down. Hannah
looked at him in his Craic T-shirt, at the planes of his
face, his mouth, and something just seemed to dissolve
inside her. He leaned forward in his chair, put his arms
around her again, stroked her hair as she cried against
his chest. When the sobs subsided, she got up and
mopped at her face with a paper towel. Then she sat
down again.

"I don't think it will really come to that, but it's obviously crossed her mind." She sat facing Liam, her
knees touching his. "Everything's such a mess. I feel as
though my mother's become my enemy."

He got up, and walked over to the window. The roses,
visible from the kitchen, bloomed in bouquets of red,
yellow and pink. He turned around to face Hannah. "I
wrote up the résumé last night. I brought it for you to
have a look at. Maybe it would reassure Margaret if she
thought…" He shrugged. "That I wasn't about to move
the two of you to Ireland."

She sighed. "I'm not sure if your getting a job is
really the answer, Liam. If you'd made the decision in-
dependently of me and Faith, it would be different,
but—"

"I wouldn't be thinking about it if it weren't for you
and Faith," he said.

"That's my point. What if you regret it a year from
now?"

"There are no guarantees, Hannah. Life's a calculated
risk."

"But how well have you calculated this one?"

"Okay then, here's the deal." He came to kneel by
her chair. "It's never going to work if we're both pes-
simistic at the same time. Last night was my turn to sing

the blues. You were the one who said we'd pull through, remember?''

She smiled slightly.

''Well, now it's your turn to wail and gnash your teeth. Go on. Do it while you can. Then it'll be my turn.''

Her smile broadened. ''You're nuts. You know that?''

''I love you. You know that?''

She nodded. Liam leaned forward to kiss her. He got up a few moments later, sat on a chair, pulled her up on his lap and kissed her again.

''Optimism alone isn't enough, though,'' he said. ''We need a plan. Tonight, after Faith goes to bed, let's have a talk with Margaret. Maybe we can get her to see our side.''

Hannah nodded. ''I guess it couldn't hurt.''

''Come on.'' He caught her hands. ''Cheer up. One of these days when we've got six kids and grandchildren running around all over the place, we'll look back on this and laugh.''

''You think so?''

''Absolutely. First, though, we need to do something about my shirt.''

''Take it off.''

He did. The shirt in one hand, he grinned at her. ''Now what?''

She laughed. Liam was wiry rather than muscular and his bare chest showed little evidence that he'd spent time basking under the California sun. But damn, he turned her on. Standing there in her mother's kitchen, blue-eyed and sexy in his black jeans that sat low enough on his belly that… ''I'll get you another shirt,'' she said. ''After you kiss me again.''

AND THEN THEY WERE OUT on the street, Liam in a yellow polo shirt Deb's ex-boyfriend had left at the house.
Walking hand in hand down Termino to Faith's school
with the sun warm on her back and the scent of orange
blossoms in the air. As they crossed Ocean Boulevard,
Hannah looked out at the strip of shimmering, postcard-
blue Pacific visible behind Albertson's market and felt a
surge of pure happiness that, like blinding sunshine,
overpowered everything but the moment. Impulsively
she brought Liam's hand to her mouth and kissed it.

"I love you," she said.

He stopped walking. "Say that again."

"I love you."

Liam smiled and looked so much like Faith that Hannah almost told him once more. They started walking
again, swinging hands, Liam humming something she
didn't recognize.

"You know something?" she said to him. "I wish we
could just take Faith and somehow…encapsulate our-
selves in our own little world. It's all the outside influ-
ences that screw things up."

"There's a spaceship parked outside Miranda's," he
said.

"I'll get packed."

"I know what you mean, though," he said after a
moment. "When I'm with you and Faith, I have no
doubt we could make things work. And then…" He
sighed. "Actually, there's some concern about the future
of the band. What with Brid out of things for a while.
Pearse thinks I've lost interest…"

"Lost interest?" Hannah looked at him. "Is he kidding?"

"Well, I've been distracted. Brid's having treatment,
so there's some excuse for her missing practice sessions,

but I've skipped a couple of sessions myself. The other night, for instance. I'd planned to go out for a quick meal, when I ran into you and Faith.''

Hannah said nothing, but a cloud drifted across the horizon. For one evening, Liam had chosen Faith over his music. How many times could he make that kind of choice and not begin to resent the sacrifice?

"Ah, to hell with it all anyway." He squeezed her hand. "To hell with everything but the three of us. If we hadn't agreed to give it a week, I'd say let's pick up Faith and drive to Las Vegas and get married."

Hannah felt her breath catch. She recalled Margaret's words. ... *you've abandoned any shred of common sense.*

"ANY MINUTE NOW," Hannah said, "those doors will burst open and a bunch of little monsters will come tearing out. If you don't stand back they'll run you down."

Liam sat on the edge of a low brick wall, his eye on the green painted double door. His assurances to Hannah aside, tension gnawed at his gut, held his neck and shoulders in a viselike grip. Hannah's mother didn't just dislike him, she was actually ready to wage war against him. And the thing was, he couldn't blame her.

He thought of his mother, blowzy and peroxided when he'd last seen her. He'd been about ten and they'd gone to Dublin on the train. A job? A man? He couldn't remember why she'd taken him there.

For hours, they'd walked about the city looking for a flat she could afford. No one would take a chance on her. She hadn't enough to pay the rent, they'd tell her over and over. It was nearly dark when they'd left the last place and he knew—and she knew he knew—they'd spend that night sleeping in the train station. He could see now that it must have been the last straw for her. She'd stood on the street screaming at him to go away.

"I can't take care of you," she'd sobbed.

And here he was, years later, sitting in the sunshine waiting for his daughter, who went off to school every day in a neighborhood of pastel-colored houses with lawns manicured to smooth green velvet and windows that glinted in the sun. Glibly telling his daughter's mother that there were no guarantees in life, but they would work things out. He looked at the knot of parents waiting for their kids and wondered who exactly was fooling whom? A blond woman in blue cotton pants and a white shirt waved at Hannah.

"Tiffany's mother," Hannah told him. "Tiffany is Faith's best friend. They argue about once a week and Faith decides Beth's her best friend and she's never going to speak to Tiffany again. The next day they're inseparable."

Liam opened his mouth to speak, but just then the doors opened. He shoved aside his gloomy musings and tried to spot Faith in the tumble of kids whooping and yelling their way out of the building. "What is she wearing?" he asked Hannah.

"Red pants and a yellow shirt. She picked them out herself."

He smiled, kept his eye out for red and yellow garments.

"Tiffany has red curly hair," Hannah added. "Bright red. If you see her, Faith will be right behind."

"What does Beth look like?" he asked.

"Beth looks a little like Hannah, actually. "Light brown hair that she usually has in a ponytail."

"Is that Tiffany?" He pointed to a girl with a mass of long curls the approximate color of tomato soup.

"Yep." Hannah peered into the crowd. "I don't see Faith, though. And there's Beth. I wonder what's keeping Faith?"

"Come on." He caught Hannah's hand, impatient to see his daughter. "Let's go and get her."

Hannah followed him, then called out to Tiffany, who was twisting her shoulders out of a dark green backpack. "Do you know where Faith is?"

Tiffany dangled the backpack from her fingers. "Her grandma picked her up."

Liam glanced at Hannah. "I don't understand," he said. "She knew we were coming to get her, didn't she?"

"Of course she did. I'm going to check in the office."

The secretary in the office had blue curls and wire-rimmed glasses. The name tag on the collar of her pale blue blouse read, Mrs. Smith. She addressed Hannah. "Your mother came by at about ten and said she and Faith were taking a little trip."

Liam stared at her. "Did Faith know this?"

Mrs. Smith, who'd ignored Liam until now, gave him an uncertain look, then raised her eyebrows at Hannah as though asking for permission to answer his question.

"This is Liam Tully," Hannah said. "Faith's father."

"Oh…" The woman's eyes widened slightly behind her glasses. "I didn't realize… No, that's the funny thing. Faith's such a little chatterbox. I heard all about her visit to the zoo, so I thought it was a bit funny when Mrs. Riley mentioned the trip and Faith hadn't said a word."

"How is it your mother's allowed to pick her up?" Liam asked Hannah.

"I gave her written permission. She picks her up most

days because I'm at work." She looked at the secretary. "You said they left about ten?"

"About that. I remember because I was taking a break. I'd just put a bran muffin in the microwave to heat when she came in."

"A trip." Hannah shook her head. "What kind of trip? Did she mention where? How long they'd be gone?"

"Sorry. I didn't even think to ask." Light from the windows glinted on her glasses. "You didn't know about this?" she asked Hannah.

"No," Hannah said. "We didn't know about it."

THEY RAN BACK to the house, neither of them speaking. Liam followed her into the kitchen, and stood in the doorway as she confronted Debra, who was sitting at the table.

"For God's sake, Hannah, calm down, will you?" Debra lifted a glass to her mouth. "Faith's with Mom. It's not like she was kidnapped by a stranger or something. Maybe they went shopping."

"Mom knew we were picking her up." Hannah stood in the middle of the kitchen. "Why would she take her out of school at ten without calling me first? God, why am I even asking that?"

She ran upstairs to Faith's room. The red suitcase she'd pulled down last night was gone. Someone, Margaret obviously, had gone through the boxes she'd started to pack. The box with the underwear had been emptied out. Hannah went into her mother's room. Margaret's overnight bag was gone. She came down to the kitchen again.

"You've no idea at all where they are?" Liam was asking Debra. "Your mother said nothing to you?"

"Nope. I'm sure she'll call in a while. You know how she likes to surprise Faith."

"Where are Rose and Helen?" Hannah asked her sister. "I thought you guys were all going sailing."

"That was Wednesday. Anyway, it kind of fell apart when you said you weren't going. I don't think Allan was too jazzed about schlepping the family along if you weren't part of the group."

Hannah closed the drawer she'd been searching. "Where's Rose?" she asked again.

"Over at Max's house and Helen's gone to some crafts thing," Debra said. "She's big on crafts things," she told Liam. "If you stand still for too long, she'll decoupage your head."

Hannah caught her face in her hands. "God, I can't deal with this. What the hell was Mom thinking? *A little trip.*" She peered at Liam through her fingers. "I'm sorry. This is obviously her way of keeping you from seeing Faith."

"You don't know that," Deb said. "Why don't you wait till she calls before you jump to conclusions?"

"Wait?" Hannah stared at her sister. "How long? An hour? A day? Two days? This is my daughter she's just taken off with, for God's sake." Her hands back around her face again, she paced the kitchen—over to the window, back to the fridge. She looked at Liam, who stood with his back to the sink, arms folded across his chest. "I'm calling the police," she said.

CHAPTER SIXTEEN

"DON'T BE CRAZY," Debra said. "You can't call the police on your own mother."

"I'll tell them Mom has a drinking problem. I'll tell them I'm worried about Faith's safety."

"Is that true?" Liam asked. "Are you?"

Hannah hesitated. The honest answer was no. Margaret was scrupulous about not driving even after just one glass of wine. Hannah's suggestion that Margaret cut down on her drinking had been motivated by her concern for her mother's health. Never for a moment had she believed that Margaret would ever do anything to endanger her granddaughter.

"What is wrong with you, Hannah?" Debra glared at her sister, then addressed Liam. "Mom's been picking up Faith from school from the day she first started and Hannah's never once said a word about a drinking problem. Now suddenly it's a big deal because Mom has a glass of wine in the evening."

"No, Deb, maybe it's a big deal now because Mom overstepped her bounds," Hannah said. "Maybe it's a big deal now because Mom seems to have forgotten that Faith has a mother *and* a father. Maybe it's a big deal now because Mom has my daughter, and I have no idea where she's taken her. Maybe—"

"Hannah." Liam caught her arm.

"No." She pulled away. "This is our daughter

she's…kidnapped. You want to just let her get away with it?''

''I need some fresh air.'' He turned to leave the room. ''Let's go outside.''

She nodded and followed him out of the kitchen.

''Hannah,'' Deb called, ''can I talk to you for a minute.'' She inclined her head to the hallway, where Liam was still visible. ''In private.''

''If this is about Faith, Liam needs to hear it, too,'' Hannah said.

He shook his head. ''I'll wait for you outside.''

''I hope you know you've driven her to this,'' Deb hissed a moment later. ''She's so damn worried about Faith, she can't see straight. You stand there asking what Mom's thinking and you see nothing wrong with letting Faith sleep on the floor of an empty apartment or hanging around with some guy who was too busy brawling in a bar to see his daughter. God, you've lost it, Hannah, you really have. While you were making out with Liam, your daughter nearly drowned, for God's sake. And you ask what *Mom's* thinking. What the hell are *you* thinking?''

Speechless for a moment, Hannah just stared at her sister. ''*Do* you know where Mom is?''

''No, I don't, but if I did, I wouldn't tell you. You're so damned obsessed with Liam, you'll put him before your own daughter. Mom said she tried to talk some sense into you when you guys went for coffee, but you wouldn't listen. *Someone* has to put Faith's interests first, Hannah.''

Hannah slowly exhaled. If she didn't get out of the kitchen, she was going to blow up. She walked away, found Liam sitting on the front step and sat down next to him. By now it was nearly five and the sun was low in the sky, filling the yard with long shadows.

"We need to find an attorney," she said. "I don't know where we stand legally, but that's the first thing we need to find out."

Liam said nothing and they sat in silence for a few minutes, her hand on his knee. She waited for him to say something; to put his arm around her, to indicate somehow that they were in this together, but he seemed suddenly inaccessible. *What are you thinking?* she wanted to ask him. *Talk to me.*

From where they sat, she could see halfway down the street. Margaret sometimes walked Faith from the house to the beach, two blocks away. Last summer she'd taken her to swimming lessons at the Belmont Pool. She watched the street now, willing her mother and Faith to appear. A new surge of anger at Margaret made her heart pound.

"Look, the main thing is we know Faith's in no physical danger. I mean, as awful as this is, we at least know she's with her grandmother. It's probably too late to find anyone still in their office," she said. Allan's name came to mind; he was the only attorney she actually knew. Not a good choice, she decided. Maybe Allan was in on this. "I'll call someone in the morning," she said.

Unable to sit still, she started pacing the lawn. "It's my fault." She stopped at the grouping of rosebushes at the far end of the lawn. Then she walked back down to where Liam sat. "The thing is, Mom does so much for Faith she thinks she has equal rights over her. It's my fault—I take responsibility for allowing it to happen." Back to the roses again. Her head throbbing, brain racing. "I truly don't think she recognizes that you have a claim to her."

Again she sat down on the steps. Liam sat on the top step, his feet on the concrete of the third step. His back was slightly bent, his head bowed as though he were reading something written on the ground at his feet.

"Liam."

He raised his head.

"Talk to me. Listen, I just thought of something. Jen should be home. Let me give her a call. Her sister went through this custody thing with her ex-husband last year. I could get the name of her attorney."

He scratched the back of his neck but said nothing.

"Hey, come on." She put her arm around him, and pulled him close for a moment. "Don't freeze up on me, Liam," she said softly. "I know this has got to be a nightmare for you. But we'll get through it."

"No…" He shook his head. "I don't think so."

"Sure we will. Her arm still around him, she tried to ignore the rigidity in his shoulders. "You were right with what you said last night about talking to my mom, trying to reassure her. I can see now, I didn't pay enough attention to how upset she's been. She's blown things out of proportion." She relayed Debra's comments about letting Faith sleep in the empty apartment, about falling into the water. "I don't know whether she really believes we've put Faith at risk somehow, or she's just using it as an excuse—"

"Either way, it doesn't matter," Liam said.

"Exactly. We just need to make her understand—"

He cut her off with a wave of his hand. "No, I mean it doesn't matter. I don't want to go through with this."

She sat very still for a moment. The hollowness in her stomach told her what her head refused to understand. "Don't want to go through with what, Liam?"

"This. The battle with your mother. Your family's

disapproval as though I'm this monster out to harm you and Faith. I don't need it.''

Hannah had taken her arm from around his shoulder. She sat with her hands folded in her lap. Words whirled around in her head like a blizzard of snow—settling, melting, forming patterns then immediately dissolving. ''But that's what I'm talking about, Liam—they don't really know you. If they did—''

''Neither do you, Hannah. And I don't know you. I got carried away with…'' He shrugged. ''Sex, chemistry.''

''Okay,'' she said slowly, willing reason into her voice. ''Let's put us aside. What about Faith? What about wanting to be part of her life? You said—''

''I know what I said, Hannah.''

''But this is a very small setback. How can you just let—''

''Tells you something about my level of commitment, doesn't it?''

''So you never meant any of the things you said?'' She didn't believe that. Still, she needed to hear him deny it. ''Talk to me, Liam.'' She put her hand on his arm. ''Please.''

She felt his arm relax slightly under her palm. He'd just had a temporary case of cold feet, she told herself. They'd work everything out. Maybe she'd overreacted. Her gaze drifted out to the street again. What *exactly* had the school secretary said?

Maybe Margaret had just forgotten that this wasn't one of her days to get Faith from school. Even as Hannah tried to grasp this thread, she knew there had been no mistake. Margaret had taken Faith in a deliberate attempt to keep her from Liam.

''It's a relief, actually.'' Liam's voice broke into her

thoughts. "You said all along that we could never make it work and you were right. The whole thing's been tearing me apart anyway, not knowing the best thing to do. It's a load off my mind to come to a decision."

"I don't believe you, Liam." She twisted around on the step to look at him. Their eyes met for a brief moment and then he looked away. "I don't believe you've suddenly changed your mind like this."

"I think it's best for Faith," he said. "She was doing well enough before I arrived on the scene, she'll do well when I'm gone. The pirate's dad would probably be a better father to her anyway."

"And what about you? What about what you want?"

"I'll still have my music," he said. "That's enough." After a moment, he stood, looking at her as though not sure how to bring the conversation to a close. "Well then…"

Hannah stood, too. Anger pulsed in her temple, her chest. Fists clenched at her side, it was all she could do not to strike him. "Well then, what, Liam? Well then, I'll never see you again? Well then, I only thought I wanted to be a father? Well then, I never meant any of the things I said anyway? Well then, it was a whim after all?"

"All of the above," he said. And took off down the garden path.

She sat down again, immobilized by rage. Her face felt hot as if he'd slapped it. By her left foot was a terracotta pot Margaret had brought up to the house to plant petunias in. Her hand shaking, she curled her fingers around the rim and hurled it at the gate just in front of Liam.

"Just a goddamned whim, Liam," she shouted.

BY TEN THAT NIGHT, she'd moved everything she and Faith owned out of her mother's house and into the new place. Clothes, books, a few pieces of furniture, some boxes that had been stored in Margaret's garage. Rocky and Jen had helped her load all of it into his pickup truck.

Activity helped. Dry-eyed and resolute, she moved about the apartment, unpacking boxes, hanging clothes in closets, folding bed linens. In the kitchen, she drank from a can of flat, lukewarm Diet Coke. The utilities would be turned on tomorrow. For now, she was working by the glow of the candles they'd used the other night; carrying her cell phone from room to room in case it rang.

She carried a box of toys into Faith's room. Earlier, she'd frozen in the doorway, gawking at the brand-new furniture that filled the small space. A bright red bed, a blue wooden chest with yellow drawers. Only one person would be unaware that Faith didn't really need a new bedroom suite. The one time Liam had seen his daughter's bedroom, it had been late and he probably hadn't noticed the furnishings.

Wondering how he'd got the furniture in, she remembered that she'd given him an extra key. Now that simple act of trust, the togetherness and shared responsibilities it implied, seemed a mockery. She took a deep breath and all the emotions, pent up since walking into the school office that afternoon, broke loose and she sat on the floor with her back to the wall and wept. When she'd cried herself out, she started to call the police on her cell phone, then decided she didn't want to be on the phone in case Margaret called. Fifteen minutes later, she was shivering in the air-conditioned chill of the Long Beach Police Department.

"I'm not sure if this is technically a police matter," she told the desk sergeant, "but my mother picked up my six-year-old daughter from school today, and I haven't seen or heard from either of them since."

"This is the child's grandmother." He was an older guy, maybe a grandfather himself, with a craggy, lined face and a bored expression. "She has your permission to pick up the child?"

"Well, yes. She picks her up most days, but this wasn't her day and she knew I was supposed to…and we had this big disagreement last night."

Her face burning, she thanked him and left the station. Five minutes later, her cell phone rang.

"Faith's okay," Margaret said. "I'm okay. We're in an emergency room in Ventura… No, no, let me explain. Someone rear-ended the car, Faith got a bump on the chin, and the CHP insisted we get her checked out. She's fine, really. Hannah, I'm so sorry. Everything just kept building, I could see Liam getting more and more involved with you and Faith and I'm sure I was putting my own spin on things, but when she fell in the water, I just couldn't…I had to do something."

HANNAH DROVE UP to Ventura early the following morning. Faith had a Band-Aid on her chin and slept all the way home. Margaret continued to apologize.

"Maybe the accident jolted my brain, too," she told Hannah. "Remember how angry I got when you told me about that Cuddlers program at Western? I think it was because I knew, deep down, that you were right." She smiled ruefully. "What *did* I have in my life without you and Faith?"

In Long Beach, Hannah pulled up in front of the house on Termino to let Margaret out.

"We're not coming in," she told her mother. "Everything's in the new place."

"Hannah, don't punish me."

"I'm not." The engine was still idling. She couldn't look at her mother. "We need to get home."

"Look, what I did was wrong, I know that. But I've learned my lesson. I have all kinds of plans, sweetheart. I'm going to sign up for classes at Cal State, check out the Cuddlers program. I'll stop expecting you and Deb and Faith to fill all my needs."

"Well, good. I'm glad you've got all this insight now that Liam's safely out of the picture. Bottom line though, you prevailed. Congratulations, Mom, you managed to drive him away again."

AFTER THE SHOW, in the hot, noisy pub, amidst the happily rowdy crowd, Liam tried to shake the gloom that had descended upon him in the last week. It felt like wet, heavy concrete slowly oozing through his vital organs. Gray and viscous; smothering his brain, filling his lungs so that sometimes he had trouble taking a deep breath. Hardening around his heart.

It had been a week now since he'd walked away from Hannah. A week of telling himself he'd done the right thing, that it was better for everyone, especially Faith, if he just bowed out. Better that she go on believing her daddy was in heaven than to have him let her down, disappoint her—as he almost surely would.

A week in which he'd managed to convince himself that what Margaret had done had probably been a blessing in disguise. Without it, he'd have kept traveling along the path to a life with Hannah and Faith. The kind of life, he kept telling himself now, in which he would never have been really happy. And, in the process, he would have made Hannah and Faith unhappy. *So, thank you, Margaret.* He drank some beer. *You did us all a favor.*

And things were not all bad. Brid was better. That was something to be thankful for. Or at least she'd assured him she was better. She'd worked out some sort of telephone counseling arrangement with her shrink at Casa Pacifica and claimed she was ready to go back on the road again. He'd taken her at her word and rescheduled the canceled performances.

Tonight they'd played at a college campus in Santa Barbara. The show had gone well, despite teething problems with hired equipment and no sound check. A hardcore crowd of faithfuls had filled the front of the place and sung along with the music. Afterward, they'd all trooped down to an Irish bar at the end of the street. Brid was singing now, Pearse accompanying her on the tin whistle.

Liam sat there, nursing his Guinness, telling himself this was the life. And wasn't it? Hadn't he always been happy with it? The music went from jig to reel while feet stomped on the wooden floor. The fiddle, the whistle, the drum like a heartbeat. Someone played pipes for a bit and then Brid grabbed the microphone again and the noise subsided as she began to sing. Something melancholy about desire and remorse; of being left behind, abandoned.

He listened, transfixed until she was nearly through. And then he put down his glass and pushed his way through the crowd to the door.

Outside, the night was cool and the streets were full of college kids in blue jeans. They spilled out of the taco shop across the road, congregated in groups on the sidewalk, laughing and talking and shouting out to one another. His face felt hot and flushed, and he stood with his back to the wall, trying to explain away the feeling that had come over him in the pub.

"Are you all right, Liam?" Brid stood in the doorway, the pale, flimsy fabric of her dress blowing in the wind.

"I'm fine."

"That song went well, can you hear them in there calling for more?"

He nodded.

"There's a girl in there asking about you."

"I'll be in, give me a minute."

"You sure you're all right?"

"Leave off, Brid." He pushed past her into the pub, but she caught his arm, pulled him against the wall and fixed him with a look. "What?"

"*What.*" She clucked her tongue at him. "How long have we known each other? You're a wreck."

"I'm fine. The show went fine."

"You're not fine."

"I am," he said. "Leave me alone."

"We're going to talk."

THEY WENT TO A DENNY'S a block or so away. He gawked at the plate of scrambled eggs and ham the waitress had set down in front of Brid and shook his head. "You go from one extreme to the other. You're actually going to eat that?"

"No, Liam, I'm going to fashion this—" she poked with her fork at the ham "—into a little hat and maybe I'll use the eggs for a facial. Of course I'm going to eat it. And stop watching me, or I'll dump it all on the floor."

Liam lifted the top of his bacon and avocado burger

to verify the presence of avocado. Two slices. He couldn't get enough of it. A few weeks from now, he'd be drooling at the memory of avocado. He glanced at Brid, who was busy segregating the pile of eggs from the ham. As a kid, he'd done the same thing with peas. God forbid that a small, shriveled, olive-green pea should come anywhere near his mashed potatoes.

Did Faith do that? Did Faith ever ask about him? Did she ever pick up the guitar he'd given her? Did Hannah think of him? Across from him, Brid cut a tiny corner off a piece of ham. So far he'd seen nothing go in her mouth. She looked up and caught him watching her.

"Pack it up, Liam. I mean it."

"So this therapist really said to call him anytime?"

"He did." Brid stared at Liam across the table. "His daughter died of anorexia, and he doesn't want to see it happen to anyone else, if he can do anything about it." She kept watching him. "Either that, or he wants my body."

"Skeletal as it is," Liam said, and Brid reached over and slapped his hand. "Sorry," he amended. "Fashionably slim."

"Not if I keep shoveling this stuff down." Brid had now impaled ham on the tines of her fork and was studying it as though psyching herself up to actually put it in her mouth. She put the fork down and looked at Liam. "So?"

He met her gaze. "So what?"

"So what's wrong with you?"

"Me? Nothing." She kept watching him. "Oh right," he said, pretending to understand. "The chronic moodiness and flare for melodrama, you mean?"

"No, that wasn't what I meant, Liam. Although God

knows, we're all quite familiar with those qualities, thank you very much.''

"Then I've no idea what you're getting at.''

"Haven't you?'' She carefully set her knife and fork on top of her uneaten food. "Right, then, I'm through.''

"You hardly touched it.''

"And I won't. Until you tell me what's making you behave like a lovesick cow.''

"A cow?'' He laughed around a mouthful of hamburger.

"Talk.''

"I don't feel like talking about it, Brid.''

"And I don't feel like eating.''

"I ended things with Hannah.'' He set the hamburger back down. "I thought it was the right thing to do, but it's killing me.''

"You love her?''

"I never stopped.''

"Does she know that?''

"I told her. And then…'' He couldn't bring himself to discuss the whole episode. "I changed my mind.'' He pushed at her plate. "Still lots of food there.''

Brid fixed him with a look. "You changed your mind? And is that what you told her?''

"Yeah.''

"God.'' She shook her head. "Men. The whole lot of you are scared to death to let anyone get close, so you tax your little brains trying to work out ways to stop it happening and then when it does, you wonder, all big-eyed and innocent, what went wrong and how you can make it better again.''

"The male psyche according to Brid Kelly.''

"So that's really what you told her?'' she asked. "Just that you changed your mind?''

He shrugged. "Words to that effect. I kept trying to see myself in her world, a little suburban house, mowing the lawns on Saturday. What it came down to in the end was I couldn't do it." He frowned at his plate, at the lurid green pickle slices, the congealing grease. "And then her family was putting up a lot of resistance," he admitted, still thinking about Margaret. Wondering as he had countless times since he'd left Hannah's how it had all ended up. Wondering what reason Margaret had given for taking Faith, although that one wasn't hard to guess. Wondering, too, how Hannah was coping. Thinking, as he had over and over, of picking up the phone to call Hannah. To find out, to explain. Deciding, as he had over and over, that he needed to put it all behind him and move on. "It's for the best," he told Brid.

"Right," she said. "It's written all over your face how happy you are about it all."

"I didn't say I was happy about it. I said it was for the best. Hannah's world isn't mine. By the same token, I can hardly expect her and Faith to give up everything and live like gypsies, following the band around." A waitress stopped at their table, looked at his plate, then up at him.

"You all done with that, hon?"

"I am." He glanced at Brid's plate, still some left but she'd made a dent in it. "I don't know about her."

"Not quite." Brid smiled at the waitress. "I'll have some more coffee when you have a moment." After the waitress left, Brid stuck her elbows on the table and propped her face between her hands. "We've had this discussion before," she said. "Remember?"

He frowned, sorting through all the advice he'd received since learning of Faith's existence. Advice from Brid, from Miranda, from the guys in the band.

"After your daughter's birthday party?" Brid prompted. "I told you then, you need to make a choice. It's one thing or the other. The kind of life you have now, or a different kind of life with a wife and daughter. There's no way you can have both, Liam."

"I know." The waitress brought coffee for Brid, smiled and set the check down on the table. Liam picked it up and studied it. "And I've made the choice. The next step is to convince myself I'm happy about it."

"BUT I HATE THIS PLACE, Mommy." Faith lay in bed, tears streaming down her face. "It's ugly and it smells funny and I miss Raisin. I want to go back to our old house. I want my bedroom and I want the tree-house bed."

Hannah sat down on the edge of the bed Liam had bought for his daughter, and tried to keep her voice and expression upbeat. In the week that they'd been in the new apartment, Faith's bedtime had become a nightly ritual of tears. Several times, unable to console her daughter, Hannah had brought the little girl into her own bed, where Faith would finally fall asleep, snuggled up so close that Hannah hardly slept for fear of moving and waking her up again.

"When can we go back to our house?"

"Sweetie, this is *our* home now. The old house is Grandma's."

"But I like that one better. I want that to be our house again."

"I know you do, but that's because we haven't lived here long enough for it to feel like our house." She smoothed Faith's hair. "Let's think about some things we could do here to make it feel like our house."

Faith brightened. "We could bring Raisin here."

Hannah took a breath. "Besides bringing Raisin here. What are some other things we could do? Tell you what…" Her brain scrambled wildly to think of something that would fulfill the objective, not cost too much, not involve pets or painting the walls, which was also prohibited. Faith was waiting, her expression hopeful. "How about we make some new curtains," Hannah said. "Red and blue to match your furniture."

Faith's expression darkened. "Why *can't* Raisin live here?"

"Because he lives at Grandma's house," Hannah said. "But you can see him whenever we visit Grandma."

"Tomorrow?"

"Well, maybe not tomorrow."

"When?"

"Soon, sweetie, I promise."

"But when, Mommy? I miss Grandma and Auntie Rose and Auntie Helen. I want to go home."

This time, Hannah didn't have the heart to correct her daughter. She leaned over to kiss Faith's forehead. "Listen, you need to get some sleep. Mommy needs to get some sleep. Tomorrow, we'll get the material for the curtains, okay?"

"I miss Grandma a whole lot," Faith said. "But I miss Raisin the most."

CHAPTER SEVENTEEN

AFTER SHE FINALLY GOT Faith to sleep, Hannah was too tensed up to sleep herself. She paced the tiny apartment, zeroing in on anything that would divert her thoughts from the endless playing and replaying of everything that had happened with Liam. In her bedroom, she hauled out all the clothes she'd initially jammed into the closets just to get them out of the way, and dumped them on the bed.

Order. If she couldn't impose a sense of order on her life, she was damn well going to whip her closet into shape. But as she segregated shirts and tops in color groups, further segregating them into casual and dress, she found herself thinking about Liam. As hard as she tried, she couldn't see anything good that had come from his brief involvement in their lives.

She hadn't seen or spoken to Margaret all week. She'd let the machine pick up all calls, and then ignored the red blinking message light. Each day after school, she took Faith to the park or beach, then stopped for a long, leisurely meal that didn't end until she figured it was too late for Margaret to drop by. By that time, Faith was irritable and sleepy, which added guilt to everything else Hannah was feeling.

But she'd been resolute: determined not to grant quick forgiveness, nor to slip back into the easy warmth of the family life. In the process, she'd also felt so lonely and bereft that she thought she would lose her mind.

But things *would* improve. Liam hadn't derailed her life. Not this time. He'd simply been an obstacle along the track. But she could circumvent it and move on. One small problem—she was no longer sure of her destination.

Where *had* she been headed before Liam's brief reappearance in her life? Continued employment at La Petite Ecole, coaching the Taylor Beckers of the world? Marriage, somewhere down the line, if not to Allan, to someone like Allan? A guy with comfortable, middle-class values, a guy who would feel entirely at home sitting around the family dinner table?

Even now, she still saw her mother's house when she thought about the family dinner table. Would there ever come a time when she'd think of herself and Faith as a family instead of a satellite in Margaret's orbit?

With the Goodwill bag full, she started sorting blue and green shirts, trying to decide whether each should have its own section, while also debating whether Liam had inadvertently done her a favor by making her question her destination. Deep in thought, she jumped, startled by a knock on the front door.

It seemed late for visitors, but the clock by the bed showed that it was only a little after nine. In the living room, she stood on tiptoe to peer through the glass pane at the top of the door. Rose, Helen, Deb and Margaret stood huddled together outside shooting each other uncertain looks as they waited for her to respond to the knock.

She opened the door.

"Ta-da!" Rose held out her arms. "You might think

you can shut us out of your life, but we're here to tell you you're wrong.''

Hannah stood with one hand on the edge of the door, struggling to keep her face composed. Rose, Helen and Debra all held bulging plastic grocery sacks and shivered a little in the cool night air. And on the lower step, her face a mask of anxiety, stood Margaret. Hannah bit her lip hard, pulled back the door and they all trooped in.

"Come on, Hanny." Rose enveloped her in a hug. "Tell your old auntie you still love her."

"*You're* going to be an auntie, remember?" Debra patted her still flat stomach. "Who do I talk to about morning sickness and stuff? Plus, it's not fair that I have to be the focus of all Mom's obsessive worrying."

"Now, Deb…" Margaret's wavering smile flickered and she looked from one daughter to the other. "I'm trying, I really am."

Debra rolled her eyes.

"*Girls,*" Helen said reprovingly. "Be nice to your mother." She surveyed the tiny living room. "This is…a sweet little place. I think when you get it all fixed up, it's going to be adorable. You know, you can actually staple sheets to the walls. I've seen some wonderful patterns and the beauty of it is you can take them all down when you move out."

"Grandma." Faith, sleepy-eyed but smiling, burst into the room and flung herself into Margaret's arms. "I miss you, Grandma."

And suddenly the apartment, which minutes earlier had been so silent, was full of voices and laughter. Helen called from the kitchen to announce that the freezer wasn't working properly. Rose was saying that she'd finally persuaded Margaret to go to a singles dance, and

Faith, still in her grandmother's arms, was demanding to hear news about Raisin.

"Omigod," Rose, who was in the kitchen now, said loudly. "This fridge must be older than I am. It looks *exactly* like the one we had growing up. Hey, Margaret, come and look at this. Remember how we used to defrost it with the hair dryer?"

"How big is Raisin now?" Faith asked Margaret. "When can we come home again?"

Hannah exchanged a look with her mother. Margaret had her arms around Faith's waist. Faith's legs, pale under her scrunched-up red nightgown, were wrapped around Margaret's hips. Faith would soon be too big for Margaret to pick up, Hannah thought. Tears stung her eyes and she turned away, busying herself straightening the miniblinds.

In the kitchen, Helen was still talking about the antiquated freezer and how the artichoke, feta and chicken casserole would thaw and get spoiled. Deb made some joke about pickles and ice cream and Rose was inquiring about the possibility of a cold beer. Hannah turned from the window to catch Margaret dabbing at her eyes.

"I'm sorry." Margaret looked at Hannah over the top of Faith's head. "I'm really, really sorry. God, I've missed you guys so much…"

"I know, Mom." Hannah swallowed. "We've missed you, too."

And she had.

They drove her crazy, she thought a little later as they all sat around the kitchen table—her kitchen table—demolishing the pan of brownies Helen had brought, but her mother and aunts were so much a part of who she was that she could never really sever the ties completely. They might stretch and fray—even to the point of almost breaking—but, ultimately, the ties were strong enough to endure. The thought made her feel happy and sad at the same time. Happy for herself; sad for Liam whose ties to her and Faith were so fragile, he could relinquish them in an instant. His loss, she decided.

"Grandma." Faith tugged at Margaret's hand to get her attention. "When *can* we come home?"

Hannah opened her mouth to speak, then decided to let Margaret handle the question.

"What do you mean, you want to come home?" Margaret scooped Faith up on her lap, tucked an errant strand of hair behind her granddaughter's ear. "You are home, my love. *This* is your home. And you know what? I think it's a pretty nifty home."

AND, GRADUALLY, the little apartment did begin to feel like home. Faith made friends with a girl two houses down who, she told Hannah, she liked even better than Tiffany. Hannah, with Helen's assistance, made curtains for Faith's bedroom windows, filled the window boxes with geranium cuttings from her mother's backyard and even planted a few of the hated nasturtium seeds that Margaret was only too glad to be rid off. Three or four afternoons a week, Hannah and Faith dropped by the house to take Raisin for walks along the beach.

One evening, mostly at Faith's insistence, Hannah invited Allan and Douglas over to dinner; another time, feeling lonely and a little blue, she went to dinner with Allan. At the end of the evening, she told him that she valued his friendship but wanted nothing more than that. He'd been sweet and understanding as he hugged her goodbye. "Have a happy life, kiddo."

At La Petite Ecole, Taylor Becker aced his kindergarten screening test and Deanna Becker was so thrilled she tried to give Hannah a gift certificate for a weekend at the luxurious Ventana Inn in Big Sur.

"Take your sweetie," Mrs. Becker urged. "The place oozes romance."

Hannah thanked her, but explained that La Petite Ecole's policy prohibited the staff accepting gifts from parents. Besides, she didn't have a sweetie. Which was just as well, because she'd signed up for landscape design classes at Cal State Long Beach. She wouldn't have time for sweeties.

THE WILD ROVERS PLAYED their final performance at a club in Hollywood where the audience seemed surly and bored from the first chord of the opening song. "Ah well," Pearse muttered to Liam as they trouped off stage, "you can't please them all." His sentiments exactly, Liam decided as he half listened to Pearse and Brid and some of the others talk about where to go for a few pints and something to eat. Like the audience, Liam felt surly and bored. As far as he was concerned, the moment they stepped off the plane at Shannon couldn't come soon enough.

"A lady here to see you, Liam," someone shouted from the front of the theater.

Liam stopped dead. He'd imagined this so many times since he'd walked away from Hannah. Right down to the night she'd finally appear, the last one of the tour. And now it was happening. He stood, immobilized. His shirt was sweat drenched from the show and he pulled it off, realized he didn't have another one and, grabbed a new Wild Rover T-shirts from the stack on the concession stand. Pearse's sister, who worked the table where the shirts were sold, gave him a questioning look.

He shrugged and headed back into the theater where a
few diehards were still straggling out.

"Liam."

Margaret. In a red blazer, white blouse and dark trousers, smiling but twisting her hands and glancing around
her and looking about as out of place in a Hollywood
club as any suburban granny would. Speechless, Liam
stared at her. Disappointment hit him like a blow to the
stomach—replaced immediately by fear that something
had happened to Hannah or Faith.

"Is Faith all right?" he asked. "Hannah? Is something wrong?"

"No." She shook her head. "Yes, well no, I mean
they're both fine but...is there somewhere we could
talk?"

They went to a nearby Subway, where Margaret said
she wasn't hungry but she'd have some coffee. He *was*
hungry but couldn't focus enough to decide what sand-
wich combination he wanted. Two cups of coffee in
hand, he sat down at the table opposite Margaret.

"However much you want to do what's best for your
children," Margaret said, "there comes a time when you
have to realize they're not children any longer and they
must be allowed to make their own decisions. You might
not agree with them, but..." She shrugged and a smile
flickered briefly. "They might not agree with *your* decisions, either. Usually don't, in fact."

Liam drank some coffee. A sense that Margaret had
carefully rehearsed what she wanted to say stopped him
from interrupting her.

"I should never have let you think Hannah had had
an abortion. And I should have backed off when you
returned. I should have had enough confidence to trust
Hannah to make the right decision. But as I told her, we

sometimes believe what we want to believe. I didn't want you to take her and Faith back to Ireland, so one way to prevent that was to cast you in the role of the philandering no-good. I made myself believe it and hoped that she would, too.''

''How do you know I'm not a philandering no-good, Mrs. Riley?''

She looked at him for a moment. ''I don't. But Hannah seems convinced you're not, and I need to trust her judgment.''

''How is Hannah?''

''Okay.'' Margaret stared into her coffee. ''But I think she'd be happier with you in her life again.''

''You *think?*''

''I know.'' She drank some coffee, then set the cup down again. ''I'm going to be honest with you. I would be far happier to see my daughter fall in love with an attorney who owns a house on Riva Alto Canal—''

''The pirate's dad.''

Margaret gave him a puzzled look.

''Nothing. Go on.''

''Anyway, my new resolution is to try to be supportive of whatever Hannah decides to do.''

''But you think—''

''I think she loves you, Liam.'' She shook her head in mock exasperation. ''So do something about it, for heaven's sake.''

HE ACCEPTED Margaret's offer of a ride back to Long Beach and, with forty-eight hours left on his visitor's visa, knocked on Hannah's front door step.

''Can I come in?'' he finally asked after she'd stared at him for several seconds. Without a word, she motioned him inside—where he made the mistake of telling her about Margaret's visit.

Big mistake. For the next fifteen minutes—he'd checked his watch—he sat on the couch saying nothing as Hannah paced around the room; railing on about her mother and her aunts, about how she *just* could not believe that they hadn't learned their lesson and were they ever, *ever,* going to stop interfering in her life and she could fight her own battles thank you very much and she certainly didn't need Margaret tracking him down on her behalf as if she were some desperate, pathetic woman who couldn't keep a man and if he imagined for a moment, an *instant,* that she had nothing better to do with her life than sit around waiting for him to make up his mind, he'd better damn well think again. And then she seemed to run out of steam.

"The place looks different," he said into the silence that followed her outburst. "With the furniture and everything. It looks nice."

"Liam. I want you to go, okay?"

He looked at her. Her hair was clipped up with this black-and-white plastic dog thing, and she had on a pair of baggy gray sweatpants. Beneath the faded blue shirt that read, Got My Dog, Got My Horse, Don't Need No Damn Man, he could see the outline of her breasts. No bra. He remained seated.

"I mean it."

"What if I said that I was here because I wanted to be here?"

She shrugged, walked to the door and pulled it open. "Life is full of the things that we *want.* For example, I *want,* really, really *want,* just for once in my life to be left alone. No family interference, no one breathing down my neck. But, God, what are the chances of that ever happening?''

"Come back to Ireland with me. That should help.'' It wasn't what he'd intended to say, it had just come out. But it didn't seem like a bad idea and when he saw something flicker in her eyes, it was all the encouragement he needed. "I'm serious, Hannah. Come on, close the door and let's talk.''

Her hand was still on the door. "There's nothing to talk about, Liam.''

"At least close the door then.''

She did, and sat down on the arm of the couch. "I'm not going to Ireland with you. We might as well establish that right now.''

"I just hit you with it, I know, but think about it.'' He could hear his voice speed up; enthusiasm like a whip, driving his words to move faster. "It would be great, terrific. We'll live in my house in Galway. Near the recording studio. It'll be just like a regular job, at least for six months or so. We can get Faith into a good school.''

"Liam, she's six. I can't uproot her from her family and take her off to a foreign country.''

"We're her family,'' he said, but Hannah was clearly unimpressed. "Look, it's wonderful for her to have your mother and aunts, but it wouldn't hurt her at all to know there was a life outside of Long Beach, California.''

She shook her head. "It won't work, Liam.''

"It could, if you wanted it to.''

"Well, maybe that's it. Maybe I don't want it enough to make that kind of change.''

"Or maybe you're scared to leave the nest.'' He could see he was losing, so he decided he might as well fire all his weapons. "It's comfortable for you here, isn't it?

Your mother and aunts twittering around, fussing over you. Maybe they get on your nerves at times, but on the whole it's safe and nonthreatening and you never really have to challenge yourself, do you?''

Hannah stood up. ''You're incredible, you know that? You're asking *me* to uproot my life to follow you across the world. You're talking to *me* about not challenging myself? Where the hell is the challenge for you, Liam? Huh?''

''Hannah, come on—''

''No.'' She pulled open the door. ''Go. Leave.''

''Your mother gave me a ride down here.''

''Oh really? So you just thought, 'Oh, I'll hop into bed with Hannah.'''

''Well...''

''Well, tough. *Walk* over to my mom's house. I'm sure she'll be happy to drive you back.''

OF COURSE sleep was out of the question. If the mental picture of Liam walking through the darkened streets of Long Beach looking for somewhere to spend the night didn't make her feel guilty enough, the anger at Margaret kept her brain working at a furious pitch rehearsing all the scathing things she would say to her mother once she'd calmed down enough not to actually kill her.

At one in the morning, she was wandering around the apartment, looking for something to organize. At two, she was sitting at the kitchen table trying to work out a filing system for the recipes she'd clipped from newspaper food sections. When she suddenly realized she'd been staring blankly at the same recipe for a while, she forced herself to concentrate on the title. *Irish soda bread.*

Maybe it was a sign.

Follow Liam to Ireland, bake Irish soda bread, have babies and live happily ever after. She got up from the table, and wandered into the bathroom. She looked at her face in the mirror, and pulled the stupid dog barrette out of her hair. Faith's *101 Dalmations* barrette. God, what a dork she must have looked.

Why hadn't she even considered his suggestion? She didn't love him enough? She *was* scared to leave the nest? Last spring, a little bird—a baby bird—kept flying against the kitchen window; bumping its head against the glass before it flew away, looking stunned.

She had flown the nest once, gotten a little bruised, then returned to be soothed and consoled. And Liam was right, it was pretty comfortable with everyone chirping and twittering all around. Now she had her own baby bird and it was scary to think of flying away again. Sure, she'd moved out of Margaret's house, but nothing else had really changed. Margaret, Rose and Helen—even Deb—were all there for her when she needed them. All there for her even when she *didn't* need them, which was probably more to the point. Maybe it was time to stop fooling herself. Maybe it was time to leave for real.

THE DAY AFTER Hannah told him never to darken her door again, Liam found himself driving south on the Golden State Freeway in a compact rented from Budget, and having serious misgivings about what he'd just done. By the time he turned onto the 710 heading back to Long Beach, he'd started rehearsing the reasons he would give to the Celtic Arts Collective for changing his mind about taking the position they'd just offered him.

He'd called the collective on a whim—there was that word again—after reading an article in the *Hollywood Reporter*. As luck would have it, there was a position he might be interested in. If he'd like to come up and talk to the director, he'd been told, maybe they could work something out.

So he'd made the trip to Burbank today and had accepted the job.

He'd be doing a bit of everything—developing new talent, helping to promote Irish music and culture and teaching guitar classes a couple of days a week.

"We can't pay you much," the director told him, "But you'll have the freedom to work on some of your own music and if your wife is working, too, you'll do okay."

His wife. Liam hadn't corrected the administrator's assumption and now the thought of Hannah as his wife filled him with equal parts exaltation and dread. Dread, because if she were still of the same mind as last night, he'd created a bit of a mess for himself.

And everybody else, come to that. Before he left for the interview, he'd told Brid and the fellows in the band that he was probably going to quit. And, determined to show Hannah he was serious, he'd told his manager to put an indefinite hold on plans for the European tour.

But now he felt less certain that he'd done the right thing.

In fact, by the time he pulled up outside Faith's school, he'd all but convinced himself that the best thing he could do now was let everyone know that he'd experienced a temporary bout of insanity and nothing he'd said or done in the past twenty-four hours should be taken seriously.

And then he got out of the car and walked across the road to wait for his daughter.

AT THREE, Hannah sat on the grass across the road from Faith's school, slightly apart from the knot of parents on the other side of the road. Her head lowered slightly, the visor of her baseball cap and dark glasses shielding her eyes, and—she was pretty sure—her face from Liam, she watched him take in the parents waiting by the entrance. He looked good. Terrific. Stylish in dark sage-green pants and a long-sleeved cotton jersey a shade or two lighter.

He hadn't seen her, hadn't looked across the street in her direction. Which was good, because she had no idea what she would say to him if he did. She drew her knees up to her chest, wrapped her arms around them and propped up her chin. Still eight minutes to go.

She imagined various scenarios of what would happen when Faith walked out. In one, Liam spotted his daughter before she did and he and Faith came over to where she was sitting. In another, she was the first to see Faith, she grabbed her daughter's hand and they made a quick getaway before Liam noticed them. In the third, they both spotted Faith at the same time, Liam smiled at her, birds twittered in the trees and they all walked off into the sunset, hand in hand.

Or none of the above.

She watched Liam say something to a woman in a red dress. The woman smiled up at him. She probably thought he was cute, which he was. Hannah chewed the edge of her thumbnail. God, her heart was going crazy. *I love you.* She could just walk up to him and whisper it in his ear. Cut through all the other stuff. *I love you.*

If she could get her brain past the thought that he was back because Margaret had intervened. He'd left because of Margaret. He was back because of Margaret. It was almost comical. Like a soap opera. What will Margaret do next? Tune in tomorrow for the next episode of *As*

Margaret's World Turns. Or maybe, *As Margaret Turns The World.* Better yet, *As Margaret Turns Hannah's World.*

A thought struck her. Was saying no to him last night actually an act of rebellion against Margaret? When Margaret had seen him as evil incarnate, she herself had rushed to his defense. But now that he had Margaret's blessing, could it just be that…nah. She pulled herself to her feet, brushed grass off the back of her shorts and sauntered over to where he stood. Came up behind him and tapped him on the shoulder.

"Hey."

He turned and smiled at her. "Hannah."

"You know that old saying about cutting off your nose to spite your face? Don't ask me to explain because I get a headache even thinking about it." *On the other hand maybe Margaret had been just using reverse psychology…God, no, she couldn't think about that, either.* "Anyway, I just wanted to tell you…that you look very nice. And…" She kicked at the grass with the toe of her sneaker. "I love you."

Liam made a melodramatic swipe at his brow. "Phew."

"What?"

"I've just taken a job in Burbank which I'd have absolutely no interest at all in doing if you didn't love me."

"A job?" She stared at him. "What kind of job?"

"This nonprofit group that's trying to promote Irish arts. Music, theater. That's why I'm all dressed up. I drove straight here from the interview."

"Wow." She smiled at him. "That's fantastic…isn't it? You're pleased about it?"

"Yeah…" He shrugged. "Sure. I'll still have time to write some of my own stuff. It'll work out."

She watched his face as he told her about what he'd be doing. He sounded okay about it, but something was missing from his voice. The spark she always heard when he talked about his music. "Are you sure you'll be happy? What about the rest of the band? Brid? The European tour?"

"Listen." He caught both her hands in his and looked into her eyes. "Stop worrying about whether I'm happy. Just tell me this makes you happy."

She swallowed. His expression was solemn now, his eyes dark. How could she not be happy? What more proof did she need that he loved her? "Liam, I just want to be sure…it's such a huge sacrifice for you."

"Happy? Or not happy?"

"Just—"

"Happy? Or not happy?"

"Okay, happy. Of course I'm happy. Who wouldn't be?"

"Well, maybe you won't be when I tell you what I've found out about the price of houses."

"Houses? You've already looked at houses?"

"Not in any great depth, but enough to depress me."

"We could stay in my place…" She caught herself and grinned. "Our place? The place I'm renting."

"I want Faith to have her dog," he said.

Hannah smiled then. Couldn't stop smiling. A few kids had started to trickle out of the school. If she lived to ninety, she thought, she could never repay him for the sacrifice he'd made today.

"I think I see our daughter on the schools steps." Liam put his arm around Hannah's shoulder and they started walking across the grass. "The girl with the frizzy ginger hair must be Tiffany, right?"

"Yep." Hannah squeezed him to her side and reached up to kiss the side of his neck. "Thank you, Liam. I mean it. I don't even know what else to say. I'll make you happy, I promise."

He stopped walking. "I can see I'm going to have to give you a stern talking to. And you're obviously a bit thick, so I'm going to say this very slowly. *My happiness is not your responsibility.*" He took her face in his hands and kissed her mouth. "Got it?"

She started laughing. "God, I'm getting just like my mom."

"Remember that no one forced me to do this. It was my choice. I did it because I want a life with you and Faith and…this is the way it worked out."

And since I turned down your first suggestion, Hannah thought, *what alternative did you have?* But she kept the thought to herself because Faith, in a pink polka-dot dress and white sneakers was tearing across the grass, hair and knees flying, face ablaze.

"Mommy. Liam." She beamed at both of them but saved her biggest smile for Liam. "I've been thinking about you," she told him.

"Have you?" His smile matched hers. "I've been thinking about you a bit, too."

Faith turned to Hannah. "Can we all do something fun, Mommy?"

Hannah glanced at Liam. "My plans for the rest of the day were grocery shopping and organizing my sock drawer."

He grinned.

"I've become very big on organizing lately. When

your closets and cabinets are in order, other parts of life don't seem so chaotic.''

"She's organizing *everything*." Faith rolled her eyes dramatically. "You wouldn't believe it.''

"Will your socks stage a revolt if you don't marshal them into order this afternoon?" Liam asked.

Hannah bit back a smile. "I'll risk it.'' She looked from Liam to Faith. "So what fun thing do you want to do?''

"Queen Mary," Faith said.

"I thought you didn't like the *Queen Mary*," Hannah said.

"No, I did." Faith's smile faded for a moment. "I was just in a bad mood.''

"Were you?" Liam frowned. "Hmm. I don't remember that.''

"Well, I was. But today I'm in a good mood. Want to know why?'' She smiled up at him. "Because you're here.''

FOR THE REST OF THE AFTERNOON, Liam carried his daughter's words in his head. A little gift he'd take out every so often, examine and smile to himself. He smiled while they ate ice cream on the dock and he reached over to taste Faith's bubble-gum sundae. And in the red water taxi that carried them over to the *Queen Mary*, bobbing across the bay, the wind and sea spray in their faces. And during the Ghost Ship tour of the old liner, listening to spooky accounts of ill-fated passengers reputed to still haunt the decks and cabins. Faith had gripped his hand and shivered dramatically. Hannah had smiled at him and he'd told himself he'd done the right thing. They *would* all be happy. He could live without the band and the touring. He'd sell the house in Galway, make California his home, wear the bloody barbecue apron if he had to. They'd all live happily ever. They would.

Around five, Faith had announced that she was hungry and they'd ended up in a downtown café called Super-Mex, where, Hannah insisted, they made the best carnitas tacos she'd ever tasted.

"You were right." He pushed his empty plate away. "Best carnitas tacos I've ever tasted."

Hannah gave him a skeptical look. "Have you ever had carnitas tacos?"

"No."

She pushed his arm. "Tully. I don't know about you."

He caught her hand and felt it go very still. Faith sat next to Hannah. Faith, all pink-cheeked and sleepy-eyed from the boat ride and the tortillas and beans she'd just demolished. He kept holding Hannah's hand as he addressed his daughter. "Here's the thing, Faith. I love your mum. A lot. And you're not so bad yourself."

Faith grinned. "And you're not so bad yourself, Liam," she said.

"Thanks. So anyway, I'd like to marry your mother and I was wondering what you might think about that."

"Marry her?" Faith's eyes turned saucer like. She twisted around to look at Hannah. "Hey, Mommy. Liam wants to marry you."

"My goodness." Hannah fanned her face with her hand. "A proposal."

"So what do you think about that, Faith?" Liam asked. "Your mother and me?"

"I think it's cool," Faith said. "Huh, Mommy?"

Hannah smiled as she looked into his eyes. "Way cool."

"But I want to be sure I'm doing the right thing," he

told Faith. "You don't think she'd rather that I just cleared off? Left her alone to organize her cupboards?"

"She already organizes way too much," Faith said.

"You think it's a good idea then? Marrying your mother, I mean?"

"*Yessss,*" Faith said loudly. "Now can I have another Pepsi?"

"Listen, Faith." His voice confidential, Liam leaned across the table. "I'm no expert on elocution, but I believe the preferred usage is, 'May I have another Pepsi?'"

"*May* I have another Pepsi?"

"No."

Faith grinned. "You're funny, Liam." Up on her knees, she looked at him for a moment. "So if you and Mommy get married, you'll be my stepdad. Just like when Tiffany's mom got married."

Liam exchanged a quick glance with Hannah, decided to let her respond.

"Well, this is a little different, sweetie," Hannah said. "It's a long story, but Liam really *is* your daddy."

Liam watched Faith's face as she considered this. Such a short and simple explanation of a long and convoluted journey. He wondered whether the answer would satisfy her.

"But I thought my daddy was in heaven," Faith said, after a few moments. "What happened? Did you come back?"

"Well, it's a long story," Liam said. "But you have the gist of it. I'm back and I'm here to stay."

"Cool," Faith said.

HANNAH STOOD in the doorway of Faith's room, watching Liam tell his daughter a bedtime story. Actually, he'd already told her a couple, in an outrageously broad accent that she herself could hardly understand. Most of it, she was pretty sure, had been lost on Faith, but it didn't seem to matter. Faith lay on her back, covers tucked up to her chin, smiling at Liam, clearly enchanted.

"And a knock came at the door," Liam was saying. "And Lady Wilde opened it to see a witch with two horns on her forehead and in her hand, a wheel for spinning wool."

"How come she had two horns?" Faith asked.

Liam scratched his head. "D'you think it would better if she had just one then?"

Faith grinned, sleepy now but willing to be entertained. "No, two horns are good."

"Well, the witches began to sing an ancient rhyme. Strange to hear and frightful to look at they were, those witches with their horns and their wheels. 'Rise, woman and make us a cake,' they said." He turned to look at Hannah. "I think she's out."

"That's what happens when guys tell women what to do," Hannah said.

"Is that so?" Liam followed her into the kitchen and they stood in the middle of the room, his hands on her shoulders. "You mean if I told you to take off all your clothes, you'd fall asleep?"

"Well, it depends. What would you do after I'd taken off my clothes?"

He kissed her on the mouth, guided her to the wall and pressed hard against her. "God, Hannah, I have no idea what I'd do. Have you any suggestions?"

"Yeah, a few." Still watching his face, she undid his belt buckle, unfastened his pants and slid her palm down over his stomach, beneath the elastic waist of his shorts.

"Would it have anything to do with where your left hand is right now?"

"It might." She smiled into his eyes. "Can you rise to the occasion?"

"I think I already have."

His body shuddered in a quick spasm and he buried his mouth in her neck, nipped at the skin on her collarbone. They kissed, mouths soft and open, bodies dissolving together. She felt languid, sensual, catlike. Jazz should be playing, she thought as she arched her neck to reach his mouth. Fear of Faith waking up and walking in on them stopped her from dropping to her knees and taking him in her mouth.

"We'd have to be very…circumspect. Faith isn't used to waking in the morning to find a man in my bed."

"I'm glad to hear that."

And then she took his hand and led him into the bedroom.

CHAPTER EIGHTEEN

THE NEXT DAY she drove over to Huntington Harbor to see Brid Kelly. Liam had gone up to L.A. to iron out visa details and wouldn't be back until early evening. As she pulled up to the curb, she thought of the last time she'd stopped by Miranda Payton's house. She'd been geared up to do battle with Liam for disappointing Faith. This time her mission was quite different.

Miranda Payton answered the door. She wore a short white terry-cloth robe and her hair was piled into a disheveled top-knot. Her eyes widened when she saw Hannah. "Liam's not here."

"I know. I'm here to see Brid."

Without a word, Miranda turned and called into the house. Moments later, Brid emerged at the top of the stairs. Unsmiling, she stared at Hannah but made no move to come down. Hannah looked from Miranda to Brid, but neither women spoke and she felt a definite tension.

"We've never met." She addressed Brid. "But I'm Hannah Riley, Liam's—"

"I know all about you," Brid said.

"I'd like to talk to you, if you have a few minutes."
Brid shrugged.

Hannah shifted her weight from one foot to the other and licked her lips. She wished Brid would come down the stairs and Miranda would go away. From somewhere in the house, she could hear canned laughter coming from a television set. "Can I buy you coffee or something?" she asked Brid. "Breakfast? I haven't eaten yet, there's a place on the Coast Highway."

"I don't eat breakfast," Brid said.

"There's coffee here if you want some," Miranda said.

"I wanted to talk to you about Liam." Hannah peered through the expanse of hallway and up at Brid's shadowy figure on the stairs. "About the band and everything…"

"The band?" Brid gave a mirthless laugh. "What's there to talk about? You've managed to make short work of the band. It's no big loss, as far as I'm concerned since I intended to quit after this tour anyway, but Liam might as well be cutting off his left arm."

"He's had a brain lapse," Miranda said. "Six months from now, he'll wake up and regret what he's done."

Hannah pushed at her hair. This was none of Miranda's business. Unfortunately, she was at Miranda's front door; Brid was on Miranda's stairs, making no move to come down, and Hannah had the feeling that alienating Miranda wouldn't help endear her to the singer.

"Liam's told you about his job with the Celtic Arts Collective?" she asked Brid.

"He has."

"He swears it's what he wants to do."

"It's not," Brid said.

"That's what I wanted to talk to you about."

"*Celtic Arts Collective.*" The derision in Brid's voice was clear. "Putting Liam into something like that, sitting him behind a desk to do…whatever…would be like taking one of your palm trees back to Ireland and expecting it to flourish.''

"He's got this thing about the kid," Miranda said, "and it's blinding him to what he really wants.''

Hannah looked at Miranda and decided she didn't care whether she alienated her or not. "The kid is my daughter. Liam's daughter. And her name is Faith.''

"Do you love Liam?" Brid asked. "Really love him?''

"Yes, I do," Hannah said, softly.

"Then please don't let him kill his soul."

"TELL ME ABOUT YOUR HOUSE in Galway," Hannah said that evening. She and Liam were in the kitchen of her apartment, trying to whip the stew Liam had sworn he knew how to make into something edible enough to serve the family, who were all coming over for dinner. "Is it in town?''

"Just outside." Liam shook pepper onto the browned meat. "What if we added tomatoes?''

"In Irish stew?" Hannah shrugged. "It's worth a try, I guess. So what about the schools? Are they pretty good?''

"My manager's daughter is doing well enough. Joel's always talking about all the prizes Carolyn's taking for this and that and she's a terrific reader. Last time I was at his house, she read me some bits from *Black Beauty*. Why?''

"Just wondering..." She tasted the stew. "God, Liam.''

He grinned. "Bad?''

"At least one of us had better learn how to cook.''

He opened the fridge. "Worcestershire sauce.''

"Couldn't hurt." From the bedroom, she could hear

Faith and Tiffany laughing together. "So about your recording contract—"

"Nixed."

She glanced at him. "But it doesn't have to be that way. You could—"

"I've made the decision, Hannah. Let's leave it at that." He poured a stream of Worcestershire sauce into the pan. "Maybe we should wait for your mother and aunts to get here and work their magic on the stew. Why didn't they ever teach you how to cook?"

"I *can* make cakes and lemon chicken," she said. "Actually, we should bring Faith in here to help us. My mom's turned her into quite the little cook." She threw some frozen chopped onion into the pan on the stove. "So anyway, after you're through with recording, you'd begin the European tour?"

"Right." Wooden spoon in hand, he glanced over his shoulder at her. "What's all this about, Hannah?"

"I've been thinking."

"Lie down."

"I'm serious. I'm thinking that it would be good for Faith to have a broader experience. See what it's like to live in another country."

"For a holiday, you mean?" He shrugged. "I'd have to check with the new boss. It might be a while before I could get the time off."

"I was thinking of something more long-term." She came up to stand behind him, put her arms around his waist. "Like actually moving there."

He went very still. "You're telling me you want to come back to Ireland? You and Faith?"

"Yep." She kissed the back of his neck. "In fact, the more I think about it, the better it sounds."

He turned to look at her, his expression unreadable.

"What brought about this change, Hannah? I thought we had it all settled."

"We did. Now I've unsettled it."

"I don't know what to say. You've taken me completely by surprise. What..." He shook his head. "Why?"

"Because..." She was about to tell him about her conversation with Brid, then decided against it. Besides, it wasn't the main reason. "I really want us to be a family, you and me and Faith. I want us to create new experiences together, to grow together. I'm not saying we couldn't do that here, but I like the idea of starting our new life together somewhere completely different."

Liam took a couple of beers from the refrigerator and held one out to her. "You don't have to do this for me, Hannah. I'm fine with the plan we had."

"I'm not doing it *just* for you." She took the beer. "I'm doing it for us. It's...I don't know, time to leave the nest."

He laughed. "A bit of a long flight, isn't it?"

"Maybe." *But I love you enough to risk it.* "We'll make it. Trust me."

"God." A smile stretched across his face. "You're sure you want to do this?"

"Yeah...I do. We need to sit down and talk to Faith about it, of course. But she's young, so she'd adjust pretty quickly. You wouldn't have to give up the band. If the European tour is in the summer, we could even go with you. Anyway, I have this new appreciation for tour buses."

"We'll fly," he said. "Tour buses are for the young and crazy."

She grinned.

"But what about you. Are you going to be happy?"

"Yeah." She nodded, even more sure of her decision now she'd told him about it. "I really do want to try something different. I've been in a rut for a while now. I just didn't recognize it. Faith provided me with an excuse to never leave my comfort zone."

"I doubt that you'll find much call for Mediterranean plants in Galway."

"Maybe not, but I bet roses do really well there. I'm excited, Liam, I really am. It's an opportunity for a whole new start. There are all kinds of ideas I want to explore."

"I could build you a greenhouse," he said.

"See? Next thing you know, I'll have a thriving roadside stand. Maybe a converted gypsy caravan. Who knows?"

"What about your mother?"

"Hey, she was the one who brought you back." She smiled. "Actually, I think she'll be happy for me. For us. She'll miss Faith, of course, but deep down she recognizes that we're our own family now. You and me and Faith."

"We'll invite her over for the wedding," Liam said.

EXACTLY TWO MONTHS LATER they stood in the back garden of Liam's stone cottage outside Galway. Hannah, shivering in a cream linen dress that skirted her knees, carried a bouquet of pink roses, just a shade darker than Faith's bridesmaid's dress. Margaret wore yellow silk, Helen and Deb were in blue and Rose made her own statement in a red velvet pantsuit with leopard trim. Brid, accompanied by Pearse on the tin whistle, sang as Hannah walked down the pathway to meet Liam, who stood waiting under a vine-covered arbor.

After the ceremony, they all crowded into the tiny

kitchen to drink champagne as they stood around the stove watching Helen, a navy apron tied around her waist, whisk a hollandaise sauce for the eggs Benedict keeping warm in the oven.

"Happy?" Liam had his arm around Hannah's shoulder.

"Very." She squeezed his waist. "Faith looks pretty happy, too." Through the kitchen window, she could see their daughter tearing across a stretch of brilliant emerald-green grass after Raisin and a large black dog she had named George. "I think she's going to do just fine."

"So, Liam," Margaret said. "Let's talk nuts and bolts. As soon as you get back from your honeymoon, you're going to start building the mother-in-law cottage?"

"Actually, I thought I'd get the hammer and pop outside as soon as I've finished this glass of champagne," he said.

"Now, Margaret…" Helen gave her sister a look. "Don't pressure him. He and Hannah need some time alone together."

"Speaking of being alone together," Rose said. "I just checked out the bedroom. Looks pretty cozy."

Liam winked at Hannah.

Hannah shook her head, trying hard not to smile. "What do I have to do to get away from them? I move to another continent and they're still poking their noses into my business."

"Ah well," Liam said. "That's the way it is with families, isn't it? The thing is they mean well."

"We do," Margaret, Rose and Helen said in unison.

Liam laughed aloud, and Hannah's heart swelled at the genuine happiness she heard in the sound. *I loved you when we were first married,* she thought. *But that didn't come close to how much I love you now.*

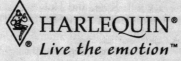

If you enjoyed what you just read,
then we've got an offer you can't resist!

Take 2 bestselling love stories FREE!

Plus get a FREE surprise gift!

Clip this page and mail it to Harlequin Reader Service®

IN U.S.A.
3010 Walden Ave.
P.O. Box 1867
Buffalo, N.Y. 14240-1867

IN CANADA
P.O. Box 609
Fort Erie, Ontario
L2A 5X3

YES! Please send me 2 free Harlequin Superromance® novels and my free surprise gift. After receiving them, if I don't wish to receive anymore, I can return the shipping statement marked cancel. If I don't cancel, I will receive 6 brand-new novels every month, before they're available in stores. In the U.S.A., bill me at the bargain price of $4.47 plus 25¢ shipping and handling per book and applicable sales tax, if any*. In Canada, bill me at the bargain price of $4.99 plus 25¢ shipping and handling per book and applicable taxes**. That's the complete price, and a savings of at least 10% off the cover prices—what a great deal! I understand that accepting the 2 free books and gift places me under no obligation ever to buy any books. I can always return a shipment and cancel at any time. Even if I never buy another book from Harlequin, the 2 free books and gift are mine to keep forever.

135 HDN DNT3
336 HDN DNT4

Name _____ (PLEASE PRINT)

Address _____ Apt.# _____

City _____ State/Prov. _____ Zip/Postal Code _____

* Terms and prices subject to change without notice. Sales tax applicable in N.Y.
** Canadian residents will be charged applicable provincial taxes and GST.
   All orders subject to approval. Offer limited to one per household and not valid to
   current Harlequin Superromance® subscribers.
   ® is a registered trademark of Harlequin Enterprises Limited.

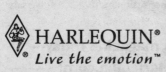

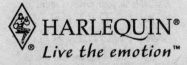

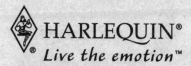

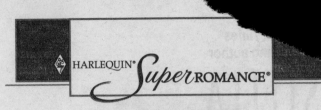

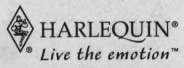